DEAD IN THE FLOWER SHOP

Blomma was dark when I unlocked the front doors. I flipped on the lights, unfolded the sandwich board, and stood it outside on the sidewalk. We wouldn't open for customers for another hour. Elin had explained that she used the time in the early morning to assemble online orders, take care of corporate accounts, and map out a delivery schedule for the day. I tossed my cell phone, keys, and purse on the workstation. My first agenda item was to prep the materials for the jewelry workshop Elin would be hosting later in the day. I headed to the workshop to grab her supply list.

The barn doors to the cottage were both open. *Odd.*

Maybe Elin forgot to shut them after the meeting last night, I thought as I stepped inside.

The space felt cold. A shiver ran up my spine. Maybe I should have worn a sweater after all. As I flipped on the lights, a new wave of chills erupted. These chills weren't from the cold. No sweater or winter parka could help. These chills were from the sight of Frank Jaffe's body sprawled on the cottage floor with a pair of shears stabbed into his chest . . .

Books by Kate Dyer-Seeley

Pacific Northwest Mysteries

SCENE OF THE CLIMB

SLAYED ON THE SLOPES

SILENCED IN THE SURF

FIRST DEGREE MUDDER

IN CAVE DANGER

Flower Shop Mysteries

NATURAL THORN KILLER

VIOLET TENDENCIES (coming soon!)

Published by Kensington Publishing Corporation

A Rose City Mystery

Kate Dyer-Seeley

KENSINGTON PUBLISHING CORP.

www.kensingtonbooks.com

KENSINGTON BOOKS are published by

Kensington Publishing Corp.
119 West 40th Street
New York, NY 10018

All Kensington titles, imprints, and distributed lines are available at special quantity discounts for bulk purchases for sales promotions, premiums, fund-raising, educational, or institutional use. Special book excerpts or customized printings can also be created to fit specific needs. For details, write or phone the office of the Kensington sales manager: Kensington Publishing Corp., 119 West 40th Street, New York, NY 10018, attn: Sales Department; phone 1-800-221-2647.

ISBN-13: 978-1-4967-0513-6
ISBN-10: 1-4967-0513-0

First printing: April 2018

10 9 8 7 6 5 4 3 2 1

Printed in the United States of America

First electronic edition: April 2018

ISBN-13: 978-1-4967-0514-3
ISBN-10: 1-4967-0514-9

Chapter One

It had to be roses. Store-bought roses no less. The kind wrapped in cellophane with sprigs of baby's breath. They didn't even smell like roses. They smelled like plastic and looked like they'd been sitting in a refrigerated cooler for way too long. That's how I found out that my husband had been cheating on me. From an uninspired bouquet of stale roses.

I'd been working a double shift that day at the wholesale flower warehouse. The only thing I wanted at the end of a long workweek was a cup of strong tea and a hot tub to warm my aching toes. Minnesota winters had taken a toll on my feet, as if the cold had permanently seeped into my bones. Even after a decade of living in the Midwest, no amount of layering with wool socks or fur-lined boots could stave off the piercing chill.

"Chad, I'm home," I called, tugging off my gloves and throwing my keys next to a stack of mail by the front door. The house felt more frigid than the wind outside.

Must be another late night at the library, I thought cranking the heat to seventy-five. Chad, my husband, had been writing the next great American novel for the last five years. He had promised that he was finally close to finishing his masterpiece. I hoped he was right because I wasn't sure how much longer we could survive on one salary. For the past month or so he had been editing late every night until the library kicked him out, which I took as a positive sign that maybe—just maybe— he really was going to finish the book.

I flipped on the kitchen lights and lit the gas stove. The tips of my fingers were numb from the cold. I blew on them as I filled my stainless steel teakettle and placed it on the burner. Working as the floral manager for a mega wholesale chain meant long hours on my feet walking between rows and rows of sunflower stems, cut mums, and mini carnations. I'd spent half of the day trying to reroute three hundred alstroemeria to a bride in Wisconsin who had accidentally been sent yellow daisies for her winter white wedding. To say the very least she was not pleased about the mix-up and threatened that if I didn't find a way to fix it she would make it her personal mission to see me fired. Part of me wanted to tell her, "Please do."

As I opened my tea drawer, which I kept stocked with a variety of blends, I noticed a vase of roses on the countertop. Chad hadn't sent me flowers in years. I almost looked past their dull color and lack of fragrance. Had he finally finished his novel? Was this some sort of celebration? Or could it be that my self-absorbed husband had rediscovered his romantic streak?

A handwritten note was tucked into the top of the bouquet. I smiled as I ripped open the envelope. What an unexpected surprise.

Darling, What a night. Your kisses are like poetry.

I paused before continuing to read. This was a surprise. Chad never called me darling, and he hadn't kissed me in weeks.

Your golden curls swirl in my dreams at night.

What did that even mean? No wonder he hadn't finished his novel. Talk about terrible writing.

And there was one major problem. My hair is brown. Dark brown. Nearly black, as a matter of fact.

The teakettle let out a shrill whistle. I jumped and dropped the note on the floor.

How could he? I thought, removing the kettle from the stove. After everything I'd given up for him? The jerk was cheating on me.

My hands shook as I poured scalding water into a mug over jasmine tea. Steam enveloped my face. Suddenly I didn't feel cold anymore. My husband was cheating on me.

I grabbed the note from the floor and ripped it to shreds. Then I threw it and the flowers into the trash. Maybe I should have felt more conflicted, but knowing that Chad had been cheating on me left me feeling strangely relieved.

Things had been less than great with us for years. I just hadn't wanted to admit it. And if I was completely honest with myself I was partly to blame. Not for the cheating. That was despicable and unforgivable. But for staying. Why had I stayed all this time when I was miserable?

Out of loyalty? No. Probably out of fear. Staying with Chad was easy. He didn't push me to challenge myself. He didn't encourage me to follow my dreams. He was quite content to follow his own and let me tag along. And I'd done it willingly.

My tea had steeped to perfection. I pulled a barstool over to the kitchen counter, sat down, and cradled the warm mug in my hands. The scent of jasmine had a calming effect. I took a deep breath, letting the smell of sweet flowers infuse my pores.

I hadn't been happy in years. In fact, I'd been miserable. Working at a soulless flower warehouse was never what I imagined for my future. Maybe this was the kick in the gut that I needed. I breathed in the tea.

When was the last time I was happy—really happy? I took a sip of tea and reflected on the past decade. My fondest memories were from when I was living with Elin in Portland.

Elin raised me after my parents died. Originally from Sweden, she had moved to Portland, Oregon, when I was seven. The Rose City's laid-back European vibe was a perfect match for her and her floral boutique Blomma. I grew up surrounded by flowers and Elin's impeccable eye for design. I'd always planned to return and help Elin with her busy shop, but then I met Chad. We were both students. I was attending the Floral Institute and he was studying creative writing. He used to whisper poetry in my ear while I sewed garlands of greenery together until late in the night.

In those days his dedication to finding the right words to express himself and crafting a superb sentence seemed romantic. We shared an artistic passion. My medium was flowers. His was words. It wasn't until I followed him to Minnesota that I began to realize that his words were really empty promises. He couldn't get a real job—like me—because crafting brilliant literary prose took hours of concentrated time and focus. Despite working two jobs, at the warehouse and filling in as a part-time designer and delivery girl for a local FTD shop, the cooking and housework fell to me because Chad insisted that his days be free in order to strike whenever the muse appeared. The muse rarely appeared. Usually he spent his days lounging on the couch watching reruns of highbrow television like *Saved by the Bell.*

I didn't need a muse to inspire me. Mother Nature does just fine in that department. She provides ample material to work with. I love blending nature into bouquets. Like a winter wreath adorned with snow-white lilies and delicate red holly berries. Or a simple summer bunch of blushing pink roses, snipped free of thorns and wrapped tightly in rustic twine.

Chad and I had discussed starting my own shop when we moved to Minnesota, but we were short on cash, so I got a job working for the biggest floral distributor in the Midwest. The pay was decent, but there was no room for creativity. My boss didn't care when the carnations' color was off or that the mass-produced roses we peddled had no scent. He would remind me time and time again that flowers were a *business,* not an art.

I tried to save as much as I could in hopes that

in a year or two I'd have a down payment for my own store, but Chad's writing expenses constantly ate away at my dreams. He needed cash for writers' conferences, a faster new laptop, "how to write" books, and his daily trip to the coffee shop. I took a second job waiting tables to make ends meet, and shoved my visions into the back corners of my mind.

It was only late at night, when I'd soak my feet in a warm tub and drink my tea, that I allowed myself to dream. Just a little. Just enough to stay sane. Every time I came close to leaving, Chad would promise that the novel was nearly done. As soon as it was finished and he sold it, it would be my turn to thrive.

That was never going to happen, Britta. Never, I thought as I finished my tea. It was time for me to do something different. Time to do something for me. And I knew where to start—Portland.

I deposited my mug in the sink, picked up the phone, and punched in Aunt Elin's number. My pulse rate was steady as I explained that I wanted to come home. Elin quickly agreed. The timing was strangely synchronistic. For months Elin had been renovating the space adjacent to Blomma to become a place where she would host couture workshops and classes. She was preparing to launch her new cottage in spectacular style with a floral fashion show. The party was less than three weeks away, which meant that she was eager for another set of hands and any help I could offer.

Within the hour I booked a train ticket to Portland and packed my bags. I couldn't believe how clear my decision seemed.

Chad came home sometime after midnight. I heard him unlock the front door and tiptoe down the hallway to our bedroom. When he asked if I was still awake I pretended to snore. In truth, I didn't sleep most of the night. I stared at the popcorn ceiling without a trace of regret. My stomach flopped with excitement. I hadn't been back to Portland in almost a decade. I couldn't wait to see Elin and finally have a chance to test out my artistic ability—if I still had any.

I wouldn't even have to change my name. Traditionally, Swedish women didn't take their husband's last names—it wasn't until the end of the nineteenth century that women began adopting them. My grandmother and mother had retained their original surnames after marriage, and I had followed suit, paying tribute to a strong line of women who came before me.

It was still dark outside the next morning as I lugged my suitcases through the dirty snow and left for the train. Chad hadn't stirred when I got up. I wondered how long it would take him to figure out that I was gone for good.

At the station the conductor took my ticket and showed me to my sleeping compartment. The little money that I'd managed to save was mine and I decided I was going to be comfortable on my journey into my new life, so I splurged on a sleeper car and a glass of red wine and double chocolate cake for dessert on my journey west.

I spent the next two days watching the landscape change outside the window. Flat prairies coated in a deep layer of snow gave way to hills and mountains. As the train chugged closer to the Pacific coast the sky began to shift. Gone was the blanket of white. I'd made it into the land of color—majestic evergreen trees, cobalt rivers, and a striated sky. I grinned as I pressed my nose to the window and took in the sight of Portland's vibrant colors. Crayons would be jealous of Portland's complexion. From peppermint striped climbing roses to gardens of neatly blooming rows of tulips, the Rose City looked as if it had been brushed by the hand of a master painter. Henri Matisse's words came to mind, "There are always flowers for those who want to see them." I felt like I was awakening, emerging from a cocoon of darkness, and ready to really see the flowers around me.

Chapter Two

"Hej!" I recognized the sound of the Swedish greeting before I spotted my aunt. "Britta!" Elin waved through the clad of travelers wearing raincoats. She stood next to the platform of Portland's historic brick Union Station. "Over here!" She held a bundle of pale purple peonies in her arms.

The years have been kind to her, I thought as I walked toward her. Her pale hair fell to her shoulders in a blunt bob. She walked with a casual elegance and her bright blue eyes sparkled with delight.

I look like my father. No one ever believes that I'm half Swedish. My mother, like Elin, had been tall, thin, and blond. They were both born in Sweden, but moved to Portland as young children. Living in the Pacific Northwest didn't stop them from keeping their Scandinavian traditions or language alive. I grew up speaking Swedish exclusively to my grandparents and Spanish to my dad, who was Argentinian. I inherited his dark hair and olive eyes.

Although my pale skin definitely came from my Scandinavian side.

"Aunt Elin!" I hugged her tight, smashing the peonies.

"Britta, darling. Let me look at you." She took a step back, holding onto my arm. "You look absolutely beautiful. You're glowing."

I laughed. "I don't know about glowing. Maybe more like glowering with anger."

She fluffed the flowers and handed them to me. "You know that peonies are flowers of good fortune. They're meant to support your future and bring healing."

"*Tack!*" I thanked her in Swedish and took the bouquet. "I could use some of that right now."

"That's what I thought." She kissed both of my cheeks.

"Where did you find them this time of year? They're not in season."

"Not here, no, but my suppliers can get me almost anything. I put in a special order for these when I learned that you were coming home."

I sighed. "That's the nicest thing anyone's done for me in a long time, *Moster.*" I fell into using an old Swedish term of endearment for my aunt.

She shook her head. "Well we're going to have to do something about that, aren't we, *lilla gumman?*" She too lapsed into Swedish. Loosely translated, *lilla gumman* meant my little darling. Warmth spread up my body. It was good to be home and back with someone who knew and loved me.

She motioned to the parking lot. A light drizzle fell from a patchy gray sky. "Bundle up. There's a chill in the air today."

"A chill?" I grinned. "This is beach weather compared to Minnesota." I craned my head upward and let the rain mist on my face. "It feels blissful."

Elin helped me with my bags and directed me toward a black Jeep with the Blomma logo printed on the sides. Like everything that Elin touches, the logo was a simple understated design. The word *Blomma* was written in a pale mint green modern script that reminded me of whimsical ivy vines.

We put the bags in the back. Elin turned the heat on, while I shrugged off my winter parka. Hopefully I wouldn't need it again. Ever.

"Do you mind if we go to the shop first?" Elin asked as she maneuvered the Jeep onto Broadway and headed toward downtown. She wore a cable-knit sweater, jeans, and rain boots. Standard Portland attire. I couldn't wait to ditch my Midwest layers for good.

"Not at all," I replied staring out of the rain-splattered window. "I'm dying to see the workshop."

Elin pointed out a variety of new buildings and high-rise condos as we made our way through downtown. Portland had grown dramatically since I last visited.

I glanced toward the riverfront, where bikers and joggers exercised despite the rainy sky. I couldn't do that back in Minnesota right now, I thought.

After a quick drive, Elin steered the Jeep into Riverplace Village. My heart thumped with excitement. This was the home that I remembered.

Riverplace Village is like its own little city within the city. It's easily accessible by foot or bike from downtown. The Willamette River is just steps away from the village of eclectic shops, restaurants, and the famed Riverplace Inn. It's a favorite stop for tourists, as there's no need to leave the village. You can spend the afternoon reading a book and watching the geese on the grassy hill next to the river, stroll along the riverfront footpath, stop for an espresso, and of course grab a gorgeous bouquet of flowers or glass of Oregon pinot noir at Blomma.

When Elin emigrated from Sweden she brought her European culture with her. Blomma is the only flower shop–wine bar in town.

"It's just like I remember," I said, squeezing Elin's hand as I stepped out of the Jeep. Blomma's front windows were draped with olive leaf garlands intertwined with clementines, lemons, and gold LED lights. Forest green awnings hung above windowed garage doors that had been painted deep red. A sandwich board sat near the entrance. Elin had written a quote in her lovely handwritten script: *"Deep in their roots, all flowers keep the light."* ~*Theodore Roethke.*

I adjust the bundle of peonies. "What a wonderful quote."

Elin smiled. "It's true. Wouldn't the world be a much kinder place if we all held more flowers and light, yes?"

"Yes." I glanced at the blooms in my hand and then down the long cobblestone path that connected the other shops in Riverplace Village. Two doors down the windows of Demitasse, an artisan coffee shop, were thick with steam. Torch, a candle and specialty gift shop, sat on the other side of the street from Blomma. Farther down there were a hotel, an Italian restaurant, and an American bistro. Cherry trees strung with twinkle lights and antique lampposts flanked the path. Every storefront had tempting window displays, collections of outdoor seating, giant planters, and welcoming signage. I'd forgotten how quaint and homey the village felt.

Thank you, Chad, I said to myself.

Elin paused before unlocking the door and looked down at her feet. She bent over and picked up what looked to be a dead bundle of roses.

"What are those?" I asked, pointing to the shriveled black roses.

"Nothing. A silly prank." She immediately unlocked the door and tossed the roses in the trash.

Odd prank, I thought, following after her.

She flipped on strategically placed lights and chandleries inside the flower shop. They cast a warm glow on Blomma's gleaming hardwood floors. "I want to show you the cottage," she said, smiling and waiting for me to take everything in. The shop was a sensory delight. Much had changed since I'd been away, and yet it was equally familiar. Elin and I had made a pact to stay in touch when I left for Minnesota. We had spoken every Sunday evening and she had constantly sent me photos of her progress in the cottage and pictures of her designs and arrangements.

Branches wrapped in twinkle lights adorned the ceiling. Tins with fresh-cut flowers were placed on countertops, and antique furniture had been artistically arranged throughout the bright space with a cozy seating area near the front. Large butcher-block tables housed woodland creations and seasonal designs. A concrete workstation with all of

the tools of the trade—wire cutters, thorn strip-
pers, shears, and floral knives—took up the middle of the open-concept studio. The back of the
shop had floor-to-ceiling windows looking out on
the Willamette River and a wine bar with a collection of Northwest wines.

Most flower shops, like Blomma, had a specific
flow. Fresh-cut stems were positioned in buckets
and tins in the front of the store and near the
garage doors in order to catch customers' eyes as
they walked past. The seating area for client meetings was tucked in the front corner. Glass case
coolers with prearranged small vases and boutonnieres were located near the workstation, as was
the intense wall of blooms and textures—curly
willows, white ranunculus, blue iris, and blushing
red roses—all waiting and ready to be made into
spectacular bouquets. One of the differences in
owning a European flower boutique was that in
Europe flowers were considered part of everyday
shopping, not a luxury. Elin made it easy and af-
fordable for her customers to handpick a collection of stems or to create a custom masterpiece.

I closed my eyes for a moment. "It's gorgeous.
Even better than I remember it."

"Wait until you see the cottage." She grabbed
my arm and pulled me toward the back.

Elin had purchased the space next door a few
years ago. She'd been working tirelessly on trans-
forming it into a cottage where she would teach
workshops on floral design. Every time we'd spoken on the phone, I could hear the excitement in
her voice when she filled me in on her progress.

The cottage would officially open in two and a half weeks, and Elin had a celebratory bash planned that would rival Hollywood movie premieres and the most elegant wedding reception. Everyone in Portland from the mayor to the press had been invited to the grand opening party, where Elin intended to dazzle guests with floor-length gowns made entirely out of flowers and massive floral headpieces and costume art. In her words, my timing—actually Chad's—was impeccable. She needed help with Blomma and I needed a job.

We weaved our way through the shop. I stopped to admire the collection of wine she'd amassed on the wall. The Pacific Northwest had become one of the premier wine producers in the world in the last few decades, and it looked like Elin had a bottle of every wine produced. I'd have to spend some time familiarizing myself with our offerings. That shouldn't be a difficult task.

I rested the peonies on one of the far tables and watched as she slid two massive barn doors open to reveal her workshop. Once we stepped inside I gasped and rested my hand over my heart. No wonder her classes were so popular.

The cottage was like something out of a fairytale. Old-growth timber beams crossed the ceiling. The walls were crafted out of stone. Ribbon, twine, design wire, and floral tape hung from wooden pegs. A large table constructed from barn doors sat in the middle of the room. An antique dresser housed drawers with shears, pruners, and wire cutters. Berries, dried flowers, leaves, glitter glass, ice and snow, grapevines, pinecones, shells, rocks, moss, fishnets, and every other possible floral design element were tucked into vases, pots, and furniture throughout the space.

Wow. I had a feeling I could definitely rediscover my creativity in this space.

"It's amazing," I said to Elin.

"Do you like it?" She gave me an expectant look. "I still have a few kinks to work out, but I think it has come together well."

"I *love* it! It is seriously the most beautiful space I've ever seen."

"*Tack!*" A smile spread across her cheeks. "Oh, I'm so glad."

"It's like a dream," I said, running my fingers along the smooth tabletop. "I feel like I'm on the set of a play."

There was a single dead rose at the end of the tabletop. Elin noticed me spot it and quickly swept it into her hand. "See, this is why I need you, Britta. I can't even keep up with the flowers." She tossed the dead rose into the garbage.

Her words surprised me. Elin was meticulous when it came to her blooms. Once when I was in high school she had me purchase samples of old roses from every vendor at the wholesale Portland Flower Market so we could watch them to see how they opened. We kept each rose in a vase for two weeks and tracked how long it took them to wilt or drop their petals. I remember her instructing me not to pull off the guard petal on a rose that had started to droop. "Never go against nature, Britta," she had said. "Mother Nature knows what she's doing. Those petals are in place to protect the rose. The longer the petals are intact the longer the rose will last."

In her quest to provide her clients with the freshest blossoms she spent hours studying the life cycle of each stem and how best to preserve them.

Could the dead flower have something to do with the black bouquet she had just tossed? "Is that part of the prank?" I asked.

She shook her head. "Oh no, it's nothing." After discarding the dead bud, Elin removed a pair of shears from the dresser and changed the subject. Placing the shiny shears in my hands, she said, "I had these engraved for you."

My initials were etched into the carbon steel. "You didn't need to get me anything, *Moster*."

She pulled a pair of matching shears from her back pocket. They were worn and engraved with the letters E and J. "You need professional tools to run Blomma. This blade is good for flowers but also trimming small branches." She pointed to a bundle of grapevine.

"What do you mean, running Blomma?" I asked, admiring the thoughtful gift.

"My work is here. I need you to manage the front shop."

"Wait? Manage?" I placed the shears on the table. When I had called Elin to tell her I was returning to Portland she said she needed help with the shop, but she never said anything about managing it. "I can't manage Blomma. I'm not ready for that. You don't understand how lame my life has been. The most creative thing I managed to do at my old job was convince my boss to wrap our fresh-cut bouquets in butcher paper instead of plastic."

She chuckled. "Britta, you don't give yourself enough credit. You're a talented floral artist."

"Floral artist? I wish." I ripped a piece of dried lavender from one of the tin vases and rubbed it between my fingers. It smelled sweet with subtle balsamic and earthy undertones. "Really, I'm not trying to be self-effacing or anything. I honestly haven't done anything interesting with flowers in the last decade." I sighed.

Elin stepped closer and patted my arm. "It doesn't matter. I know what you're capable of and I need you." She motioned to a mannequin that she had strung with wire to create a hoop skirt. "That dress alone is going to take me at least a week to put together. Not to mention the floral jewelry, headbands, and shoes I have to finish before the launch."

Before I could protest further the sound of a soft knock on the barn door interrupted us. "Elin, are you back there?"

"Come in, come in!" Elin turned to me. "That's Nora. She owns Demitasse."

Nora entered the cottage balancing two cups of coffee in her hands. She kissed me on both cheeks. "You must be Britta." Holding up the coffee, she continued. "I wasn't sure what you liked so I brought a latte and an Americano."

"Either sounds delicious."

"Your aunt has taught me that you Swedes need a daily *fika*—coffee break, right?" She handed me a paper mug. "Take the latte. It's our house specialty."

"Right." The latte was warm and smelled rich, not like the watered-down coffee that Chad brewed at home. I took a sip. "This is fantastic, thank you."

Nora waved me off and delivered the Americano to Elin. "That's nothing. Come by the shop tomorrow and I'll have one of the kids do a pour-over for you."

I didn't want to ask what a pour-over was. "Sounds great." I took another long sip of the creamy latte. "Usually I'm more of a tea fan, but I might have to switch allegiances if Demitasse's coffee is this good. How long have you owned the coffee shop?"

Nora wrinkled her brow. She and Elin looked to be about the same age, but that was where the similarity ended. Nora was short and slightly plump. Her hair was dyed platinum blond and cut in a cropped spiky style. She wore a black leather jacket and knee-high black boots. She could pass as Pink's mother. "How long have I been here, Elin?" she asked. "Seven, eight years, maybe?"

Elin nodded. "That sounds about right."

"I've heard all about you, Britta. You aunt is so excited to have you here. We all are." She winked at Elin. "I've been telling her to hire help for years now. You couldn't have picked a better time to come home."

"I'm happy to be home." I smiled. That was true, but I wondered how much Elin had said about why I was back.

Elin removed the lid from her Americano and took a sip. She caught my eye and gave me a slight nod. I hoped that meant she hadn't said much. Not that it mattered, but I didn't want to have to go through a lengthy explanation about my cheating husband to everyone I met. At least not yet.

"It will be good to have another set of eyes up

front here." Nora's expression shifted. "Have you heard anything more from you know who?"

"No." Elin's lips tightened.

"I thought I saw his delivery truck earlier," Nora continued, but Elin gave her head a quick shake as if to signal Nora to stop talking. Nora looked surprised, but shrugged and dropped the subject. She glanced at her watch. "Listen girls, I've got to jet, but enjoy the coffee and be sure to come by tomorrow."

With that she waved as Elin and I called "*tack,*" in unison.

"What was that about?" I asked after Nora left.

"It's nothing." Elin busied herself stringing more wire around the structure of the hoop skirt. "Another florist in town who is trying to get under my skin. But it's nothing to worry about. We have much to do and must keep our focus on the flowers."

I dropped the subject but couldn't help wondering if there was more to the story. I knew Elin didn't want to worry me, and yet if there wasn't anything to worry about why had she cut Nora off like that? For more reasons than my own well-being and sanity I was glad to be back in Portland. My aunt wasn't telling me everything, but we had time. I would—as Nora had suggested—keep my eyes open and find a way to get Elin to open up about whatever was going on between her and a rival florist.

Chapter Three

I spent the next two weeks taking extensive notes on Elin's process, customer order forms, delivery schedules, and the other details of running a successful floral boutique. By the time we called it quits every evening, my head was swimming and my hands were clammy. I felt a rush of excitement that I hadn't experienced in years mixed with a gnawing anxiety that there was no way I was going to be able to do this. The launch party was three days away and we were kicking things off with a soft opening for Blomma's best customers tomorrow night. There was so much more to be done before the soirée. Blomma was practically swimming in arrangements, boxes upon boxes of floral jewelry, and mounds of garland decorations.

Elin didn't appear fazed, despite my insistence that I wasn't sure I could manage the shop on my own. I attributed her confidence to our Scandinavian roots. Swedes tend to be a bit more stoic. Not

in a negative way. More like in a highly capable
way. Maybe it was due to the climate of Sweden—
the arctic winters and long dark days bred a steadfast resilience in its people. Chad had accused me
of being standoffish and cold. I used to wonder if
he was right, but watching Elin made me realize it
just might be my genetics. Except that internally I
was freaking out.

Nora interrupted my thoughts when she danced
into the shop on the day before our soft opening.
"Fika!" she called, entering through the roll-up
garage door. "I thought you might need your daily
coffee fix, girls."

Elin placed her shears on the countertop and
momentarily abandoned a sherbet centerpiece
with pops of fresh mint and blackberries. It
looked good enough to eat.

While I might have been craving raspberry sherbet, settling on Nora's latte certainly was no mere
consolation prize.

"Are you all set for tonight?" Nora asked, offering each of us a coffee.

"Yes."

She paused and looked at me. "You're probably
exhausted after the past couple weeks. I'm happy
to run you home before the meeting."

"I'm fine," I said, holding up the frothy latte.
"Especially after this. I'll be awake for hours. What
meeting? I thought the soft opening was tomorrow
night?"

Nora ran her fingers through her funky hair.
"We're having the Riverplace Village business owners' meeting here tonight. Your aunt kindly agreed
to let us use the store." She glanced to the wall of

wine. "It's a good thing you have plenty of wine on hand. We're going to need it. I have a feeling things are going to get intense."

"Why? I thought everyone in the village got along well." The latte tasted better with each sip. I wondered if Nora had added an extra shot. The espresso flavor was intense, but without any bitterness. If Nora kept stopping by with coffee my tea-drinking days were going to be a thing of the past.

Nora shook her head. "We do. Well, most of us." Rolling her heavily lined eyes, she made a face and picked up a sprig of mint. "Except for Frank Jaffe."

I looked to Elin, who nodded in agreement. Could Frank Jaffe be the rival florist that Nora had alluded to a while ago? "What business does Frank own?"

"He doesn't. He owns a real estate firm, Jaffe and Associates." She locked eyes with Elin and scowled. "He thinks he owns all of us. He wants to bulldoze Riverplace Village and put up luxury condos. Portland has tough land-use laws, and waterfront property is hard to come by. He's dangling a bunch of cash in front of us in hope that he can get the association to sell."

"You wouldn't sell, though, would you?" I turned to Elin. I was surprised that she hadn't mentioned anything about Frank Jaffe since I'd been back.

"This?" She motioned to the cottage workspace. "Not for a million dollars. I've put so much work into this space. Blomma is my life."

Nora chimed in. "None of us are going to sell. We've told Frank Jaffe he can stick it where the sun don't shine—if you know what I mean—about a hundred times. He needs the entire Riverplace

Village Business Association to agree, and none of us have any intention of selling. He just can't seem to get that through his thick skull."

I noticed a look of concern flash across Elin's face, but she quickly recovered, readjusting the lid on her coffee cup and walking Nora toward the door. "I'll have wine and cheese ready by five. It'll be a nice opportunity to officially introduce Britta to everyone."

Nora gave us both hugs and promised to be back in time to help set up. Elin seemed distracted as she finished the sherbet centerpiece. We had a dozen more to make before the launch party. They would be placed throughout the shop and cottage, along with matching garlands, which would be strung from the ceiling and draped over the windows and doors. We were constructing a floral archway for guests to enter through and a flower carpet. Elin had opted for a pastel color palette to launch her spring line, complete with succulents, huge boughs of pink dogwoods, passion vines, kumquats, and poppies. The pink, tangerine, and peach tones brought a romantic and fragrant vibe into the shop. I couldn't wait to see it all come together.

"Are you worried about Frank?" I asked Elin as I tucked a kumquat into a bouquet.

"No. Don't let Nora get you riled up too. I love Nora, but she has a tendency to inflame things, unintentionally perhaps." She snipped a peony. "Frank isn't taking up any space in my head."

I had the sense from her weighed-down tone and the way she was focusing her complete attention on the single stems waiting to become bouquets that she was holding something back. Was it

Frank Jaffe, the mysterious competitor, or something else? The truth was that I wasn't sure how to get her to open up. Despite our weekly phone calls and email chats, we were forging new ground. When I left I was still growing up—trying to make my way in the world. Things were different now. Elin had done so much for me, from taking me in to raising me and encouraging my passion for nature and design. Flowers were our point of connection, and I could only hope that as we continued to create bouquet after beautiful bouquet that our relationship could shift from niece-to-aunt to friend-to-friend. For the time being I let it go and concentrated on sherbet goodies.

As promised, Nora returned a little before five with a platter of cookies and biscotti from Demitasse. She was followed in by a tall thin woman wearing a navy blazer, silk blouse, and a short narrow skirt. The skin around her eyes had been subtly smoothed. Probably the work of an expensive plastic surgeon, I thought, wondering if she was older or younger than Elin. She rolled a cart of wine behind her.

"Serene! I didn't expect to see you tonight. Did your flight just arrive? How was Italy?" Elin greeted her with a kiss on both cheeks. "Meet my niece, Britta."

I extended my hand. Serene placed her flawlessly manicured hand into mine. "Lovely to meet you. I've heard all about you from your aunt." She smiled at Elin and Nora. "What wouldn't we do for young skin again, right, ladies?" She touched the smooth skin beneath her eyes. "I expected you to be a blonde, what with your Swedish roots, but wow, that skin and your dark hair. Elin, you didn't tell us that your niece was a beauty." Serene winked at me but her eyebrows didn't move.

"My dad was Argentinian." I shrugged off the compliment.

"Ah. Lucky."

"Serene is my sommelier," Elin said, helping Serene with her cart. "She knows more about Northwest wine than anyone around. However as of late she's been in Italy sampling the best that Tuscany has to offer."

"I wouldn't say that I know more about wine than anyone around, but I do appreciate the growing region and, after last summer's heat wave, the spring releases are going to be talked about for years to come. And I have to tell you that Tuscany has quite a lot in common with the Willamette and Yakima Valley growing regions. In fact almost every winemaker I spoke with would say things like, 'Don't drink our wine. Your wine in the Northwest is much better.' Can you believe that? Italians telling Americans not to drink their wine!" She laughed and removed a bottle from the cart with a simple black label and the word ERA stamped on the front. "This is one of my favorite local wines," she said, handing me the bottle. "Do you know much about Northwest wine?"

"Not really." I ran my fingers over the label. "I grew up in Portland, but I was too young to appreciate good wine back then. Elin sends me a bottle for my birthday every year, so I've sampled a few."

"I do believe that calls for uncorking a bottle, don't you think, ladies?" she said twisting her long highlighted curls into a knot. Then she took the bottle and walked back to the wine bar. The sound of her navy pumps tapping on the hardwood floors reverberated through the room. I suddenly felt underdressed in my jeans, rain boots, and gray hoodie. Serene, on the other hand, looked right at home behind the elegant distressed wood bar, against the wall of sparkling wine bottles and crystal stemware. The bar wasn't particularly long—about eight feet with four barstools carved from reclaimed barn wood. A black iron candelabra hung above it, casting soft halos on the hickory wood.

We followed and watched her expertly uncork the wine and pour four tasting glasses. "I think you'll love this." She motioned for us to take a glass. "There's so much we can do. My time in Italy was beyond inspiring. I'm thinking a vines and vino class where we pair flowers and wine. The possibilities are endless."

Nora reached for a glass and took a quick swig. "Nice, girl. Forget the Italians. Viva America!"

Serene held her glass under the flickering light and studied it. Then she pointed to the collection of chairs that had been rearranged for the meeting and the platter of cookies. "Am I interrupting something? I thought the launch party wasn't for a few more days."

Elin swirled her wine. "Not at all. We're having the Riverplace Village business owners' meeting tonight. You know most everyone who's coming." She turned to me. "Serene is highly sought after for her exquisite palate and knowledge of wines."

At that moment the door swung open and a guy about my age wearing a suit that was slightly too big burst inside. His ash white hair was slicked back with a slimy gel and he had a cell phone stuck to his ear. He held up his index finger to indicate that we should keep quiet while he finished his call.

"That's Kirk Jaffe," Elin whispered. "Frank Jaffe's nephew." She ran her finger along the rim of her wineglass.

"Ah. I see." I breathed in the wine. It smelled of oak and cherries.

"Where is he?" Kirk shouted into his phone. "Not acceptable. I want him over there right now. Otherwise it'll be your head." He clicked the phone off and shoved it in his suit pocket. Making eye contact with me, he straightened his tie and sauntered toward the bar.

"Hey ladies." He flashed a shockingly white grin. His teeth looked unusually bright and matched his hair. "Who is Snow White, here?" He made a clicking sound out of the side of his mouth.

Elin stepped between us. "Kirk, this is my niece, Britta."

"Britta." He massaged my hand. "Mind if I call you Snow?"

I pulled it away. "Uh, Snow?"

He ran his eyes up and down my body. "Dark hair. Pale skin. Sexy eyes. You look like Snow White."

"Thanks, I guess?" I looked to Elin for help.

She set her wineglass on the bar. "What can we do for you, Kirk?"

"I'll take whatever you ladies are drinking, for starters." He stared at Serene. She shot Elin a look of irritation, but poured him a taste.

He drank it in one gulp. "Can you top me off?"

"This wine has been barrel aged. It's meant to be sipped slowly." She frowned as she poured the wine into his glass.

"I thought wine was meant to be drunk." He chuckled and nudged me.

Serene carefully poured each of us a full glass of wine. "What do you think?" she asked me.

"It's excellent." I took another sip. "I can really taste berries."

"Yes." She nodded with approval. "It's a fruit forward wine. The finish is so smooth and nicely balanced. They're doing some amazing things in Walla Walla, Washington." She placed the bottle on a cocktail napkin on the counter. "It's one of the best growing regions here. If you like that wine, I'll come in one day later this week and have you taste some blends from the area."

Elin held up her glass in a toast. "Perfect. Britta is going to be managing Blomma, so the more she knows about wine, the better. *Skål!*"

"*Skål!*" Serene and Nora clinked their glasses to mine.

I swallowed hard, trying not to let my nerves get the best of me. "*Skål.*"

Kirk tapped his glass on mine. "What's *skål?*"

"Cheers in Swedish," I said, taking another hearty sip of the wine.

The front door opened again. A handsome man in an oversized black jacket with the Riverplace Inn logo embroidered on the front stepped inside. His jacket was splotched with rain. An older man in a cashmere trench coat followed him in. And then a young woman who looked drenched and frazzled raced in after them with a notepad tucked under her arm.

"Come in, everyone." Elin waved the new guests toward the bar.

Serene finished off the bottle of wine and opened a new one while Elin introduced me to everyone. The man in the Riverplace Inn jacket was Mark Sanders, general manager of the hotel and president of the Riverplace Village Business Association. The man in the cashmere coat was Frank Jaffe, the real estate developer who was pressuring Elin to sell Blomma. The wide-eyed girl who looked terrified of him was introduced as his personal assistant, Lawren.

I cringed as Elin raved about my floral design skills and the new vision that I would be bringing to Blomma. Frank muttered something under his breath that sounded like, "Not if I get my hands on this place first."

He took a drink of the wine Serene offered and made a gagging sound. "This is swill. What are you serving here, boxed wine?"

Serene pursed her lips and folded her arms across her chest. "That happens to be *Wine Magazine*'s wine of the year."

Frank pinched Lawren on the waist. "Go get that bottle I brought in the car, honey. We'll give everyone a taste of real wine." Frank was old enough to be her father. I cringed at his treatment of her and caught Serene glaring at him too.

Lawren startled, but followed his order and went back out into the rain.

Serene gave Frank a piercing look. "I'm going

to head out, Elin. I'll be back tomorrow with your new order and to do a more formal tasting with you, Britta."

Elin kissed her on both cheeks.

Frank grabbed her wrist as she rolled her cart past him. "Don't you want to stick around and give my wine a taste?" His skin had an orangish hue, as if he had spent too much time in a tanning bed. His hair had a similar look. It wasn't a natural orange, more like dyed chrysanthemums.

Serene threw his arm off her and shot him a nasty look.

Lawren returned breathless. She handed Frank the bottle of his special reserve. He cradled it in his arms for Serene. "This is imported from Tuscany." They shared a strange look like I couldn't quite decipher. Was it mutual love for wine or disgust with each other?

Serene looked at the label and shrugged. "1972? That was a terrible growing year in the Tuscan Valley. It rained all spring." Without another word she headed straight for the door.

Frank made a grunting noise and thrust the bottle at Lawren. "Take it back to the car, sweets."

No wonder Elin had seemed worried about him when his name came up earlier in the day. He was one of the least pleasant men I'd met in recent history. That was saying a lot considering I'd just discovered that my husband was cheating on me.

After filling their wineglasses the rest of the business owners, along with Kirk, Frank, and Lawren, gathered around the grouping of chairs we had set up in the front of the shop. Elin and Nora circulated around the space with snacks and wine. Mark started the meeting with a recap of the last meeting's minutes and announcements about upcoming events in the village. After he finished general business, he cleared his throat. "As most of you know, the reason we're here is that we've had a generous offer from Jaffe and Associates Real Estate. Frank Jaffe has come to speak to us tonight about his plan for development and incentives for a group buyout."

Murmurs of discontent sounded from the business owners.

Mark quieted them down. "I know many of you don't want to sell, but it's only fair that we hear what Frank has to say."

Kirk jumped to his feet. "I'd like to show you the design plans our architectural firm has drawn up. I think you're going to be super impressed." He started to unroll a large poster.

Frank cut him off. "That can wait, Kirk."

Kirk looked like an injured child. He rolled the poster back up and returned to his chair.

"Lawren." Frank snapped his fingers. "Pass around the handouts."

Lawren nodded and hurried to each table with a stack of papers. Her tailored shirt looked like it was polka-dotted with raindrops. I guessed her to be in her mid-twenties, but due to her skittish nature and tiny stature she could pass for a preteen. She was probably cute, but thanks to multiple trips outside, her hair was stringy and plastered to her head. Shivering with cold, she darted between the business owners and thrust the paperwork in their hands.

"If you take a look at our offer, I'm confident

you'll make the smart business choice. I know that the vast majority of you aren't bringing in the kind of cash I'm offering you."

Nora spoke up. She looked like a rocker grandma in her leather jacket. "Riverplace Village isn't just about making money, Frank. We're family. We love working here. You can't write a check and replace everything we've built here."

"Everything you've built? What sort of business mentality is that? You're not going to get an offer as generous as mine, and I want to be clear, this is a one-shot deal. I'm putting this offer on the table tonight. You have twenty-four hours to make your decision. I promise you you're not going to see a better offer than this."

Kirk stood and held up the plans. "Is this a good time to show them, Uncle Frank?"

Frank made a slicing motion across his throat. "No. They've got the information they need in front of them. Let's go."

Lawren gathered the extra papers and left with Frank. Kirk looked confused. Frank paused at the front door and glared at him. "I told you, let's go."

Kirk stuffed the poster under his arm and trudged after his uncle.

Tension hung in the air. Business owners nibbled on cookies and spoke in low tones among themselves.

Nora finally broke the silence. She jumped to her feet. "Anyone ready to vote?" She raised her hand. "I vote no!"

Mark cleared his throat. "Hold on, Nora."

They locked eyes on one another. For a moment the room was eerily still. The only sound that could be heard was the rain hitting the roof. I thought Nora and Mark might stay deadlocked in their gaze, but he gave her an almost pleading look, which, to my surprise, made her give the floor to him and return to her seat.

Mark's demeanor was calm yet firm as he addressed his fellow business owners. "As you know, the Riverplace Inn has a deep commitment to Riverplace Village's future. I've watched development along the Willamette for the last two decades. And while I don't want to see our way of life change, I also understand that Portland is changing. This could be an opportunity to be part of something great. Jaffe and Associates has a long history of projects like this, especially on the east side of the river, that have really revitalized the business community. I suggest that everyone take their offers to review independently. We can meet at Demitasse first thing in the morning, if that's all right with you, Nora?" he asked.

Nora shrugged. "That's fine, but my answer isn't go to change."

Mark gave her a warning look which again made hard-rocking Nora back off. "I want to encourage you to give Frank's offer some serious thought tonight," he said to the crowd. "In Jaffe and Associates' proposal you'll find that each of us will have first right of refusal in the new build. That could mean an upgrade of space for some of us, which I think is worth considering."

Was Mark on Frank Jaffe's side? The Riverplace Inn was one of Portland's most prestigious hotels. I couldn't imagine what his motivation for selling could be. Apparently nether could anyone else. Nora whispered something to Mark and then huffed away without saying good-bye. The other business owners milled around chatting in small groups for a while before finally agreeing to reconvene in the morning.

After everyone dispersed I helped Elin clean up. It had been a long and eventful day. I felt like I'd been in Portland for months, not days. The business owners in Riverplace Village had made me feel so welcome and part of something special. I hoped that none of them would be swayed by Frank Jaffe's offer. I didn't want to see my new home crumble before I'd even had a chance to settle in.

Chapter Four

I woke to the sound of rain on Elin's roof the next morning. My feet were actually warm under the covers. That never happened in Minnesota. I used to go through a ritual every morning before getting out of bed that involved layering with three pairs of wool socks and racing to the hallway to crank up the heat. Chad insisted that he couldn't sleep unless our bedroom was like an icebox. That wasn't hard during Midwest winters when windchills would drop to fifty below zero.

Elin's guest room reflected her style. It was outfitted with birch furniture from IKEA. There was a small desk next to the window with a plush chair and comfy bright yellow and orange pillows, a reading lamp, and a delicate perennial paperwhite. The walls were painted in a pebble stone gray with glossy white trim. Elin had emptied the dresser and stocked the closet with hangers for me. I'd been so exhausted every night since I had arrived in Portland that I hadn't even bothered to unpack. It was oddly refreshing to fall asleep the minute my head hit the pillow. For the first time in many years my creative juices were flowing and bringing me restful sleep. I hadn't realized the impact the distance between Chad and me had had on my sleep.

I tugged on a pair of cozy red striped socks and got to work arranging the few belongings I'd brought with me. It didn't take long to organize my clothes and the handful of important items that I had stuffed in my suitcase in my haste to leave, like my collection of design books, my flower bible, and my favorite photo with me and my parents. The photo had been taken six months before their accident and shows the portrait of a happy family. My father is holding me on his hip while my mother is kissing my cheek and leaning into us. They look joyful and free. It's how I've always remembered them and how I wish my marriage could have been.

Running my fingers along the edges of the silver frame, I let out a sigh and placed the photo on the top of the dresser. There was a collection of family photos resting on the homey birch wood— pictures of me and Elin at flower shows, a snapshot from my college graduation where I'm tossing my cap in the air and wearing a lei of orchids Elin had made for the day, and a collection of photos from my childhood. As I made room for the picture of my parents I noticed a small frame near the back. It contained a photo of Elin with a man who I didn't know but seemed slightly familiar. She had to be young at the time the photo was taken, maybe in her late twenties. The man looked to be about the same age with a tall frame and muscular build. His arm was wrapped tight around Elin's shoulder while she was staring up at him with dewy eyes and holding a dozen red roses. I didn't remember ever seeing the picture, and I knew with certainty that Elin had never mentioned a boyfriend or former love. Who was the man? I would have to ask Elin later.

My cell phone buzzed on the nightstand. I returned the picture to its place and went to see who was texting me. No surprise. It was Chad. He'd been jamming my phone with messages since I passed through Montana. The latest message was a lament about how sorry he was, how he had received the divorce paperwork and wouldn't I please reconsider. For a brief moment I felt sorry for him. But then I read on as he pleaded for financial support and complained about how he was going to have to get a job to afford rent and groceries. Welcome to my world.

I deleted the texts and pulled on a pair of jeans and a turtleneck. Portland's mild winters meant that I probably didn't even need a sweater. What a concept. Had it really only been a couple of weeks ago that I was tugging on extra layers to walk down the hall?

See you never, I said to my winter parka as I hung it in the back of the closet and headed downstairs.

Elin was dressed and boiling eggs when I came into the kitchen. "Good morning, how did you sleep?" She handed me a steaming mug of coffee.

"Great. Really great." I took the coffee without mentioning that I typically started my days with a cup of Earl Grey. I had a feeling that being back in Portland was quickly going to make me a coffee convert. With the steaming mug wrapped between my hands I sat at the circular dining table. Her kitchen reminded me of her cottage. The windowsill was lined with pots of fresh herbs. A rustic chandelier with taper candles hung above the dining table. The space was small and free of clutter. "Can I help you with something?"

"No. No, you sit. I'm making eggs and toast."

"It smells delicious. I can't remember the last time someone made me breakfast."

Elin turned and frowned. "I'd like to have a little conversation with Chad."

I chuckled. "I'd like that, too. You know he's terrified of you."

She lifted an egg from the boiling water and set it in a ceramic egg cup. Memories of my childhood came flooding back. My favorite part of breakfast used to be cracking the top of the egg with a tiny spoon. Chad didn't like boiled eggs so I'd given them up. That seemed to be the theme of my life—giving up what I wanted for him. Why had I done that for so long?

"Terrified of me?" Elin interrupted my moment of self-pity as she placed the egg in front of me and handed me a spoon. "Why?"

I shrugged and tapped the top of the egg. "I think he's intimidated by strong women."

"You're a strong woman, Britta." She sat next to me.

"I haven't been." I shook my head.

Elin deftly cracked her egg in one fluid motion. "We'll have to work on that too, won't we?"

"Yeah." I scooped a bite of the hot egg into my spoon and devoured it. It tasted like stepping back in time. "Hey, I noticed an old photo of you and a very handsome man on the dresser upstairs."

Tucking her hair behind her ears, she forced a smile. "That was a long time ago. An old friend."

I could tell she didn't want to say more, so I dropped it for the moment. "Did you look over Frank Jaffe's offer?" I asked, changing the subject.

She rubbed her temples. "There's nothing for me to consider. I'm not selling Blomma to Frank or any other developer."

"Do you think any of the other owners are seriously considering selling?"

Elin rose and walked over to the oven. She removed a tray of golden brown toast. "I don't know." Her shoulders slumped. "I don't think so, but you know how people get with money."

"Are you worried?"

She returned to the table with a stack of toast, butter, and honey. "I have a bad feeling about it. I'm not sure why."

I buttered a slice of toast. "I'm here to help however I can, so just let me know what you need me to do."

Reaching across the table, she laid her hand on top of mine. Her hand was rough and calloused from years of using gardening tools. "This isn't your worry, Britta. I'm so pleased to have help at Blomma. That's all I need from you."

We dropped the subject and chatted about the floral jewelry workshop she was hosting in the cottage later. The class would be our test run before the launch party. Some of the participants would

have a chance to model their designs at the bash.
Elin had been creating botanical rings, necklaces,
and earrings as an alternative to corsages or as ac-
cessories for bridal parties and runway shows.
Using succulents, tendrils from passion vines, and
small blossoms, she weaved gorgeous floral jewelry
that was as visually stunning as it was fragrant. She
was credited with starting the trend, not just in
Portland but throughout the international floral
community. Being a leader in the industry took a
certain kind of person, a person like Elin. She was
confident in her skill and knowledge, willing to
share her expertise and celebrate her students'
success.

She was highly sought after, receiving invitations
to teach in Tokyo and Paris. Opening the cottage
would allow her to expand her reach and having
me to run the shop would mean that she could actually travel and bring her designs to far corners of
the world.

After breakfast we gathered our things and
headed to the waterfront. When we arrived in
Riverplace Village, I unloaded a box of dried herbs.
"I'll open Blomma and get everything in order while
you meet with everyone at Demitasse."

She frowned and glanced down the cobblestone
street where a few business owners had already
begun to gather. "Wish me luck."

"*Lycka till!*" I called, wishing her luck in Swedish.
Hopefully she wouldn't need it.

Why would anyone give this up? I thought, pausing
to admire the view. A misty fog hung above the
river. Winter finches flitted between cherry trees.
Candy-colored raincoats broke through the shim-

mering sky. A running club, clad in matching yellow spandex, sprinted past me, waving and calling "good morning." I smiled and returned their greeting.

It was a good morning. It was the first morning of my new life.

Blomma was dark when I unlocked the front doors. I flipped on the lights, unfolded the sandwich board, and stood it outside on the sidewalk. We wouldn't open for customers for another hour. Elin had explained that she used the time in the early morning to assemble online orders, take care of corporate accounts, and map out a delivery schedule for the day. I tossed my cell phone, keys, and purse on the workstation. My first agenda item was to prep the materials for the jewelry workshop Elin would be hosting later in the day. I headed to the workshop to grab her supply list.

The barn doors to the cottage were both open. *Odd.*

Maybe Elin forgot to shut them after the meeting last night, I thought as I stepped inside.

The space felt cold. A shiver ran up my spine. Maybe I should have worn a sweater after all. As I flipped on the lights, a new wave of chills erupted. These chills weren't from the cold. No sweater or winter parka could help. These chills were from the sight of Frank Jaffe's body sprawled on the cottage floor with a pair of shears stabbed into his chest.

Chapter Five

This couldn't be happening. Was this some kind of practical joke? A bizarre form of initiation to welcome me home?

I scanned the fragrant cottage. It smelled of roses and death. No, Elin would never do something like that to me. Frank must really be dead.

I stepped closer, inching around a pile of discarded rose stems. It wasn't like Elin to leave the cottage a mess. I knew I'd been away for a while, but I also knew that my aunt was meticulous when it came to design and cleanliness. My foot kicked a scarlet red rose. I looked down and realized that roses were scattered all over the cement floor. Each bloodred rose had been snipped off and beheaded. I recognized the heirloom variety as Deep Secret. Deep Secret was the darkest of all roses, with buds the color of night. It bloomed with a perfect scarlet finish, velvety petals, and intense fragrance which made it highly sought after for flower arrangements.

Seeing the tea roses scattered around Frank's lifeless body gave them a new and sinister feeling. I shuddered and moved closer to him. Black, dead roses were mixed in with the Deep Secret roses. Where in the world would dead roses have come from? We don't keep dead flowers in the shop. I tried to wrap my mind around what I was seeing.

I bent over. Upon closer inspection I realized that Elin's garden shears had punctured his stomach. Blood, the color of the roses, seeped from his abdomen and pooled on the floor. Sweat dampened my brow and my neck began to flush and tighten. How could Frank be dead? I'd just seen him last night. And why was he in Elin's cottage? He had stormed out of the meeting early. Had he come back later?

Was this really happening? I couldn't focus. The room looked fuzzy and off-center.

Breathe, Britta, I told myself, as I blinked and concentrated on Frank. The color had drained from his face. His lips had a blueish tint. For a brief second I considered trying to administer CPR, but something inside me nudged me toward the telephone instead. A glass bowl filled with shiny pebbles had been knocked on the floor, leaving shattered remnants and tiny rocks everywhere. Had Frank been in some kind of a fight before he was stabbed? Maybe a lovers' spat? From the looks of the cottage he must have. Elin's supplies were strewn about on the top of the oversized workspace. Scissors, ribbons, garland, pinecones, and shredded flowers littered the floor. I almost slipped on a piece of broken glass as I made my way to the back of the cottage where Elin had set up a small desk.

Did she have a phone back here? I'd left my cell in the front. For a brief second I considered leaving Frank, but then I spotted a vintage rotary phone on the corner of the desk. Did it work? I picked it up and brought the receiver to my ear, not knowing whether it was functional or simply another of Elin's design touches. To my surprise I heard the low, dull buzz of a dial tone. I quickly looped my finger through the holes and dialed 911.

A dispatcher answered on the first ring. "Nine one one, what's your emergency?"

"I'm at Blomma and a man has been stabbed," I burst out.

The dispatcher slowed the cadence of her speech. "Take a breath. Let's start with your name and location."

I tried to mimic her tone and inhaled through my nose. Glancing at my hands I realized they were trembling. "I'm Britta Johnston and I'm at Blomma."

"What's the street address or nearest cross street?"

I glanced out the leaded glass window. What was the address? I should have known it, but I didn't. The Willamette River was the only thing I could see from the window. "It's a flower shop on the waterfront," I said to the dispatcher. "But I'm not sure what the address is. We're in Riverplace Village."

"Okay. I'll find it," the dispatcher continued to speak in a calm, even tone. "You said that someone has been stabbed?" she repeated.

I explained my early arrival and finding Frank. She asked me a handful of questions about Frank's condition that I couldn't answer, like whether he had a pulse. Maybe I should have been more thorough before I called for help.

"There's an ambulance on its way, but I need you to stay on the line and help assess the patient with me."

The word "patient" made me cringe. Frank looked more like a victim to me. "I can't," I said into the receiver.

"Can't what?" The hum of background conversations and ringing phones in the emergency services department came through the line.

"I can't stay on the line," I replied, examining the foot-long cord attached to the vintage phone. "I'm on a rotary."

"Portland hipsters," I heard the dispatcher scoff under her breath.

I wanted to tell her that Elin and her European style boutique were distinctly *not* hipster, but she instructed me to put the phone down and check for a pulse. Getting any nearer to Frank's body wasn't high on my list. It had been evident since I opened the cottage door that Frank was dead, but I obliged and sidestepped the roses and debris. Kneeling next to Frank made me almost lose my morning coffee. His wrist was cold to the touch as I felt for any trace of a heartbeat. Unsurprisingly there wasn't one.

He smelled of expensive cologne. I didn't remember him wearing cologne last night. After years of working in the floral industry I had honed my nose to be able to pick out almost any scent. The spicy cologne mingled with the delicate roses and metallic smell of blood, making for a surreal combination. Much like this morning thus far, I thought to myself.

Frank wore the same cashmere overcoat that he had had on last night. The coat was stained with blood spatter. I tried to avoid looking at the shears gashed into his abdomen as I reached up and placed two fingers on his neck. I knew that finding a pulse was a futile effort, but I wanted to be thorough for the dispatcher. Like his wrist Frank's neck was like ice. How long had he been like this?

I was about to return to the phone when I noticed a Deep Secret rose tucked into the breast pocket of Frank's coat. There was so much blood that I hadn't seen it earlier. Nor had I seen a note written on a ripped piece of paper. Could the note be a confession left by Frank's killer, or was it possible that Frank had stabbed himself?

Without thinking I reached for the note and opened it. The note had been written by hand on a piece of stationery from the Riverplace Inn. It read: "You are my one and only."

What did that mean? Had Frank been meeting a secret lover in Blomma? Nothing made sense.

I tucked the note back in his pocket. The dispatcher had said that an ambulance and I assumed the police were on their way, and while I'd never seen a gruesome death up close like this, I knew enough from watching detective movies that tampering with any potential evidence was a bad idea.

"He's not breathing and doesn't have a pulse," I reported to the dispatcher.

Thankfully she didn't ask me to do anything else with Frank's body and stayed on the line until I heard sirens wailing on the street in front of

Blomma. The next few minutes passed in a blur. A crew of EMS workers raced into the cottage and immediately began surveying the scene. They were followed shortly after by a young police officer wearing a standard blue uniform and a distinguished man, who I presumed to be a detective, wearing a charcoal gray suit. The man in the suit made eye contact with the police officer and nodded in my direction.

While everyone huddled around Frank's body the police officer made his way to me. My mouth felt dry and my throat tightened even more. Suddenly everything became very real. Frank was dead and I had found his body.

I tried to swallow but my tongue was like sand.

"Are you okay, Ma'am?"

Ma'am? I thought, swallowing again and trying to force my scratchy throat open. I knew I wasn't in my twenties anymore, but Ma'am?

"Do you need some water or something?" the policer officer asked, glancing around the room.

"I'm fine." I cleared my throat.

"You sure? You look kind of . . ." he trailed off.

I wondered what he was going to say. Thirsty? Shaken? Both were true, but I coughed and managed a smile. "I'm okay, really."

"All right well, I'm Officer Iwamoto here assisting Detective Fletcher." He pointed to the guy in the suit. It wasn't hard to deduce that Detective Fletcher was in charge. He strolled around Frank's body making notes on a yellow legal pad. "Did you place the 911 call?" the police officer asked.

I nodded. "Yeah, I'm Britta." I held out my hand, which was still twitchy.

Officer Iwamoto shook my hand and gave me a reassuring smile. He was of Asian descent with a cherubic face and bright brown eyes. I would guess that he must be a recent graduate of the police academy from his boyish face. "Your first crime scene?" he asked, releasing my hand.

"Is it obvious?" I stuffed my hands in my jean pockets in hopes of masking my nerves.

He leaned closer and whispered. "To tell you the truth, this is only my third official crime scene. I mean, I did a bunch of training on simulated scenes while I was at the academy, but seeing someone like that in real life is totally different." He motioned to Frank's body.

Detective Fletcher caught us looking at him and gave Officer Iwamoto a look that meant business. "Right." He reached into his uniform and removed a small spiral notebook and pen. "I get teased all the time for being old school, but my dad is—well, was—a cop too, and he never went anywhere without a notepad. He taught me everything I know, and always says that everything you need to solve a case you can find in your notes."

I liked Officer Iwamoto, but sensed he lacked a bit of focus. I also wondered if Detective Fletcher agreed with Iwamoto's philosophy because he rolled his eyes and shook his head.

"Start from the beginning and tell me everything that happened leading up to finding the deceased." Officer Iwamoto clicked a ballpoint pen. "Oh wait, do we have a name or identity for the deceased?" he asked Detective Fletcher.

"Frank Jaffe," I offered.

"Thanks." He smiled and made a note. His

handwriting was meticulous. He wrote in beautiful cursive as he listened.

I told him about last night's meeting with the Riverplace Village business owners and everything that had happened before they had arrived. Officer Iwamoto took extensive notes, stopping me every now and then for clarification. My throat relaxed slightly as I told him about Frank's demeaning attitude and explained my observation that none of the business owners in the village had appeared to be interested in Frank's offer.

When I finished he asked me to stay put and went to speak privately with Detective Fletcher. I couldn't help but want to eavesdrop, especially when the detective removed the rose and note from Frank's coat pocket and sealed it in a plastic evidence bag. Had he read the note already? I'd been so wrapped up in my conversation with Officer Iwamoto that I hadn't paid attention. I also had left out the part about reading the note. I figured I should probably mention that considering my fingerprints were already on it.

The men spoke in hushed tones for a few minutes. Officer Iwamoto carefully flipped through the pages in his notebook while Detective Fletcher listened. Still feeling off balance I pulled out the desk chair and plopped myself down. Elin's class schedule was plotted out on an oversized desk calendar. Tonight's jewelry workshop was slated for seven p.m. I wondered if we would have to cancel the class in light of Frank's unfortunate death. What about the launch party? It was only two days away. We'd put so much work and effort into preparing, I couldn't imagine having to cancel or postpone that too.

I sighed and rubbed my temples. What crummy timing. Just as I had arrived to help lighten Elin's load a tragedy had struck.

"Ms. Johnston?" Detective Fletcher's deep voice shook me from my thoughts. "I'm Pete Fletcher, Portland PD." He extended his hand.

I started to get up but he stopped me.

"Sit, sit. You're fine." He pushed aside a ceramic vase with an assortment of colored pencils and leaned on the edge of the desk. Unlike his young partner I would place Detective Fletcher closer to my age. He was tall and thin with short russet hair that reminded me of an uncommon rose called Brown Velvet. A small scar ran from above his lip to the tip of his eye. His cheeks held a trace of five o'clock shadow and his eyes a sharp intelligence.

"Officer Iwamoto tells me that you're new to town, Ms. Johnston." He focused his chocolate eyes on me so intently that I felt my body pull backward.

"Not exactly," I replied. "I grew up in Portland, but took a detour to the Midwest for a while."

"And what brought you back to Portland?"

"My aunt and this shop." I motioned to the calendar. "She's getting ready to open this cottage to expand her offerings. She's teaching workshops and classes here and I'll be managing the front."

He frowned. "What's the square footage in here? Must have cost your aunt a pretty penny to get waterfront space like this. Portland real estate is at a premium."

Something in his overt attempt to appear relaxed by leaning on the desk and crossing his legs made me wonder if he was driving at something more and trying to put me at ease. "What do you mean?"

"I mean that we have a victim over there who is one of Portland's most prolific real estate developers. Don't you find it slightly odd that he ended up dead here in your aunt's newly renovated property the night after he laid out an offer to purchase the very same property?" He raised one brow and picked up a yellow pencil.

"I don't understand what you're getting at, Detective. Are you saying that you think Elin or I had something to do with Frank's death?" I sat up in the chair, feeling heat rise in my cheeks. If that really was Detective Fletcher's theory it didn't even make sense. Wouldn't it be the other way around? Frank would have killed Elin for the property. He couldn't force her to sell, so what possible motivation could she have to kill him?

He tapped the yellow tip of the pencil on one hand. "What I'm saying is that in my line of work—contrary to popular belief—they aren't that many motives for murder. Money and property are high on the short list."

I was about to push back that regardless of any motive, Elin wasn't a killer. Nor was I. That thought reminded me of the note. "Um, you're probably going to find my fingerprints on the note that was in Frank's pocket."

"And why would that be?" He frowned.

"I read the note. I thought maybe he had killed himself."

Detective Fletcher placed the pencil behind his ear. "I see. Next time don't touch any evidence on my crime scene, understood?" His words were firm.

"Hopefully there's never a next time," I bantered back without thinking. This made him smile. I was about to explain how his theory on motive had some gaping holes, but at that moment the coroner arrived. Detective Fletcher gave me a curt nod and strolled over to meet him with a parting command not to go anywhere until he was done. "I'm not finished with you yet," he said, returning the pencil to the holder.

My cheeks felt like they might burst into flames. How dare he insinuate that either Elin or I could have anything to do with this? How experienced was he anyway? Officer Iwamoto had admitted he was new to the job. Maybe Detective Fletcher was too. As soon as we resumed our conversation I was going to give him a piece of my mind. I had stayed silent in my relationship with Chad for too many wasted years. Portland was a fresh start for me and I wasn't about to let Detective Fletcher ruin that.

While I fumed, another thought crossed my mind—he had just let something major slip. Frank Jaffe had indeed been murdered. And if that was the case what did it mean for Elin?

Chapter Six

Elin arrived as Officer Iwamoto began bagging evidence. She blinked rapidly as if trying to make sense of what she was seeing and tugged off her tailored black raincoat. Light from the chandelier made her hair sparkle, giving her an almost angelic appearance. How could Detective Fletcher possibly think she could be involved in Frank's murder?

She noticed Frank and put her hand over her heart. "Oh dear." Then she swooped to pick up one of the roses from the floor. She held the rose to her nose and inhaled. Then a look of sadness washed across her face.

Detective Fletcher held out his arm. "Don't touch that. That's evidence."

Elin stopped an inch away from the rose and stared up at the detective. "Such a waste of roses," she said with a sigh and stood back up.

"Excuse me?" Detective Fletcher moved away from Frank's body and toward Elin.

"Where did these come from, Britta?" Elin asked me.

I shrugged.

Detective Fletcher pulled out his badge. "I assume you're Elin Johnston?"

Elin nodded.

"I understand that you own this property?"

She nodded again. "Yes, what happened to Frank?"

The detective frowned. "That's what we're here to find out." He pointed to the desk. "You can wait with your niece. I have some questions for you."

"Of course." Elin glanced at the floor again. "I don't understand where these roses came from. This isn't a cultivar that I keep in the shop." She stared at the scattered stems and velvety buds.

Why was Elin so fixated on the roses? I could tell from the growing scowl on Detective Fletcher's scarred face that he wasn't pleased. I wanted to jump in and say something. Between her reaction to the roses and the fact that Frank had been stabbed with her shears I was worried that she was at the top of the detective's suspect list.

"Wait," he said to Elin. "You own a flower shop. You're saying these roses aren't part of your inventory?"

"No." Elin shook her head. She stared at the roses wistfully. "No, they aren't anything I stock, but they are beauties, aren't they?"

"How do you know that these aren't yours?" Detective Fletcher continued. "I saw the front of the shop. You must have twenty or thirty different colored roses up there."

Elin tucked her hands into the pocket of her

eggplant fleece. One of the things about working with flowers is that it's always cold. Heat is a florist's worst nightmare. I had learned from a young age to dress in layers even in the middle of summer. Regardless of what the temperature was outside, stepping into Blomma was always like stepping into a refrigerator. The cottage felt particularly cool this morning.

"I handpick every stem that we sell in this shop," Elin explained. "There's nothing fake or processed here. Every living thing in Blomma has been picked with love."

I couldn't be sure but it almost looked like Detective Fletcher smiled. He quickly returned to his sober demeanor. "And you're sure you didn't order these roses?" He pointed to the floor.

"No." Elin turned to me. "Britta is the rose expert. I might stand corrected, but these aren't in season, are they?"

"Rose expert?" Detective Fletcher chuckled. "I've heard that Portland is known as the Rose City, but I didn't know I was in the presence of a rose expert."

He motioned for Elin to join him and walked over to the desk. "So Miss Expert, do tell. Can you enlighten us?"

"I'm not really an expert," I said standing and pushing the chair into the antique desk.

"She's being modest," Elin chimed in. "Britta knows more about roses than most master gardeners. She took first place in high school in a statewide FFA essay contest and won a scholarship to the National Floral Institute with a paper she wrote on Portland's rich history with roses."

"Really?" Detective Fletcher made a note.

"That was a long time ago," I said.

"Essays aside, what can you tell me about this rose?" Detective Fletcher held one of the blooms in a gloved hand.

"It's called Deep Secret. See how its blossoms are shaped like a teacup?"

Detective Fletcher held the rose out and flipped it over.

"It's a hybrid tea rose. They are known for their extremely fragrant scent and their velvet petals. They bloom from summer through fall and originate from Asia." I could have continued, but I wasn't sure that Detective Fletcher was interested in a history lesson on the crimson rose.

"See," Elin said with a half smile. "I told you she was an expert."

"Would you call this rose rare?" Detective Fletcher asked.

"Not exactly. These days flowers are shipped all over the world. It's a multibillion-dollar industry. The flowers you might buy at the supermarket were probably flown in from Hong Kong or Auckland. Like my aunt said, her philosophy has always been to stock locally grown fresh flowers. That might mean that depending on what's in season we might not have a particular color, but we guarantee our flowers will last longer and bloom more vibrantly than anything you can find at the grocery store."

Elin gave my shoulder a squeeze. "Exactly. I've always said that we're in the business of spreading love."

"It's a nice sentiment, ladies, but I'm afraid I'm

in the business of murder, and unfortunately that's what's spreading in your shop this morning." Detective Fletcher flipped through his notebook. "What was your relationship to the deceased?" he asked Elin.

"Frank?" She moved to see around Detective Fletcher. "He and I weren't friends, but I'm sorry that he's dead. Who did it? And why here?"

"My thoughts exactly." He turned his notebook to a blank page. "Where were you last night?"

"Me?" Elin pointed to her chest and then looked at me. "I was with Britta and the Riverplace Village business owners. We had a meeting here at Blomma and then I went home. Why?"

"Standard procedure." He scribbled on his notepad.

Officer Iwamoto came over and whispered something in Detective Fletcher's ear. Then he made eye contact with Elin and grinned. "Hey, Ms. Johnston. Good to see you."

"You too," Elin replied. "How's your family?"

"Fine." Officer Iwamoto looked like he wanted to say more, but Detective Fletcher cut him off.

"This isn't the time for pleasantries. You two can catch up later."

Officer Iwamoto gave us a sheepish smile and returned to his work. Detective Fletcher continued his questioning. "How would you describe Frank last night?" he asked Elin.

"He was his normal pompous self." Elin stopped herself. "I didn't mean it to sound like that. Listen, I've known Frank for years. The man is hot air. He likes to hear himself speak, and likes to stir up drama. I can't begin to count how many times he's tried to get me to sell. I've learned to let him talk. He'll throw out a lowball offer and threaten that none of us will ever see money like his again and then he'll go away for a while only to come back a few months later and do the dance all over again."

"You don't think that Frank was serious about his offers?"

"Who knows? I think part of it was a game with him, and I heard a rumor that his pockets weren't as deep as he liked everyone to think."

"Really?" Detective Fletcher's eyes perked up.

Elin doodled a picture of a rose on a sketch pad. "It could be talk, but people in the village have been saying that Frank was strapped for cash."

"Hmm." He made another note and seemed to be considering what to ask next. Before he could formulate his question the coroner came over to confer with him again. "Hold tight," he said to both of us.

After he was wrapped up in a discussion with the coroner and Officer Iwamoto, Elin leaned close and whispered, "How could this have happened, Britta? Why would someone murder Frank in our cottage? Do you think it could have something to do with last night's meeting?"

I shivered and rubbed my hands together for warmth. The temperature in the cottage was like ice. "I don't know, but I think we're going to have to figure that out, because, Elin, aren't those your shears?" I asked pointing to the pair of shears the coroner was removing from Frank's abdomen.

She clutched my hand. "Oh my, Britta, yes."

Chapter Seven

The rest of the Riverplace Village business owners had gathered outside Blomma's front door. Officer Iwamoto had been tasked to interview each of them. He allowed us to return to the shop and opened the door for everyone to come inside. Nora was the first one in, and as usual held a tray of Demitasse coffees and pastries.

"How's it going back there?" she asked me and Elin. "Take a latte. I made them extra strong. I had a feeling that no one would turn down a bonus shot of caffeine."

I took a warm paper cup from the tray and cradled it in my hands.

"Is it true? They're saying that Frank Jaffe is dead." Nora thrust the tray toward me. "Have a pastry, too. I recommend that lavender honey scone. It's to die for." She gulped. "Sorry, wrong choice of words."

Elin took a scone and latte. "Nora, did you see

anything this morning? You're always the first shop open in the village."

Nora placed the tray on a round table. "No. Nothing. It was dark when I opened Demitasse. That's the worst part of this time of year in Portland, isn't it? I open the shop in the dark and by the time I close up after five it's dark again."

I sipped the creamy coffee. It coated my throat. For the first time since I'd arrived at Blomma this morning I felt like I could swallow.

"It was my regular o-dark-thirty crew," Nora continued, breaking off the end of a buttery scone. "The early java junkies are my suits. I like to help them start their morning with a hit of caffeine and some rock and roll." She shook her petite frame. Her black leather pants were glued to her body and she wore a tight black V-neck T-shirt with a picture of a pug and the words SEX, PUGS, AND ROCK AND ROLL.

She must have noticed me staring at her shirt. She pointed to the pug and laughed. "You like it, honey? That's my best friend in the whole world, minus your aunt—Sticks. Come by the coffee shop later and you can meet him."

"It's funny to think of an artisan coffee bar like Demitasse having a touch of rock and roll."

"That's Portland, isn't it?" She looked to Elin for confirmation.

Elin nodded and smiled as she sipped her steaming latte.

"My regulars—the suits—have high-powered day jobs. They're attorneys, bankers, city council members, you get my drift. Demitasse is just for them. They feel safe to bring potential clients in for my upscale coffee, but we secretly know that the classical music playing in the background is the Rolling Stones."

"Wait, you play classical rock and roll at the coffee shop?"

"Every day, girl. Come check it out. Actually one of my regulars got me hooked on the station. He's a lawyer for the DOJ. You'd never know that every inch of his body from his wrists to his ankles were inked. He wears a three-piece suit to cover up his tattoos, but on the weekends he lets loose and can hang with any hair band."

"Okay, that is definitely not something I saw much of in the Midwest."

Nora took another bite of scone and stared at the wall of wine behind us. A strange look passed across her face. "Wait a minute. Now that I think about it, there was something out of the ordinary this morning. You know who came in for a coffee?"

Both Elin and I shook our heads.

"Kirk Jaffe. I almost forgot about it in the activity." She motioned to the windows, where blue and red police lights lit up Riverplace Village's sleepy morning streets. "Kirk came in behind my tattoo guy. He ordered two single-shot espressos to go, but he left before they were ready and never came back. Paid and everything. I thought maybe Frank had sent him to scope me out, but do you think Kirk could have seen Frank and attacked him?"

Elin finished her scone. "How did either of them get in? We locked up last night, right, Britta?"

Before answering I played out last night's events step by step. After everyone had left Blomma Elin walked me through her point of sale and pricing systems. Since Blomma sold flowers by the stem, we didn't have any set prices. Elin believed that every bouquet that passed through Blomma's front door should be organic and unique. She'd ask each customer for their budget and then two or three questions, like what was the occasion for the flowers and whether the recipient had a favorite color or particular scent they were drawn to. From there she would design an arrangement on the spot. Last night she had given me background on the corporate accounts I would be working on, and then like she said to Nora, we locked up and headed for home.

"Yeah, I definitely remember locking up." I scanned the shop. The abundant sherbet bouquets stuffed in the glass cooler and tiny twinkling lights overhead seemed out of place against the backdrop of murder.

Nora sighed. "Well do you think there's any way that Frank could have gotten his hands on a key?"

"No!" Elin appeared to surprise herself with the force of her response. "Sorry, but no. How could he? That would be illegal, for starters."

"Right," Nora agreed. "I don't trust Kirk. There's something about him that is seedy."

"Seedy?" Elin asked. She walked to the workstation, picked up her spray bottle, and began misting the plants. "I'm listening. I have to do something, though."

Nora nodded. "I got you, and I don't mean seedy as in seeds that you plant. I mean cagey. Don't you think so too? He's cagey. I thought that last night. He kept moving around, trying to push the plans on us. Even Frank seemed annoyed with him. Maybe Kirk wanted more power that his uncle wouldn't give him. I wonder who stands to inherit Frank's business now that he's dead."

Nora's question made the three of us stop and ponder. Who would inherit? Kirk? Like Detective Fletcher had said earlier, there weren't many motives for murder, but money was high on the list. What if Kirk killed his uncle to take control of his company? A chill ran up my arms and not just from the cool air blowing out the vents overhead. That could be a clear motive for murder. I was confident that Detective Fletcher would be considering every angle given his professionalism, but when he questioned me again I would have to remember to mention it.

As if on cue, Detective Fletcher appeared from the cottage and strolled over to us.

"Yowza, he's a hot one," Nora said a bit too loudly. "If only I was your age, Britta, I'd be all over that hunk of a rocker."

"A rocker? He's a detective," I replied, smoothing my turtleneck and twisting my ponytail higher.

She winked. "Trust me, honey, I know a rocker when I see one."

I had a feeling that Nora thought that everyone she met was a secret rocker, but I didn't say more.

"Latte?" Nora asked Detective Fletcher, grabbing the tray and pushing it on him. "I'm Nora. I own Demitasse, the best and oldest artisan coffee house on this side of the Willamette."

"Nice shirt," Detective Fletcher said, taking a coffee. "I used to have a pug."

Nora batted her eyes, which were lined in black

and dusted with silver shadow. "Thanks. You should come by and meet my little four-legged friend, Sticks. He's the cutest thing you've ever seen. I call him my handsome little devil because the canine loves caffeine."

"Caffeine?" I interrupted. "Sticks drinks coffee?"

"I don't let him, but if I'm not watching he'll try to slug down the stuff."

"A pug who drinks coffee. Now that I have to see." Detective Fletcher caught my eye and winked. "Sorry to break up the party, but I need a few minutes of each of your time."

"Ooooh, I'll go first," Nora said, looping her arm through the detective's and winking playfully at me.

Detective Fletcher held his coffee cup up to me in a form of acknowledgment and led Nora to the cottage.

"She's hilarious," I said to Elin. "I can see why you've been friends for so long. I would guess there's never a dull moment when Nora is around."

Elin nodded. "It's true, but don't let her feisty exterior fool you. Nora is a steadfast friend. She would do anything for me and for Riverplace Village for that matter. She's been here longer than any of us. Nora knows every square inch of the village and every storefront. She's been a lifesaver more than once when I've had deliveries to do and been short on help. Nora will let herself into Blomma and bring in packages or grab an arrangement for Demitasse. We trade coffee for flowers. Actually we all trade. It's wonderful to be part of such a caring community. Everyone has keys to each other's shops. We jump in and help whenever we're needed. Like Valentine's Day last year. Half of the village was here taking walk-in orders and tying last-minute bouquets for me." She squirted a hanging fern and moved toward a collection of potted plants near the garage doors.

"I'm so glad you've made long-lasting connections," I said, following after her and feeling a twinge of sadness. Why had I wasted so many years in a loveless marriage and a place I didn't love? I wanted what Elin had.

She must have picked up on my wistfulness. "How are you holding up, Britta? This must be awful for you. I'm so sorry you had to be the one who found Frank this morning. It should have been me."

"No, don't even give it a thought. I'm fine. I mean, I'm shaken, but I'll be okay. You couldn't have known something like this was going to happen."

She attempted a reassuring smile, but it didn't reach her eyes. "No, not something like this, but I've had a bad feeling about Frank Jaffe for some time now. I should have acted on my instinct. If I had, maybe none of this would have happened."

Now it was my turn to console her. "You can't blame yourself, Elin. Whoever did this to Frank is responsible." I paused, a thought forming in my mind. "You don't think that anyone in Riverplace Village could have intentionally tried to set you up, do you?"

She looked shocked. "No, why?"

"I don't know. It seems too convenient. Frank was trying to force you to sell. You were vocal about holding your ground, and then he's murdered in your shop."

Her face blanched to match a bunch of white lilies. "Who would do something like that to me? I can't imagine anyone in the village wanting to do anything to harm me or Blomma."

I felt bad for bringing it up. Elin was obviously distressed, so I changed the subject and polished off my latte. The Riverplace Village owners certainly seemed to be a tight-knit group, but was there a chance that one of them had it in for Elin or Blomma? I was going to do everything in my power to protect my aunt and the shop I had already fallen in love with, even if that meant digging into who had been leaving her the dead roses and if there was a connection with Frank's murder.

Chapter Eight

"Well, he's all business," Nora said with a sneer when she finished her questioning session with Detective Fletcher. "Never trust a man who doesn't flirt."

I laughed. "But I thought he was a closet rocker?"

Nora ran her fingers through her spiky platinum hair. "Oh, he is, but he refuses to admit it. Don't you worry, I'm going to make it my mission to get him to take off his tie and let loose. Mark my words, when I'm done with Pete Fletcher he could body double for Mick Jagger."

Mick Jagger? Detective Fletcher couldn't resemble anyone less than the aging British rocker. He reminded me more of an older Prince Harry, but Jagger—no.

"Listen, girls, I've got to get back to Demitasse," Nora said picking up the empty tray. Her lattes and scones had been devoured. All that remained were a few crumbs and a couple of recycled paper napkins. "If you need anything, just holler. And good luck with Mr. Suit, see if you can get him to unbutton the top button of his overstarched shirt. That would be an early win." Her flippant tone changed when she kissed Elin's cheek. "I know this is terrible, but we've got your back. Don't you worry."

With that she shimmied her narrow hips and danced toward the front door. Elin walked behind the workstation and began misting each flower stem, even though they were already submerged in buckets of her love juice. I remember when I was a kid Elin used to say that a spray bottle was a florist's best friend. She gave each plant and flower a healthy spray at least fifteen or twenty times throughout the day.

"What do we do now?" I asked following after her, and studying the buckets of single-stem roses that she was spritzing. There were pale lilac roses with variegated edges, brilliant sunny yellow roses, and peachy roses with deep red tips. I knew that each rose had its own meaning and significance. To send someone a bouquet of cream roses indicated charm and thoughtfulness, making them perfect for saying, "Thank you." An orange rose symbolizes passion and romance. As a purveyor of flowers I had always believed it was my responsibility to understand each of their meanings, and was surprised that so many of my fellow florists didn't bother to steer clients toward a rose that perfectly captured the message they intended. Blomma's stock of roses was vibrant and intoxicatingly fragrant, but as Elin had explained to Detective Fletcher, there wasn't a single Deep Secret rose in the bunches.

"I suppose the only thing we can do is wait," Elin

said as she examined the stem of a two-foot-long pussy willow.

"Should I get started on the corporate arrangements?"

She glanced toward the doors leading to the cottage. "I think we had better wait until Detective Fletcher gives us the all clear. I'm not even sure that he'll allow us to open today."

"I didn't even think of that." Would Frank's murder have an impact on Blomma's business? What if customers were put off or nervous about coming into the shop when they heard the news?

Officer Iwamoto appeared at the doorway and waved to Elin. "Detective Fletcher is ready for you now, Ms. Johnston."

Elin placed the spray bottle back on the concrete slab countertop. "Would you do me a favor, Britta?"

"Sure, anything."

"Could you walk down to the Riverplace Inn and let Mark know that we might not be able to deliver new arrangements today? Maybe you can even spruce them up. Take out any dead stems and change the water?" She handed me a plastic caddy with a set of shears, twine, floral tape, and packets of love juice.

"Of course." I grabbed my knee-length brick red raincoat from the hook near the front door and pulled the hood up. The cobblestone pathway was slick with rain. A bank of heavy gray clouds hung overhead. Gray stretched from the sidewalk to the sky. The only thing breaking up the dreary mist were the line of emergency vehicles parked along the pathway. Their lights cut through the gloom in rhythmic flashes.

I glanced at Torch, the candle shop across the
street, which was still dark. Elin had mentioned
that the gentleman who owns it was on vacation.
As a candle fanatic I couldn't wait for him to return. Torch's window display with taper candles
hanging from invisible strings had been tempting
me since I'd returned home. A black van with
tinted windows was parked in front of the candle
shop. Maybe it was just my frayed nerves from finding Frank, but I got the feeling that someone was
watching me from behind the tinted windows. I
paused for a second and squinted to see if I could
make out who—or if anyone—was inside.

Was that movement in the driver's seat? Or was
my imagination playing tricks on me?

A shiver ran down my back. While I could ratio-
nalize that I was most likely being paranoid, a man
had been murdered. What if the killer had returned to the crime scene?

I wasn't about to take any chances so I picked
up my pace and continued on past Demitasse,
where Nora waved from behind the espresso bar. A
handful of businesspeople with briefcases and coffee to go ambled along the sidewalk, but it was too
early for families or tourists to be up and moving.
Rain dripped from the red-and-white-striped awnings of Gino's, the Italian restaurant. I wiped a
drop from my nose.

The four-story Riverplace Inn sat at the end of the
river walk. Yellow antique street lamps and hardy
green oak trees flanked the path that led to the marina. A few of the six-paned windows, some with
iron balconies, glowed like welcoming beacons on

such a dismal day. Otherwise the majestic hotel had cocooned its guests in a gentle slumber.

Rose City red bikes with wicker baskets and old-fashioned bells were parked in cheery rows in front of the hotel. Guests could hop on a bike and explore the riverfront path on two wheels, or if they preferred they could curl up in one of the many wooden rockers on the marina side of the hotel with a cup of tea and watch sailboats drift by.

A doorman greeted me with a half bow and opened the door for me. Inside, the lobby was warm and inviting. Low orange flames burned in a stone fireplace surrounded by hickory bookcases, an arrangement of comfortable high-back leather chairs, and a massive log coffee table. There were touches of the Northwest everywhere, from tapestries to framed clippings of native Oregon plants like pink flowering cherry blossoms and leafy ferns. Plush Pendleton carpets and blankets were scattered throughout the spacious lobby, as were Elin's arrangements.

In a small room adjoining the entry a side table had been set up with silver tea and coffee kettles, packages of spicy Oregon chai, and a kaleidoscope of assorted teas—peppermint, chamomile, and Oregon berry. There were baskets of airy croissants and a bowl of organic fruit. Newspapers, magazines, and travel brochures were stacked at the end of the table. What a wonderful way to start a morning, I thought as I imagined myself with a steaming mug of tea, flipping through the paper in front of the earthy, crackling fire.

Alas, I had a job to do and more questioning to face when I returned to Blomma, so with a wistful glance at the lobby I made my way to the reception desk.

"Is Mark in yet?" I asked the concierge.

"Mark who?" she asked with a friendly smile.

To be honest I didn't know Mark's last name or what his official title was. "I think he's the owner—maybe general manager. I'm with Blomma, and I need to talk to him about the floral arrangements."

"Oh, you mean Mark Sanders." She typed something into the computer and then looked around the lobby. "I don't have him signed in yet, but I swear I heard his voice a few minutes ago. He may be in his office. Let me call up there."

I studied a black-and-white photo dated from 1912 of a family in a Ford jalopy while she placed the call. The women in the vintage photo wore bonnets of roses and every inch of the car was draped in garlands and wreaths of pine boughs, ribbons, and roses. Only the tires and headlights were visible beneath the showy display of Portland's most abundant flower. Someone had handwritten a note at the bottom of the photo that read: *Annual Flower Fete, Portland, Oregon.* The photo was from one of Oregon's first Rose Festivals.

The Rose Festival was Portland's grand party of the year. When I was growing up it rivaled Christmas and Halloween. The festival takes place in early June and draws over a million visitors to the waterfront for the Starlight Parade, dragon boat races, carnival, fireworks, and the pièce de résistance, the Grand Floral Parade, featuring jaw-dropping all-floral floats along with marching bands, Royal Rosarians, dancers, and elegant equestrian riders.

The Parade took center stage at Blomma from late winter through spring. Elin would transform the shop each year to match the theme of the festival. She had consulted on float designs and always volunteered to decorate the floats, and had been the florist of record for the Grand Marshal's and Rose Princess's corsages and boutonnieres. I had missed the Rose Festival for too many years, and the thought of getting to participate again almost made me forget about finding Frank's body.

"Mark's not answering," the concierge said as she hung up the phone. "You might try the ballroom. They're setting up for a conference, and he could be in there." She pointed down the hallway.

"Thanks, and if I can't find him I'll go ahead and give the arrangements a little spruce-up, so don't worry if you see me plucking old flowers out of vases."

She chuckled. "Sure. Have at it." Then she craned her neck and peered out the front lobby windows. "Is it true that someone died at Blomma this morning?"

So much for getting swept into the fairytale of float design for Rose Festival. My throat swelled. Was I having some sort of Pavlovian response each time someone mentioned Frank's murder? I tried to swallow but my mouth dried up like a sponge. "Yeah, I'm afraid so."

"That's terrible. Were you there?"

I nodded.

She bit her bottom lip. "Wow, I would probably lose it if that happened to me. I'm impressed that you're upright and functional."

"It's kind of a blur. It doesn't even feel real," I admitted.

"Did you know the person?"

"Not exactly. My aunt did, but I only met him for the first time last night."

"Who was it?" She offered me a sheepish grimace. I wondered if she felt bad for asking. Was it human nature to be curious at times of tragedy? I also wondered if I should say anything. Detective Fletcher hadn't said not to, plus I had a feeling that Nora was probably peppering all of her customers with details about Frank's demise. Unless things had changed dramatically, news—or gossip—in Riverfront Village spread faster than the winter ice on a Minnesota lake.

After thinking about it for a moment, I replied, "Frank Jaffe."

"Good riddance," she said in a high pitch. "Sorry, I don't mean to sound crass. That's terrible that he's dead, but that man was a nightmare. He pranced around here like he owned the place. I can't tell you how many times I had to warn him not to reprimand staff. And for the record, he didn't own the place. He was constantly hounding Mark too. Followed him around like a jail warden. Poor Mark, he's too nice. I told him not to put up with it, but Mark seemed to think that Frank was hot air."

"Really?" I was surprised to hear that Frank had been tailing Mark. Had he been putting on the pressure to try to get Mark to sell? From the looks of the high-end hotel, Mark had a good thing going. I couldn't imagine him wanting to sell, but like the concierge I couldn't imagine why he would put up with Frank's tactics. And Mark had been the only business owner to suggest that everyone at least consider Frank's offer.

"Yeah," she continued. "He was such a jerk. Two days ago I had to spend hours consoling a member of the housekeeping staff because Frank yelled at her and made her come clean the baseboards. He's not even a guest at the hotel. Such nerve."

She paused for a moment and turned the edges of her lips down. "His nephew was even worse."

"Kirk?" I asked.

"You know him?" She nodded. "He decided that he should provide feedback on everything we could be doing to improve as a staff. You're not going to believe this. He delivered a six-page document of every violation he noticed in the hotel. Does he think he's a city inspector or something? I told Mark that I wasn't putting up with any of it. In fact Kirk was here about an hour ago, helping himself to free coffee and croissants, and I kicked him out." Her smile was smug.

Kirk had been at the hotel as well? Thus far Kirk had been at two businesses in Riverplace Village before most people were even out of their pajamas. What was he doing lurking around? Was he really on a snooping errand for his uncle or could he have killed Frank?

I thanked the concierge for her help and started down the luxurious hallway to find Mark. Kirk's early morning activities had my curiosity piqued, but I was equally confused by Mark. Why would he have let Frank and Kirk have the run of the hotel? Could it be that there was more to their relationship that I was missing?

Chapter Nine

The ballroom was painted in a rich caramel color with a mahogany chair rail that ran the length of the spacious room. Floor-to-ceiling windows looked out on the Willamette and an intricate dogwood vine mural brought a touch of nature inside.

A crew was setting up round tables and draping them with lavender linens. There was no sign of Mark, though. I knew I hadn't been gone from Blomma long, maybe ten minutes, but I didn't want to end up on Detective Fletcher's Most Wanted list if I wasn't there when he finished questioning Elin.

I could come back and talk to Mark later, but for the short term I needed to check the arrangements. As I returned to the lobby the sound of voices startled me. The sound was coming from a small boardroom across the hall from the ballroom. I wouldn't have thought much of it except for the fact that I heard a man shout, "Kirk, I've had enough. I told your uncle the same thing. You need to get off these premises before I make you regret it."

Was that a threat? The concierge had said that Mark was too nice, but nothing in his tone sounded friendly.

"Whatever. I own the company now, so you had better back off before I make *you* regret it," Kirk shot back.

"Get out!" Mark shouted.

I tried to sneak into the ballroom, but I wasn't fast enough. The boardroom door flew open and Kirk Jaffe stalked out. He didn't notice me. I watched him stomp down the hall. He stopped before he got to the lobby and punched the wall. Then he grabbed his hand and disappeared out of sight.

"Sorry you had to see that." Mark's voice made me flinch.

I looked up to see him leaning in the doorframe staring after Kirk. "No, I'm sorry, I didn't mean to eavesdrop." I pointed behind me to the ballroom. "I was looking for you, but then . . ."

"Then Kirk Jaffe decided to show you just how immature he is." Mark stepped to the side. "Come in."

I hesitated for a second and then followed Mark into the boardroom. It contained one large mahogany table with twelve matching leather swivel chairs. There was a projector in the center of the table and a white screen on the far side of the room.

"It's Britta, right?" Mark pointed to one of the chairs. "I'm not always great with names, but your aunt has been talking about you forever. She thinks the world of you."

When I sat my body sunk into the cushy leather. "The feeling is mutual."

Mark sat and folded his hands on the polished wood. "I'm sorry to hear what happened this morning. You must all be in shock." With his height he didn't sink into his leather seat.

I nodded, internally begging my throat not to tighten.

"The Jaffe family must be upset. I tried to give Kirk the benefit of the doubt this morning. I know that grief can make people act in ways they might not otherwise, but he refused to listen to reason."

"I heard him say something about owning the company. Do you know what he meant by that?"

Mark sighed and unfolded his hands. "Who knows? Kirk likes everyone to think he has power. He could just be saying that. Or I guess it's possible that Frank left the company to him. As far as I know Kirk is Frank's only living relative. If that's the case then with Frank dead, Kirk would stand to inherit everything."

My mind flashed once again to my conversation with Detective Fletcher. Could there be a bigger motivation for murder than "inheriting everything"?

"But you're not here to have me loop you into my personal drama, are you?" Mark offered a half smile. "Many apologies. I promise that we are typically very professional here at the Riverplace." He looked the part of a professional hotelier in his crisp navy slacks and white dress shirt with the Riverplace Inn logo stitched on the breast pocket. His dark hair was slicked back with styling gel and his cheeks cleanly shaven.

"Not to worry. I'm impressed with the hotel. It's stunning. I remember it being fancy when I was a kid, but you've added such lovely touches."

This time Mark actually smiled. "Thank you. It's been a labor of love. We went through an entire overhaul two years ago. We redesigned everything from the shower curtains to the light fixtures. We want our guests to feel at home, pamper them, and give them a real Northwest experience."

"I think you've succeeded." I nodded at the Oregon pine curtains that framed the windows.

"You'll have to stop by for happy hour one afternoon. It's an open invitation to any of our fellow business owners in the village. We pair Oregon wines and cheeses with locally sourced nuts and meats from a butcher who smokes everything in house."

My stomach rumbled. "That sounds amazing."

"Come by. It's free and we host happy hour for guests every day of the week." He cleared his throat. He ran his hand over the polished tabletop. "Aside from Kirk and our delicious wine tastings, what can I do for you?"

"Right. Elin wanted me to let you know that we might not be able to deliver your arrangements today. We're not sure if we'll even be allowed to open, but while I'm here I'll do my best to give each arrangement a quick refresher."

"Don't even worry about it. I've told your aunt a million times that Blomma's bouquets last ten times longer than any other flowers. We could easily go for another week before they need to be swapped out."

"I'm glad to hear that. We pride ourselves on having the freshest flowers. I know that my aunt guarantees every bouquet she creates." It felt odd and comforting to talk about Blomma as if I was part of it. It had been a long time since I was part of anything I was proud of or excited about. Now I was. And despite the crazy events of the past few hours, knowing that I was welcomed and would be encouraged to put my creative energy to work was heartwarming. Maybe after all of those frozen Minnesota winters my heart would start to thaw. I knew that I wasn't speaking out of turn when it came to Elin's guarantee.

Since she opened Blomma over twenty years ago she had a weekly tradition of going to the Portland Flower Market. Every Wednesday she would wander the halls and chat with local growers, picking only the most beautiful and bountiful organically grown stems. Then she would return to the shop, where she would process each stem by hand. This involved snipping off the end to give the stem a fresh cut. Then it would be dipped in a bucket of warm water enhanced with floral food. This had to be done within five to ten seconds, otherwise the flower would form a scab. From there she would peel off any greenery so the water didn't produce rotten bacteria, and allow the stem to drink heavily.

Processing was the most important part of owning a floral boutique, according to Elin. Many shops sold "lab flowers": lifeless, stale stems that had been bred in greenhouses the size of small cities. These mass-produced flowers were flown from continent to continent and trucked to neighborhood flower shops. Not at Blomma. Processing was a labor of love. It required dedication and took hours of work but the results were evident in every bunch of flowers

or bouquet that left Blomma's doors. Flowers purchased from a mass-market shop might begin to
droop and wilt after a few days, but Blomma's
arrangements stayed fresh and vibrant for a week
or more.

"Is there anything you need from me?" Mark
asked in a subtle dismissal. I saw him glance at his
watch.

"No. I'll let you get back to work. I just need a
sink and some water." I patted the supply bag I had
brought along containing plant food, shears, and
twine.

Mark stood and showed me to the door. "Straight
down this hallway and third door to your right you'll
find a utility sink. If you need anything, holler and
my staff will help." He held the heavy door open
for me. "And please tell Elin that I'm here for
whatever she needs. I'll be by later to check in."

"Thanks," I said with a wave and headed to the
lobby to get the first arrangement. There are a few
simple tricks for preserving cut flowers. The first is
keeping them out of the heat and away from windows where they will bake in the sun. I always tell
my floral clients to store their bouquets or fresh
cut flowers in a cool basement or garage at night.
That alone can extend their bloom for a few extra
days. Another professional trick is to replace the
water in the vase every few days. Any greenery left
on the stem can produce a rotten bacteria and
fungi that smells disgusting and creates a slime on
the stems. Fresh water, a dash of floral food, and a
quick trim of the stem can bring new life to a wilting or drooping bouquet.

I picked up a massive arrangement of Stargazer

lilies and carried it to the utility room. The water in the clear glass vase had turned murky and terrible. I carefully removed any dead stems, dumped the water, and replaced it with clean water mixed with floral food, or as Elin says, "love juice." We include a packet of floral food with every sale and recommend that clients use half of the package when they initially place their blooms in a vase and save the other half for when the water begins to get gunky.

Floral food can easily be made at home by adding a teaspoon of sugar, bleach, and lemon juice or vinegar to lukewarm water. Tepid water allows the stems to drink heavily. The only exception to that rule is when working with tulips and a handful of other spring bulbs that much prefer ice-cold water.

I continued the process with each arrangement in the lobby, dining room, and ballrooms. It didn't take long before each stunning display looked bright and cheery. Mark was right, with a little TLC the flowers could easily last for another four or five days. Pleased with the results, I packed my supplies back in the pouch and said good-bye to the concierge.

As I made my way back to Blomma I noticed that the ambulance had left, as had two of the squad cars. Only one police car and one unmarked vehicle remained. I assumed the unmarked black sedan must belong to Detective Fletcher. Three satellite vans blocked the sidewalk and competing news reporters stood with their microphones at the ready in front of Blomma.

Fortunately the black minivan that I'd seen parked in front of Torch was gone. Crime scene

tape had been stretched across the entrance and
a small crowd gathered across the street trying to
get a glimpse of any action. I waved to Nora as I
passed Demitasse. The windows of the coffee shop
had begun to sweat as more onlookers had con-
gregated inside. Coming closer I could hear one
of the reporters rehearsing her intro.

She paced on the cobblestone walkway, checking
her appearance on her phone and repeating, "Flowers turn fatal this morning at historic Blomma in
Riverplace Village. Portlanders know the artisan
flower shop for its charming location and involvement in the Rose Festival every year, but today instead of the aroma of fragrant flowers this idyllic
village has the stench of death."

Stopping in midsentence she turned to her cam-
eraman. "What do you think? Is that too much?"

I didn't wait to hear his response. My stomach
dropped at her dramatic intro. Now more than
ever I was convinced that Frank's murder was
going to be bad for business. Really bad.

Chapter Ten

"How is it out there, Britta?" Elin asked when I opened the front door. The reporters had yelled after me when I ducked under the police tape and hurried toward Blomma. I ignored their calls and showed the officer positioned at the front door my ID.

"Uh . . ." I glanced out the window. "It's a little crazy. The press are here."

"I noticed." She frowned.

"You're done with questioning, I take it?" I walked to the back counter and placed my supply pouch on the concrete slab.

She took her eyes off the reporters. "Yes, he said to send you back as soon as you returned." Her voice sounded faraway, as if she wasn't even connecting with her words.

I wanted to console her. I couldn't begin to imagine how she must be feeling. Having only been home for two weeks I was reeling with the tragedy at Blomma. Elin had invested her entire life in being an integral part of her clients' lives. She wasn't just a florist. She listened with an open ear and an ever-ready box of tissues during the darkest days of her clients' lives like planning arrangements for funerals and pick-me-up bouquets to be delivered to sick children in the hospital. She was with them at their weddings, birthdays, anniversaries, and baby showers. She knew each client by name and often knew every generation of the family. Blomma wasn't a shop—it was her home.

"Are you okay?" I asked, patting her back.

She brushed a tear from beneath her eye. "I'll be fine." She turned away from the window. "It's unsettling, seeing so much negativity around the shop, you know."

"I know." Without hesitating I wrapped her into a hug.

We held each other tight. I could smell a hint of tea and her honey lemon soap on her skin. "What would I do without you," she said finally releasing me and wiping more tears from her eyes.

The sound of someone clearing his throat made us both jump slightly. "Ladies, sorry to keep breaking you up like this, but I have some further questions for Ms. Johnston." Detective Fletcher had opened the door leading to the cottage and motioned with his index finger for me to come with him.

"I'll be back in a few," I said to Elin. "Why don't you go sit down? Maybe make yourself another cup of tea."

"Britta, I'm fine." Elin gave me a reassuring nod. "It's not every day that someone ends up murdered, that's all, but having you here is going to make getting through this much, much easier."

Detective Fletcher cleared his throat again. "Ms. Johnston."

"Coming." I gave Elin a final once-over to make sure she wasn't in any danger of passing out or something and then went with the detective.

To my surprise Frank's body had been removed from the cottage floor. A chalk outline, like I'd seen in police procedurals on TV, was left in its place. Small yellow numbers were scattered throughout the floor and on the barn door worktable. I surmised that they must be marking evidence. Officer Iwamoto circled the room with the digital camera and snapped a bunch of shots.

"What possessed you to leave my crime scene, Ms. Johnston?" Detective Fletcher said pulling out his notebook.

"What do you mean?"

He let out an exasperated sigh. "What do you think I mean? You seem like a reasonable and intelligent adult. In fact Iwamoto seems to think you're the most reliable witness he's ever seen, and yet I tell you not to go anywhere until I give you the all clear, and I learn that you've taken it upon yourself to sneak out of my crime scene to go *fix flowers*?" The disdain in his voice was evident.

"It wasn't like that," I started to reply, but he held up his index finger to stop me.

"Not another word. I don't want to hear any excuses, especially anything pertaining to flowers. Now if you were a heart surgeon I might give you a pass, but in what world do you live in to think that checking on a bunch of daisies warrants leaving the scene of the crime? You know I could arrest you right now."

My heart pounded in my chest. I could feel sweat start to form on my brow. Detective Fletcher made a fair point, but it wasn't as if I went far. I thought about telling him that daisies weren't in season, but one glance at his severe face made me bite my tongue. "Sorry, you're right. I shouldn't have left. I've never been on the scene of a crime before. I assumed you meant don't leave the village."

"I didn't." He scowled, but I caught a hint of amusement in his steely eyes. "If you try anything like that again, Ms. Johnston, you're going to get yourself a ride in the back of one of my squad cars to the station, understood?"

"Understood."

Officer Iwamoto stepped over a pile of roses. He caught my eye and winked, then made a goofy impression of Detective Fletcher. I ignored his antics. I was already on the detective's bad side, I didn't need any more help in that department.

Detective Fletcher flipped through his notebook and landed on the page he wanted. "Now, let's go over the timeline once more. I want you to walk me through every step you took from the time you left Blomma last night until the time you called EMS this morning."

I wanted to remind him that I'd already gone over the timeline with him and Officer Iwamoto, but instead I repeated everything I had told them earlier. Why was he so fixated on the timeline? It must be important, or maybe it was his strategy to try to catch me in a lie. I knew that I wasn't lying, but he didn't know that. Perhaps criminals slipped up in multiple retellings.

As I replayed my movements he made check-marks in his notebook. Once I had finished I added in my own observations, explaining how Kirk Jaffe had been at Demitasse and the Riverplace Inn this morning, seeing the strange black van parked across the street, and about the argument I'd overheard between him and Mark.

Detective Fletcher made note of what I told him, but finished by saying, "Thanks for your theories, Ms. Johnston, but let's leave the speculation and rumors alone. You're not trying to go all Jessica Fletcher on me are you?"

"No." I didn't add that having a man killed in my aunt's flower shop with her shears would most likely make any rational person interested in the case.

Officer Iwamoto took one final photo of the outline of the body and then joined us. "That's it, boss. I catalogued them all."

"Good work, Iwamoto."

"Does that mean we can start getting the cottage cleaned up and open?" I asked.

The officer who had been guarding the front door interrupted our conversation. "Sorry, sir. There's a young woman up front who is saying she left her wallet here last night. She wants in, what do you want me to do?"

Detective Fletcher sighed again. "What do you think I want you to do?"

"Uh, tell her she has to wait, sir?" the officer replied.

"Exactly." Detective Fletcher dismissed him by turning his back.

"It's just that, sir, she says she has important information about the case. She's claiming to be the deceased's personal assistant."

Lawren, I thought. I didn't remember her leaving a wallet at the meeting last night or seeing one in the shop this morning, but then again I hadn't been looking for one either.

Detective Fletcher clenched his jaw and said something undistinguishable under his breath. "Next time, lead with that. If she has information regarding the case, by all means send her back here."

Iwamoto stifled a laugh. The other officer turned red and made a quick exit.

"Sometimes I wonder if I really landed in Portland because everyone around us seems to be operating as if we were in some tiny small town," he said to Office Iwamoto.

"Welcome to Portland, sir." Iwamoto said with a grin.

"It's true," I chimed in. "Portland may be growing, but we're a small town at heart, especially here in the village."

"That's great, but not when it comes to police procedures." Detective Fletcher tapped his notebook with the tip of his pencil. "In terms of your question, Ms. Johnston, my team still has work to do. The cottage is going to be sealed for a while. I can't make any promises, but after we finish sweeping the front, I don't foresee a problem opening that later. Officer Iwamoto will keep you posted, and in the meantime when I say don't leave the premises, I mean DO NOT leave Blomma, understood? I've informed your aunt of the same thing."

"Understood." I scooted away before he could continue to reprimand me. Did he think I was a suspect, too?

Lawren was being escorted into the cottage as I left. She looked terrible. Her hair was tangled, her skirt twisted and wrinkled, and her eyes looked bloodshot.

"Oh, hi," she mumbled as she passed me.

I wondered what important information she could have on the investigation. As Frank's assistant she must have access to his personal files. Did she know who would inherit the company? Could she have proof that Kirk Jaffe was Frank's sole heir?

I tried to silence the many questions forming in my mind, but it was almost impossible. Was this a normal response? Having never witnessed a murder or a dead body for that matter, I had no baseline of how to operate or respond. Question after question battered my brain. Who could have killed Frank and why at Blomma? As much as I didn't want to entertain the thought of someone being out to get Elin, I couldn't help but wonder if Frank's killer had intentionally murdered him here to get at her. If that was the case, I would do everything in my power, whether Detective Fletcher approved or not, to clear Blomma's name and get back to the business of spreading love in the form of flowers.

Chapter Eleven

Elin had taken my advice and was resting in a cushy chair at the front of the shop. One of the many charms about Blomma's airy space were the different cozy areas Elin had designed. The sitting area at the front housed four antique plush chairs in eggplant and gray. A low coffee table with notebooks showcasing Blomma designs anchored the space. Elin used it to meet with potential clients, serving brides-to-be and their fiancés, mothers, and bridesmaids tea and scones as they flipped through photos of elegant and earthy displays. There were swatches of fabric and pressings of greenery. Elin believed in the power of touch. She wanted prospective clients to have a tactile experience along with a sensory one.

She made a mini bridal bouquet for every client she met with, offering it as a token of her goodwill (regardless of whether or not the bride ended up choosing Blomma for her big day) and as a sample of her artistic ability. It was simple, yet personal touches, that drew nearly every person who walked through Blomma's front door to want to work with her.

"How did it go back there?" Elin asked, patting the empty chair next to her. "I felt like I was in a wolf den. You wouldn't believe how many questions he asked me about my shears."

"I'm sure it's standard procedure." I sat next to her.

"It's tough being back there though, isn't it?" She grimaced.

"Yeah. It's unsettling to say the least."

She placed her head in her hands. "Oh Britta, how are we ever going to get that terrible energy out of the cottage? I poured so much love into that space, and now this."

I squeezed her knee. "I know. I was thinking the same thing while I was talking to Detective Fletcher, but we'll find a way. Once the police leave, we'll open up every door and window and fill the cottage with as many calming and peaceful flowers as possible."

She gave me a half smile. "You know what flowers best serve that occasion."

"Yeah. I'll do some thinking. I've never had to name a flower for a murder scene before, but Blomma is *you*, and we'll recapture that vibe, I promise." I released her knee.

"Poor Frank." She stacked a collection of flower magazines on the coffee table. "I never thought I would be saying that about Frank Jaffe, but I can't shake seeing his body on the floor. Who could have done such a thing? And here, in our village?

We've had a few disagreements over the years, but nothing like this. Nothing."

"I know. It's terrible." I considered how I could broach the subject of whether any of her fellow business owners might be holding a grudge against her or Blomma. What about the competitor Nora had mentioned the other day? What if they were trying to set Elin up? After considering it for a moment I decided my best option was simply to put it out there. Elin was a straight shooter and one of the strongest women I knew. She could handle it.

"And you're sure there's no chance that someone could be trying to sabotage the shop?" I asked. "Nora made it sound like there's another florist in town who has been bugging you."

"No, that's nothing." She scooted her chair closer and looked thoughtful for a moment. "Although for the past few months I've had the sense that someone was watching me when I was working in the cottage at night."

"Really?" I thought about the black van I'd seen in front of Torch.

She nodded. "I didn't think anything about it. I thought maybe I was being paranoid. There were construction workers coming and going from the cottage and I would often stay late after they finished to review their progress and do anything I could to help move them along. You know how it goes trying to keep a project like that on track."

"I can only imagine," I agreed.

Elin stared at the garage door window that opened onto the cobblestone walkway. "It's so light in here. Most days, even when it's raining I open the garage door and then of course we get light coming through on the river side too. But the cottage isn't like that. It only has two small windows. I could swear that someone was peering into the window on the riverfront a couple of times, but by the time I went outside to look around there was no one there."

Her words made the tiny hairs on my arms stand at attention. Had someone been stalking Elin? And why was she so dismissive about the florist Nora had mentioned?

Elin tucked her hands into her fleece sweater. "So many people use the waterfront path—tourists, families out for bike rides, couples picnicking on the lawn, and even the occasional homeless person. I blew it off. I figured I wasn't used to working in a more enclosed albeit cozy space, or that it was probably just people who were curious about what was going on in the shop," she continued. "The cottage had been empty for years, as you know, so I'm sure seeing any activity made people interested."

That theory made sense and sounded reasonable, but still I felt a sense of cold consume my body. Could Elin have been in danger? What if whoever killed Frank had actually been after her? What if the killer snuck into the cottage expecting to find Elin and ran into Frank instead? Maybe his murder had been a mistake. He could have simply been at the wrong place at the wrong time.

"Britta, are you okay? You look as gray as the clouds outside."

"Sorry." I gave my shoulders a shake, trying to

drive away the invading thoughts. "You don't think there's a chance someone could have really been spying on you?"

"Well, I didn't, but now with Frank and everything that's happened, it has been top of my mind again. I can't imagine why anyone could possibly be sneaking around the cottage. It's hardly like we keep much cash on hand or house highly valuable flowers."

"True." When I attended the Floral Institute I had witnessed a handful of knock-down, drag-out fights break out at the wholesale flower market trading floor over highly coveted rare stems. Rare flowers had fetched massive amounts of money in the global market, like the Juliet rose, which sold for nearly sixteen million dollars or the Shenzhen Nongke orchid, which only blooms every four to six years. The rarest bloom in the world is the Kadupul flower, which is actually a cactus. It can only be found in Sri Lanka and it only blooms at night for a few short hours. Catching a glimpse of its stunning, dainty white petals would be like stumbling upon the Holy Grail for a florist. The Kadupul flower had reached almost mythical status in the flower world, and given that it has never actually sold it's considered priceless.

But like Elin said, Blomma didn't stock anything that valuable or rare. No local florist could afford that kind of expense.

"It's probably nothing," Elin repeated. She sounded like she was trying to convince herself.

"What about the other business owners in Riverplace Village. Were any of them interested in the property?"

She considered my question for a moment. "No, I don't think so. If someone was, no one said anything to me. The cottage had been empty for at least ten years. If someone wanted it they easily could have beaten me to it. It just took me that long to save up."

"Right." I nodded. "You should at least mention it to Detective Fletcher though. It might be nothing, but it could be related to Frank's murder."

She patted my knee. "I already did."

"Good." I smiled. Then I followed her gaze toward the garage doors. The camera crews and reporters were still camped out front. It looked like one of the reporters was accosting every poor bystander for a comment. As the morning had worn on the crowd had grown and the rain became steadier. It fell in sheets and pooled on the cobblestone path. The wind kicked up too, sending wet leaves sailing in the air and raindrops into Blomma's windows.

"I don't know about you, but the minute the police give us the go-ahead to get back to work I can't wait to start putting some bouquets together and bring some cheer and color to this dreadful day."

I understood that Elin's words contained a double meaning. It had been a dreadful day so far, and it wasn't even halfway over yet.

Officer Iwamoto escorted Lawren to the front. If possible she looked even more shaken than before. "Detective Fletcher has given her permission to look for her missing wallet," he said and then returned to the cottage.

"Let me help you look," I said getting up and walking toward the back wall of wine.

Lawren made a sound like an uncomfortable laugh. Or maybe it was a whimper. I couldn't be sure. She stared at the wine lined up in neat rows along the wall. Elin had had custom shelves made to house her vast collection of wine. There must have been at least three hundred bottles on display. Wine was organized in four categories—sparklings, whites, rosés, and reds. Each artistic label faced toward the shop, making the wall look like a miniature art gallery.

"Did you leave your wallet back here?" I asked approaching Lawren.

She shrank back as if she expected me to throw a punch. "What? No, uh. No, I don't think so. I mean I'm not sure."

I didn't remember Lawren being anywhere near the wall of wine last night, and I also wondered where she could have possibly tucked her wallet. In between a bottle of merlot and a Malbec?

She continued to stare at the elegant glass bottles. Her eyes stayed focused on one particular spot.

"Are you sure I can't help you look?" I asked.

"No, I must have left it in the car, or maybe I dropped it on the sidewalk." Lawren rubbed her shoulders. "It's chilly in here." No wonder. She wasn't wearing a coat. Her T-shirt was paper thin, as were her leggings.

"We keep it cool for the flowers." I pointed to the opposite wall where foot-high black buckets bursting with colorful stems were stacked on vintage tables and rustic pallets.

"Sure," Lawren replied giving the wine one final

glance. "I should go. Sorry to bother you. I've got to go."

"Not a problem." I followed her to the door. "We'll let you know if it turns up here. Are you sure you don't want some help?"

"It's fine." She raced out the door and ducked her head to avoid the waiting reporters' questions.

"That was odd," I said to Elin as the breeze from the opening door blew in rain.

"Very odd," Elin agreed. She motioned toward the back. "Let's check out the wine. Was anything missing?"

I grabbed a forest green towel hanging on a low glass doorknob by the door and used it to mop up the floor. Elin kept the towel along with a drinking and treat station for dogs, and an assortment of flower-themed umbrellas by the front door. Dogs were always welcome at Blomma and Elin made sure their drinking bowl was full of fresh water and their treat dish (a ceramic vase with hand-painted blue variegated hydrangeas) was always brimming with crunchy dog bones. The umbrellas were free for any customer to use as they strolled through Riverfront Village. Each business had umbrella return stands at their front door. That way a customer could pick up an umbrella at Blomma and return it the Riverplace Inn at the far end of the village.

"What was her obsession with our wine?" Elin mused, picking up a bottle of a red blend with a pretty hummingbird label.

"Your guess is as good as mine. She could have stored her wallet up there, but I don't even remember her being back here, do you?"

Elin ran her hand over the smooth label. Her hands had definitely seen years of work. Her fingers were calloused. She had a couple of scars from previous cuts and a few more recent scrapes. There was something symbolic in her hands, as if a trace of every flower and stem that she had snipped lingered in her skin. "No. In fact, if my recollection is correct, she barely made it halfway through the door before Frank was bellowing for her to leave." Elin returned the bottle to its place.

"That's what I remember too."

"Then why show up in search of a wallet?"

Why? That was the question of the moment. Why had Frank been killed? Why was he at Blomma? Why was Kirk Jaffe in Riverplace Village before dawn? Why had someone been spying on Elin? And why had Lawren really come to Blomma?

Chapter Twelve

Waiting for Detective Fletcher to clear us to resume work felt like agony. Sitting around with dozens of questions competing for space in my head only made things worse. Elin wasn't faring much better. She had started pacing around the shop. I was about to head to the cottage and ask if we could at least walk over to Demitasse for a tea when Officer Iwamoto appeared with a smile and two thumbs up.

"You are good to go. Detective Fletcher says it's fine for you to open for business, but he doesn't want you to talk to the media. They'll try to get you to talk—just say, 'no comment.' And he also said that no one is allowed in the cottage until you hear from one of us directly."

"Finally some good news." Elin sounded relieved.

"It's not all good news, Ma'am." Officer Iwamoto's face faded. "It sounds like it might be longer than we originally expected before we're going to be able to give you access to the rest of the property."

"What about my class tonight and tomorrow, not to mention our launch event the next day? We've invited the press and everyone in the Portland floral and event industries!" In addition to the jewelry workshop Elin had planned on teaching tonight she had scheduled a natural garland class for tomorrow. Garlands had become popular in any season. They were most known for their use during the holidays. Clients came to Blomma at Christmastime for Elin's gorgeous layered evergreen garlands that she adorned with vibrant holly berries, oranges, lemons, winter herbs, and even ornaments. But recently the trend in Portland's upscale markets had been to decorate with seasonal garlands. Lavender and rosemary garlands twisted together with twine and dotted with pink sedums in the spring. Fall garlands made from the seasons' changing leaves and layered with pinecones and acorns. And winter garlands crafted with salal, cedar, and boxwood and decorated with dried tallow berries and larkspur. Garlands could be draped above fireplace mantels, hung from stairwells, and arched around entryways, bringing a festive touch to any season.

"I'm afraid tonight's workshop will have to be postponed," Officer Iwamoto replied. "We're going to do everything we can to get you back in business for the launch party, Ms. Johnston. My mom is planning to come, by the way. But I don't know about tomorrow either."

Elin pursed her lips, but nodded. "I understand.

May I come get my class list? I'll need to call everyone to let them know."

"Of course." Iwamoto shot me a smile.

While they went to find the class list, I got to work on the corporate accounts. I knew that we had permission to officially open, but I wanted to wait until Elin had finished getting in touch with her clients and we were both ready to face the onslaught. I had a feeling that every person in Riverplace Village would find their way into the shop at some point during the day. And to be honest I wasn't sure I could face the press alone.

The first order was for a law firm four blocks away. I reviewed Elin's notes. She kept copious notes on all of her repeat customers—both personal and corporate. The law firm's file mentioned that one of the legal aides was allergic to lilies and that they preferred low arrangements for their conference room table.

I turned classical music on the overhead system and got to work. When I start on any design I let my intuition guide me. Sometimes I might be inspired by a single stem, or perhaps from an intricate lacy vase. From there I add color and texture as the arrangement begins to take on a life of its own. Some florists, in fact most florists, tend to overstuff their bouquets. I think in part because that way clients feel like they are getting the most bang for their buck, so to speak. But I like negative space in my floral designs. If too many plants and flowers are crammed into a vase, none of them have a chance to shine.

For this arrangement my eye was drawn to an antique silver bowl. Elin's assorted vases ran the gamut from traditional crystal stems to mason jars and ceramic teacups. I packed the base of the bowl with damp floral foam. Since the law firm didn't want height in their arrangements I planned to create a cascading design in the low container that would allow for easy conversation around the table.

I built from the outside, starting by dangling white strawberries from the edge of the bowl. Then I placed three pale pink roses in the center and interspersed more roses, sweet peas, and pink pansies to fill in the rest of the arrangement. When I was done I stepped back to examine my work. Usually the flowers guide me. It's as if they tell me when they know the arrangement is complete. I liked the subtle pink tones and texture. The antique silver bowl gave the arrangement a nostalgic vibe, while the white strawberries made it feel spring-like.

"Britta, that is stunning!" Elin exclaimed as she returned. She walked over to the cement worktop and studied my arrangement from every side. "See, this is why I'm so happy to have you home. How long was I gone? Ten, fifteen minutes? I can't tell you how many assistants I've trained for years who never could create something like this. I leave you alone for almost no time and you've already designed one of the most beautiful arrangements I've seen in years. You have the touch, my dear."

"Thanks." My neck felt warmed. I was sure it was probably starting to splotch with red. "Do you think it's enough? Does it need something else?"

She held her arms up in protest. "Don't even think about touching it. It's perfect. Absolutely perfect just as it is."

"If you're sure you like it?"

Her eyes narrowed. "Britta, I love it. I wouldn't let it out the door if I didn't. What are we going to do to boost your confidence? There used to be a time when you would immerse yourself in flowers and not give a second thought to what anyone else said, do you remember that?"

I looked at my feet. "Yeah, that was a long time ago."

She placed her hand around my waist. "Listen to me, the flowers know. They're alive. They're part of us. You are part of them. Don't you remember when you were a young girl? You would spend hours wandering around the park picking weeds and dandelions and tying them into tiny bouquets with long pieces of grass. You were meant to do this. You have a gift, and it's your job to share that with the world."

My eyes felt damp. "Thanks, *Moster*. I guess you're right. I've kind of lost my groove. I've got to find a way to get it back."

"You've got your groove back right there." She released me and pointed to the arrangement. "What did Chad do to you, Britta? I want my strong Scandinavian girl back."

"Me too." I sighed. "Elin, can I confess something?"

"Anything. You know there's nothing you can say to me that would ever make me love you less."

"I think I did this to me. It wasn't all Chad. I keep wondering what would have happened if I didn't catch him cheating? Would I have stayed there and been miserable forever? Why did I stay for so long?" I twisted a piece of twine around my pinkie.

A knowing smile passed over Elin's face. "I don't know, Britta, but one thing I do know is that there isn't much point in beating yourself up. You're here now and that's all that matters. Instead of wallowing in the why, what if you celebrated the now?"

"It's a good idea." I forced a smile. I appreciated her pep talk, but while her theory resonated with me I still had some tough questions to ask myself. I was excited about the now, yet if I didn't do some serious self-reflection I was worried that I would be doomed to repeat my past. That could wait, though. I wasn't likely to come to a point of understanding overnight.

"Good." Elin picked up the arrangement. "I know one easy way to get you back in the now and build your confidence. You can deliver every single bouquet, arrangement, or special order for the next few days. I want you to see the expression on customers' faces when you hand them your designs. I want you to feel the joy you're going to spread through flowers. If that doesn't get your groove back then I don't know what will." She winked.

I returned to crafting more low arrangements for the law firm and mulled over our conversation. I hoped that my aunt was right. She made it sound easy. If only delivering a few fresh bundles could change my state of mind. I did believe that flowers could brighten a mood or bring a calming visual and sensory comfort in times of trouble, but whether or not they were the answer to my personal crisis remained to be seen.

Chapter Thirteen

As Elin predicted, the paralegal I delivered the finished arrangements to gushed over the design. A tiny bit of pride welled inside as she called one of her colleagues over to admire the flowers. Maybe I did have something original to offer.

I packed up the old arrangements and returned to Blomma with a slight spring in my step. The minute I rounded the corner and saw the buzz of activity and flashing lights I was reminded of Frank's body and my feet fell heavier on the ground.

Detective Fletcher and Officer Iwamoto were examining different roses with Elin when I held the door open with one foot and stepped inside. Officer Iwamoto noticed me and came over to help with the damp box of old flower arrangements. "Wet out there, huh?"

"Just a bit." I took off my dripping raincoat and hung it by the door.

"We were going over some rose facts with your

aunt." He nodded toward the pile of blush, violet, and burgundy roses on the concrete slab.

I showed him where to put the box and then joined them at the workstation.

"Britta, I was telling Detective Fletcher that you really are much more knowledgeable than me when it comes to roses."

Detective Fletcher held a two-toned tangerine rose in his hand. The color made the subtle auburn streaks in his hair look more pronounced.

"That's not true. Everything I learned about roses I learned from you," I said to Elin.

"I think we have what we need for the moment," Detective Fletcher replied, smelling the rose. His face shifted as he inhaled the scent. I'd witnessed a similar transformation many times over when customers were perusing the shop. They would stop to smell the roses—literally—and I could almost always predict their reaction. The words might be a cliché, but the act of pausing and breathing in the scent of a flower had the power to positively impact someone's day. My instructor at the Floral Institute had shared a study that noted people who stopped to smell the roses were happier and reported being more satisfied with life. The simple act of taking a minute to appreciate a flower's sweet scent or cheerful bloom had a direct impact on health and well-being.

Maybe you should start sniffing more flowers, Britta, I told myself and then focused on the conversation.

"I'm leaving you in Officer Iwamoto's capable hands," Detective Fletcher continued, stuffing the rose back into a bucket of water. "If you need anything, here's my card." He placed a basic white business card on the slab. "I'll be back later." He gave me a curt nod and strolled out the front door.

Officer Iwamoto watched him go. "I'll get out of your way, ladies." He started toward the cottage, but Elin stopped him.

"I have a question. How long has Detective Fletcher been on the force?" Elin asked, wiping down the far end of the counter. "I know your father, of course, and a number of Portland's police officers from my work with the Rose Festival, and because so many have them have become clients over the years since the precinct is so close. I don't remember ever seeing Detective Fletcher before."

"That's because he's new." Officer Iwamoto stared in the direction of the door. "He moved up from LA."

"A Californian, I knew it!" Elin snapped her fingers together. "He has a California look about him."

I wasn't sure I agreed with her about that. Detective Fletcher's reddish hair and short beard blended in more with the Portland vibe than California in my opinion. But native Oregonians had had an ongoing debate about California transplants. It first began in the 1970s when Oregon's governor, Tom McCall, infamously gave voice to the slogan, "Come visit, but don't stay." The feud had raged ever since. Californians had raced to buy up property in Portland, which until recently had been a steal. Elin had told me the battle had heightened as the real estate market exploded. Yard signs could be found throughout the city reading, "For sale, except to anyone from California."

"Right?" Iwamoto grinned. "It shows, doesn't

it?" He pointed to his earlobe, where there was a tiny hole. "I'm not wearing it now while I'm on duty, but usually I have a stud in. You know, to make a statement."

"How?" I interjected, trimming stalks of rosemary. The earthy scent infused the room.

"It's how my generation expresses itself. Tattoos, plugs, nose rings. Anything goes. Detective Fletcher, he's by the book, as we say in the field."

I rubbed a sprig of rosemary between my hands. "Don't you need to be 'by the book' when investigating a murder?"

Iwamoto laughed. "I guess, but he's more buttoned up. We're laid back here in P-town."

Elin nodded in agreement. "It's a serious issue, Britta. I welcome Californians with open arms, but the problem is the influx of people moving north has priced so many Portlanders out of the market. It's complicated, and so far the city hasn't figured out a solution."

"She's right," Iwamoto agreed. "My parents keep joking that they want to sell and move to Alaska." He scratched his head. "I hope they're kidding. If they sell I won't have a place to live."

"You live at home?" I asked.

"Yeah, everyone my age does. I couldn't afford anything in the city on my salary."

"Really?" I couldn't believe the housing market was so tight. Good thing Elin had invited me to stay with her for as long as I needed.

Elin returned the single stems to their buckets. The racks of blooms waiting to be made into colorful masterpieces called to me. "It's reached critical mass, which is yet another reason I was fortunate to get the cottage. Commercial real estate is also in high demand."

Iwamoto headed to the cottage and I considered Elin's words. The Portland real estate market was hot. How could that tie into Frank's murder? Could he have been killed by an angry client who had been priced out of the market? It sounded far-fetched in my head, but I supposed stranger things had happened.

At that moment the door swung open and Serene, the wine distributor, burst in wheeling a cart of wine behind her. "My God, it's obnoxious out there. I thought I was going to be taken down by reporters begging me for a comment. A comment on what? What happened?" She cinched the belt around her tailored gray raincoat. Her hair was tied in a messy bun and her makeup was flawless.

"You haven't heard?" Elin said, catching my eye.

Serene wheeled the cart of wine toward us, leaving a trail of wet tire tracks behind her. When she reached the workstation she brushed rain from her coat and set the cart upright next to the counter. "Heard what? Did you have a break-in or something?" Her eyes strayed to the wall of wine.

"Worse, I'm afraid," Elin began.

"What could be worse than a break-in?" Serene asked.

Elin looked to me, and then said in a soft tone, "Murder."

"Murder?" Serene sounded repulsed. "Here?" She glanced around as if looking for evidence that a crime had occurred.

"In the cottage," Elin replied. "Britta found Frank Jaffe this morning."

Serene blinked rapidly. "Frank is dead?"

I couldn't exactly read her reaction. The rosemary leaves had left a slightly sticky but powerfully calming residue on my fingers. I brushed my hands on my jeans and then held them under my nose to breathe in the scent.

"Frank Jaffe is dead?" she repeated. Was it my imagination or was her mascara starting to streak? Maybe it was from the rain, but she brushed something from her eye.

Elin nodded.

"That's impossible." Serene twisted the belt tie on her stylish raincoat. "It's impossible. I saw him last night."

"We all did," Elin agreed. "It's a shock, isn't it?"

Serene rubbed one temple with her finger. "I can't believe it. You're sure he's dead?"

"Very sure." Elin nodded. "Would you like a cup of tea? I know that it's dreadful news."

"No, I'm fine." Serene waved her off and began unloading bottles of wine. "Do they know who did it?"

"The police are here investigating now," Elin said, taking a bottle of pinot gris from Serene.

Serene's hands slipped. She nearly dropped a bottle of merlot on the concrete floor, catching it on her hip at the last second. "Frank is really dead," she repeated almost under her breath.

I was surprised that Serene was taking the news so hard. She and Frank hadn't appeared to be particularly close last night. In fact if anything I had gotten the impression that she couldn't stand him.

"We don't need to do this now," Elin offered.

"No, it's fine," Serene replied, holding up two opened bottles of wine. "I brought a number of things for you to taste, Britta." She looked at me, placed the wine on the counter, and then pulled two more bottles from the cart. "We have to get your wine selected for the launch party."

A sip or two of wine might take the edge off this terrible day. However I was more than curious as to why Serene was so on edge. She was trying to keep her composure, but it was evident in her quaking hands and stilted responses that she was upset by Frank's murder. Was it because like me she'd never known anyone who had been killed in such a dramatic fashion, or could there be something else to her reaction?

Chapter Fourteen

Elin declined being a part of Serene's tasting so we left her at the workstation and I helped Serene carry the open bottles over to the wine bar. She stopped in midstride and whipped her head around. "Was someone back here?"

"I don't think so. Why?" For some reason I didn't want to tell Serene about Lawren. I felt protective of the young assistant.

"It looks like things have been moved," Serene replied with a frown, but she dropped it and began unloading her cart.

She was certainly at home behind the bar. She lined up six sparkling glasses and even produced two bowls of crackers and biscuits. "I like to use these with the sweet wine," she said as she positioned the biscuits next to our tasting glasses.

Then she poured a buttery white wine into the first glass. She handed me the glass and then poured a taste for herself. Holding her glass up to the base of the chandelier she said, "Isn't that a lovely color? Get your nose in there and tell me what you smell."

I followed her instructions and took a whiff of the fruity wine.

"You should be good at this," Serene commented, watching me. "Your aunt says that you're a flower expert. Flowers and wine have so many commonalities."

"This one almost has floral notes to me," I said, taking one more inhale. "I'm getting peaches and apricots."

"Exactly." Serene untied the belt on her raincoat, removed the coat, and stored it under the distressed wood bar. "Now taste it and see if you pick up anything else."

I took a leisurely sip of the aromatic wine. It was sweeter than I expected. I tasted hints of peach and even pear. Serene closed her eyes and swished a bit of wine like mouthwash. "It's good, isn't it?" She opened her eyes. "I definitely taste the peach, as well as butter and brown sugar."

Passing me the bowl of biscuits, she said, "Now eat one of these and taste it again."

I crunched the dry cookie and then took another sip. The cookie had altered the flavor of the wine. It didn't taste quite as sweet this time.

"Well?" Serene waited for my response.

"I like it better after the biscuit. It toned down the sugar and almost gives it a new crispness, like underripe fruit."

"You are good." Serene tapped her fake nails on the bar. "Should we move on?"

"Sure." The sip of wine had warmed my throat.

While Serene poured tastes from the second bottle, a dry Riesling, I decided to see if I could prod a little on the subject of Frank. "You sure know your way around here. How long have you and my aunt been working together?"

"Oh, let me think, at least six years, but maybe even seven by now." She handed me the next glass. "As I'm sure you've already figured out, everyone in Riverplace Village adores your aunt."

"I got that impression." I took the glass and repeated Serene's tasting instructions. "Except for Frank."

At the mention of Frank's name Serene spilled a splash of wine on the bar. She looked flustered for a moment, but dabbed the wine with a paper cocktail napkin. "Why do you say that?" she asked, holding the wine bottle steady with both hands as she poured.

"The meeting last night. Frank was pretty aggressive."

Serene didn't meet my eye. She studied the Riesling in the light. "That was Frank. He was like that with everyone."

"Did you know him well?"

"Me?" She stuck her nose in the glass and then shook her head. "I guess I knew him as well as anyone. He had me do a few special orders and private tasting parties for his high rollers."

"That must have been a lucrative account." I tasted the Riesling, picking up backgrounds of fresh-cut grass and green apples.

"Not really." She clutched the stem of her wineglass as she spoke. "Frank was notoriously cheap. He liked to put on a big show to impress his clients, but he would make me funnel less expensive bottles of wine into expensive bottles. He didn't pay for anything."

I could hear the bitterness in her tone. "Did he do that because he was cheap or do you think that he was in some kind of financial trouble?"

"Where did you hear that?" Her voice was sharp. She dabbed the corner of her eyelid with her pinky. It looked as if she was trying to readjust one of her fake lashes.

"I'm not sure," I lied. "The police have been floating a bunch of theories around this morning. I know that they mentioned they would be reviewing his business account."

She knocked back her Riesling and set her glass on the bar with such force that I thought it might shatter. "If Frank was broke I know who is to blame for that."

I finished my wine and waited for her to pour the next. "Who?"

"His nephew—Kirk. Kirk blew through cash. He was constantly spending money. Frank liked to look like he was spending money, but Kirk actually did spend money."

The next wine was a pink rosé. It even smelled slightly like roses. "Really? What did Kirk spend money on?"

She shrugged. "Who knows? Everything. Wine, women."

I puzzled this over as I drank in the rosé. If Serene was correct and Frank had been cheap and Kirk was a spender, how did that play into his murder? The piece of Frank being frugal matched what I had learned at the Riverplace Inn. That could be why Frank hung around the hotel, munching off of Mark's complimentary European breakfasts and afternoon happy hour, but what did that mean in terms of Kirk? Could Kirk have killed his uncle because Frank had cut off his spending?

Serene and I finished our tasting session. She stocked the wine bar with the other bottles she'd brought. I still wasn't convinced that she'd been entirely honest with me. Her reaction to Frank's death was surprising. But the more I learned about Kirk Jaffe the more convinced I was becoming that he must be the killer.

Chapter Fifteen

It was midafternoon by the time Detective Fletcher returned. Serene was on her way out when he arrived. She rolled her wine cart toward the front door, and called good-bye to Elin and me.

"I'll be by tomorrow," she said with a wave. "Unless I get a case of that Walla Walla blend in early. If it arrives I'll swing by tonight and stock the bar."

Detective Fletcher had been holding the door open for her. He frowned and held up his index finger. "I'm sorry, Ma'am, and who are you?"

"Serene," she replied with a subtle bat of her lashes. Was she flirting with him? Nora had had the same reaction to the detective. Sure, I had to admit that he was handsome, but flirting with a stranger wasn't my style, especially the lead detective in a murder investigation.

He closed the door and stepped inside. Serene looked put out. "I'm going to need more than that," he said removing his badge and flashing it at her. "Especially because it appears that you work here."

Serene shook her head. "I don't work here. I just supply Elin with wine and sometime I use the space to host private tasting parties."

"Which means that I assume you have a key or some other way to access the property during non-business hours?"

"Yeah." Serene looked to Elin and threw her hands up in disgust. "I'm not sure I understand your point, Detective."

"I'm sure that you are aware there has been a murder here and I'm going to need you to come with me and answer a few questions." He motioned to the cottage with his thumb.

Serene stood her ground and protested. "Right now? I have other deliveries to make."

Detective Fletcher didn't even blink. "Right now." His brow furrowed, making his scar more pronounced.

Serene's heels clicked on the concrete as she trailed after him. Her ever-changing demeanor bothered me. When I first met her she came across as polished and a consummate professional, perhaps even a tiny bit snobbish. Today she seemed on edge and bitter. Maybe it was simply her way of responding to stress, but it left me feeling unsettled. The other thing bothering me was how many people had access to Blomma.

At the workstation Elin stood back and appraised a bouquet of morning glories and purple fuchsias. "Does it need something more?" she asked as she took the flowers out of a vase and placed them into a mason jar filled with clear pebbles.

I studied the wall of blooms. The arrangement was lovely but needed some height to add a touch of drama. "How about these?" I reached for a bundle of grapevine and offered it to her. "Hey, can I ask you something?"

"Yes. That is it!" She placed three of the earthy branches into the mix. "Ask away."

"How many people have keys to Blomma?"

"What do you mean?" She looked thoughtful.

"Hearing Detective Fletcher ask Serene about having a key got me wondering how many other people might have keys."

Elin set the rest of the grapevines on the counter. "Hmm. Let me think. Nora of course. Serene. I believe Mark has a key. Come to think of it, most of my fellow shop owners have a key. We've all swapped them over the years."

She had said something about that earlier but I hadn't realized how important that could be. Nora, Mark, and Serene each had keys to Blomma, which meant that in theory any of them could have let themselves in, killed Frank, and slipped out unnoticed.

"What about the Jaffes? You said that Frank didn't have a key, but what about Kirk?"

"No." Elin scrunched her face. "Never."

I had suspected that was what she would say, but found myself disappointed by the news. Kirk Jaffe was my number one suspect, but he was also the only person who didn't have a way in to Blomma. However I reasoned that he could have easily swiped someone else's key. It sounded like common knowledge that the business owners in Riverplace Village had granted each other access to their individual properties.

"Too bad it isn't that simple." Elin finished adding the reedy grapevines. They gave the bouquet height and a woodsy texture which contrasted beautifully with the dainty fuchsias and delicate morning glories.

What if it was? I mused internally. Everything I had learned thus far pointed to Kirk. The rest of Elin's colleagues all seemed genuinely supportive of one another. I couldn't picture any of them killing Frank. Then again, maybe one of them was lying or putting on an act.

I tried to concentrate on designs. I had to find a way to get out of my head, and flowers were the only solution. There was still plenty of work to be done before the launch party, so I threw myself into making wrist corsages out of pink champagne rosebuds and hops. Concentrating on creating something beautiful helped, but as the morning wore on I became more and more distracted. Elin decided against opening the shop. "Do you think it's even worth it, Britta?" she asked when Detective Fletcher showed Serene to the door. "I don't think I'm up for it. Not today."

"Me neither," I agreed. "Why don't we finish these orders and call it a day?"

"I like that plan."

We worked in relative silence, snipping stems and tying raffia ribbons. Within an hour we had twelve arrangements boxed and ready for delivery.

"I'll check in with the police," Elin said as she placed the last bouquet in a cardboard box. "We can drop these on our way home. I don't know about you but I could go for a hot bowl of soup and a bath."

"That sounds divine." I swept a handful of discarded flower debris into a recycling bin. "I'll finish cleaning up."

Elin returned less than five minutes later. "They said they would be here a few more hours. We're free to go. Detective Fletcher will give us an update in the morning."

We loaded the flower boxes and turned off the lights. Despite Blomma's inviting spaces and evergreen floral displays the space felt different. Had it only been this morning that our floral oasis had been turned upside down? I thought about finding Frank's body, the dead black roses, the mysterious note, and the cottage that Elin had worked so hard on designing being left in complete disarray. Everything felt out of balance. I hoped the feeling was temporary. Today had been awful. Tomorrow we could start fresh.

Chapter Sixteen

The drizzle continued the next morning, although the rain had let up a bit. Elin and I shared a leisurely breakfast of Swedish pancakes smothered with homemade lingonberries and a pot of dark coffee. Elin always joked that she drank her coffee as black as a Scandinavian winter sky. I sensed that we both shared the same feeling of trepidation about returning to Blomma.

"Would you like another cup, Britta?" Elin asked holding up the empty coffeepot. "I can make us another."

"No, I shouldn't. I'll be shaky all day," I teased, wiggling my fingers. "I'd forgotten how much coffee Portlanders consume. It might be hard to trim roses with the caffeine shakes."

Elin smiled, placed the coffeepot in the sink, and then wrapped a creamy blue and red blanket scarf around her shoulders. She was a striking woman with her pale hair, tall and thin stature, and intelligent eyes the color of cornflowers. "I suppose that means we have to face the music, doesn't it?"

I got up to help her clear the breakfast dishes. "Well, we could hide out here for the day, drinking copious amounts of coffee, but I don't know about you, I think just sitting around worrying about Frank's murder would be worse."

She rinsed the plate that I handed her and put it in the dishwasher. "Yes, you are so right. I wish you weren't, but you are."

With the dishes cleared and loaded she squared her shoulders and looked at me. "Ready?"

"Let's go spread some joy."

"Yes." We looped arms and headed for the Jeep. I had dressed in layers again, opting for a pair of well-worn jeans, a red long-sleeved T-shirt, red and black plaid vest, and my rubber boots. Not having to bundle up in my faux fur parka or have a biting wind and blowing snow hit my face every time I stepped outside was a welcome change. The drippy sky didn't even bother me. Neither had missing Chad. That had to say something, didn't it? I was still angry with him for betraying me, but other than questioning why I had stayed when I'd been unhappy for so long, I didn't miss anything about my old life in Minnesota. In fact I couldn't wait for Chad to sign the divorce papers. I was ready to put him and my past behind me and fully embrace Portland.

The damp evergreens and muddy, swollen waters of the Willamette River might have appeared dismal and gloomy to some people, but to me there had never been a more welcoming sight. This was the only home I'd ever known. The only place where I felt free to be me. I reflected on my choices—determined not to repeat the same mistakes—as Elin navigated through Portland's one-way streets. Bike commuters whizzed by in the shared lanes, which were painted green to alert drivers of two-wheeled traffic. Royal red banners announcing the Rose Festival hung from light posts along Front Street.

Everywhere I looked there were cranes and massive construction projects in the works. Sleek modern buildings made entirely of glass and eco-friendly high-rises manufactured with recycled wood were sprouting up along the waterfront. Known as the bridge city, Portland had recently christened its newest bridge, the Tilikum Crossing. The bridge connected the east and west with tracks for light rail, bike lanes, and pedestrians. Its brilliant white pentagon-shaped suspension cables lit up with rotating colors at night based on the flow and temperature of the Willamette River below.

When we turned into Riverplace Village I felt an immediate sense of relief. The police cars and media vans were gone. Yesterday's crowd had dispersed and Blomma sat in a peaceful early morning slumber. Nor was there any sign of the creepy van that had spooked me. I wondered if Detective Fletcher and Officer Iwamoto had finished their investigation in the cottage last night. Maybe today really could be back to business as usual.

"It looks like the novelty of a murder must have worn off," Elin commented as she pulled into an angled parking space reserved for her Jeep. "That's a relief."

"I was thinking the same thing." I unloaded stacks of empty delivery boxes from the Jeep. Elin was a

conservationist. She, like the vast majority of Portlanders, believed in recycling and composting. It
was an important part of working in the flower industry. She had seen firsthand how fragile plant
and flower ecosystems were, and how easy it was to
throw things out of balance. For example declining honeybee populations had had a direct impact
on the wholesale flower market. Flowers aren't
simply beautiful, they are an integral part of the
ecosystem, attracting birds and insects that polli-
nate the flower itself, releasing seeds, and even
providing shelter.

Elin supported small growers and family farms,
and was fanatical when it came to recycling and
reusing whatever she could in the shop. Like the
delivery boxes. Many florists left the boxes they
used to transport flowers with the arrangement,
but not Elin. She reused the boxes until they fell
apart or disintegrated. Many of her clients knew
this about her and would leave their used vases on
Blomma's front doorstep or bring her old spools
of yarn or used garden art. Thanks to her eye for
design and artistic talent she would find a use for
everything her customers left for her. Portland
had become known for its green policies in recent
years, but Elin had been silently leading her own
movement of protecting the city's natural resources
for decades.

She went in first. I stopped to pick up an empty
turquoise vase, assuming it had been left by one of
her clients. When I peered inside the vase I nearly
dropped it. Another black rosebud was tucked inside. There had to be a connection with Frank's murder. And I knew there was something Elin wasn't

telling me. Someone had to be stalking Blomma. Why did she keep blowing me off?

I decided that I was going straight to the police with this one, and shoved the dead bud into my vest pocket before following her inside.

Elin turned on the overhead lights and went around the room plugging in strands of twinkle lights. Then she immediately filled her spray bottles and began spritzing the plants and flowers. I stored the boxes under the workstation and reviewed the day's orders. In addition to fulfilling a few corporate orders there were two birthday bouquets, an anniversary, and a baby shower delivery. There were also two consultation sessions scheduled. One with a bride and another with an event planner. "Are you going to do custom mini-arrangements for today's meetings?" I asked.

She squirted a potted fern. "Oh, right. I almost forgot about potential client meetings today. Yes, I'll do those if you want to tackle the corporate accounts."

"Sounds like a plan to me." I noticed that police caution tape had been stretched over the cottage door. I guessed that was Detective Fletcher's way of telling us they weren't finished with their investigation.

Elin flipped the chalkboard sign on the front door from CLOSED to OPEN. The open side had the word *Blomma* written in a pink and green flowery script with bunches of open tulips. The closed sign was the same, only the tulip blooms were closed. Then she rolled open the garage doors, allowing fresh air and the early morning chill to roll in.

She erased the chalk sandwich-board sign and

looked thoughtful for a moment. "Yes, this is the one," she said, reaching for a piece of chalk and writing on the board. When she had finished she turned it to face me. The quote read: *"The Earth Laughs in Flowers" ~Ralph Waldo Emerson.*

"It's perfect, but how do you keep so many quotes in your head?" I asked placing the new pair of shears Elin had given me on the workstation.

She smiled and shrugged. Then she placed the board on the cobblestone sidewalk and brushed her hands on her jeans. "Are you ready for this?" she asked, coming back inside and turning on classical music and warming a kettle of tea. "I have a feeling we are going to be in high demand today, and I do mean *we*, not our flowers."

"Yeah." I searched through her collection of containers before deciding on five cobalt blue glass vases for the corporate order. It was for a bank on 5th Street and Broadway. The note mentioned that their colors were silver and blue. I thought I could use pale blue hydrangeas as my starting point and accent the arrangement with *Convolvulus cneorum*, also known as silverbush, a small evergreen shrub with silvery leaves and white trumpet flowers.

The door burst open as I started filling vases with warm water and "love juice." Nora led a parade of business owners in who pounced on Elin for details. "The cavalry has arrived," Nora announced, balancing a tray of Demitasse coffees and shortbread. *"Fika!"*

I kept my head down and focused on my design while Elin filled everyone in on yesterday's developments. The thought of more coffee made my stomach gurgle in an angry warning. And these were Elin's friends. I was still getting a lay of the land and the shop. I didn't need to be part of the gossip. I was so intent on my project that I didn't even notice that Kirk Jaffe had slipped in. He startled me by slapping a fifty on the workstation and saying, "Hey, Snow White, I want to place an order."

"Excuse me?" I looked up from my pile of blue and silver petals to see Kirk staring at me like an ogre. His slick hair was matted on his head and the way his eyes traveled up and down my body made me want to take a shower.

"Remember me, Snow? I need some flowers for a special lady. Can you help a guy out?" His pudgy fingers had two matching class rings made of gold and adorned with red and orange stones. He didn't strike me as particularly athletic, more like bulky. But the rings made me wonder if he had played football in high school. Defensive end, probably.

"Yes, I remember you, Kirk, and like I told you before, my name is Britta, not Snow." I folded my arms across my chest in my own line of defense.

He gave me a cheesy wink. "Right, but you're Snow to me. You're like a beautiful queen."

Was this guy for real? Who talked like that? I'd never been called Snow White before and I wasn't about to let someone as sleazy as Kirk Jaffe stick a nickname on me.

"Who are the flowers for?" I asked, reaching for an order form and a pencil.

"A special lady friend, although, if you want they could be for you."

I tried not to roll my eyes, but he was too much. "You want me to make flowers for myself?"

"That would be a fun story to tell the kiddies one day, huh?"

I couldn't decide if I wanted to vomit or walk around to the front of the concrete slab and give him a swift kick in the shins. "As tempting as that sounds, I'll pass." I tapped the pencil on the order form.

He shrugged. "Fine, just give me fifty bucks of your best stuff." He pushed the bill toward me.

"We don't really work like that here. It would be helpful to understand a bit more about your intentions. Are you wanting to send romantic flowers, an apology? Does the recipient have a favorite color, favorite scent? Any allergies?"

"Geez, I'm not marrying the flowers. Can't you just stick fifty bucks' worth of roses in a vase and call it good?" He kept glancing to the front of the shop where Elin and her friends were chatting.

"If that's what you want." I didn't even try to mask the irritation in my voice.

"Yeah. I don't care what they look like," he snarled and hit the fifty with his knuckles. "Just give me some flowers already."

What a romantic sentiment. I wondered who the unlucky lady was.

He paid no attention as I began to gather flowers from their buckets on the wall. His gaze was focused on Elin. "Hey, what's going on up there? Are they having a Riverfront Village meeting or something?"

"I don't know." I bundled a pale purple, yellow,

and white rose together. "How about something with this color combination?"

Kirk didn't even bother to turn around. "Sure, sure, that's fine. I didn't hear that there was going to be a meeting this morning. Someone should have told me."

"Why?" I gathered a dozen roses and began removing their thorns.

"Because I'm in charge now. I should have been invited." He glared in Elin's direction.

The sweet scent of the roses helped to keep me calm. "In charge? I don't understand. How would you be in charge? You don't own any property here in the village, do you?" I asked, snipping a thorn from the stem.

A gleeful look crossed his face but he didn't answer the question. He just shrugged.

I wasn't sure if it was residual anger over what had happened with Chad, pent-up frustration, or the fact that Kirk was nauseating, but I decided to push him. "I'm surprised to hear you say that you're in charge, because I've heard a lot of people saying that your uncle was broke. In fact I heard that he was about to declare bankruptcy." The latter part was an exaggeration, but Kirk didn't need to know that.

His smug smile evaporated. He leaned across the countertop. "Where did you hear that?" he said in a seething tone.

I kept my composure by concentrating on snipping each thorn. Plus I figured my shears could act as protection in case things turned ugly. "Everyone's saying that."

"Everyone?" He whipped his head around and stared at the group chatting in hushed tones in the front. "Are you serious right now? Are you being straight with me?"

I plunged a yellow rose into a simple glass vase. "Yeah, why would I lie?"

He pounded his fist on the counter. "Seriously everyone knew that my uncle Frank was broke? How can that be? He swore that no one knew."

My stomach flopped, but this time not because of Kirk's unwanted advances. I couldn't believe my lie had worked. Had Kirk just admitted that Frank was broke? If Frank Jaffe had been about to declare bankruptcy what could that mean in connection with his murder? I wasn't sure, but I knew that I had to tell Detective Fletcher.

Chapter Seventeen

I couldn't believe that Kirk Jaffe had let something so important slip. Placing a lemon-colored rose in the vase, I asked, "Wait, so your uncle was having financial trouble?"

Kirk shot a look at the Riverplace Village crew and then back to me. "Yeah, but no one was supposed to know. He was worried it would threaten his deal if it got out. He needed this deal."

Tucking more roses into the vase I tried to quickly think through the ramifications of Frank's money troubles. Did this make Kirk less likely to have killed his uncle? Or more? He must have wanted—needed—the Riverplace Village deal to go through, too. Unless he wanted the deal to himself. Or maybe he stood to inherit a large sum from Frank's life insurance? What if the only way out of bankruptcy was to murder his uncle?

You have to stop, Britta, I told myself, pinching

the top of my thigh and trying to stay in the moment.

"I still don't understand," I said to Kirk. "How could the deal go through if Frank didn't have the cash to buy out everyone? His offer was for millions of dollars. Where was he going to get the money to pay for his vision of the waterfront redevelopment?"

Kirk's eyes lingered on the vase, which was now brimming with roses. Their pastel hues reminded me of a collection of Easter eggs. "That's really good. You put that together fast."

"Thanks." I would take that as high praise from someone so detached from artistic endeavors like Kirk.

He shocked me by leaning down and smelling the flowers. His jaw slackened slightly and he gave me a semi-impressed nod of acknowledgment. "Those actually smell good, too."

"We pride ourselves on having the freshest and most fragrant flowers at Blomma." I finished the roses by wrapping alternating ribbons of matching purple, yellow, and white around the base until it was completely encased in satin.

"Like I said," Kirk continued, watching me work. "The deal was solid. Cash wasn't going to be a problem. We have a silent partner." He picked up one of the discarded rose stems and stabbed one of its thorns into the palm of his hand repeatedly.

A silent partner with extremely deep pockets, I thought to myself.

Kirk seconded my thought. "Sure, Uncle Frank

136   *Kate Dyer-Seeley*

hit a rocky patch when the housing market tanked. He had a few bad investments, but that's real estate. This deal was going to put him on the map. It was worth it for him to partner up. Normally that wasn't his style. But this development project stood to make him and his partner crazy rich. The long-term revenue from rent was insane. We're talking millions upon millions. I mean think about it. Imagine a ten-story multiuse complex here." He motioned to the ceiling with the rose stem. "Retail clients on the ground floor and condos the rest of the way up. That's a lot of rent money."

I didn't want to think about Blomma being torn down in favor of a ten-story high-rise, but Kirk had a point about the proposed development's revenue potential.

"Where do things stand now?" I asked, pushing the roses to his side of the tabletop. For a bouquet that started with Kirk's "I don't care what it looks like" attitude, I was pleased with the final product, and hoped whoever his mysterious woman was would be too.

He tossed the stem and picked up the vase. "Nothing's changed. I'm going to continue my uncle's legacy, but I'm not going to be secretive about it. This deal is happening and I know it because I talked to Frank's silent partner yesterday and he's still fully invested in making this go."

"Is the silent partner anyone I know?" I'm not sure what made me ask the question, but I had the sense from Kirk's cocky attitude that it was someone connected to Riverplace Village.

"Yep." He smirked. "Everyone around knows him

and now they're going to understand why I'm confident that we'll be bulldozing the village soon."

I wanted to snatch the roses out of his hand.

"Don't worry," he continued in a demeaning tone. "In addition to a very lucrative purchase price every small business here on the waterfront will have first right of refusal on the ground floor retail space."

Never. I couldn't imagine Blomma confined to a boxy, soulless high-rise.

"Who is the partner?" I asked again.

Kirk grinned like a creepy clown and nodded toward the front. His eyes landed on Mark.

"Mark?" I asked.

"Mark."

"Wait, Mark from the Riverplace Inn?" I repeated. No way. Why would Mark want to sell and why would he be willing to front that kind of cash?

"That Mark." Kirk shifted the vase.

At that moment Detective Fletcher and Officer Iwamoto arrived. Kirk looked cagey and patted his fifty that was resting on the concrete. "We're good, right? I have to jet." He headed for the door, but then turned, blew me a kiss, and yelled for everyone to hear, "Catch you later, Snow."

Detective Fletcher nodded at Officer Iwamoto, who followed after Kirk. He greeted the Riverplace Village owners and then strolled toward me. His lanky, casual stride somehow managed to exude confidence with each step. Today he wore a pair of black slacks and a white button-down shirt. I found myself straightening my shoulders and adjusting my hair as he approached.

"Morning, Ms. Johnston." He gave me a short nod.

"Good morning." My heart pulsed in my chest. I hoped it was a natural reaction—a reminder of yesterday's tragedy—but Detective Fletcher's gold-flecked brown eyes made me feel slightly unsettled.

"Snow?" He raised one eyebrow and stared at me.

"Don't ask. For some reason Kirk has decided that I look like Snow White and has taken it upon himself to nickname me Snow."

Running his fingers over the stubble on his cheek Detective Fletcher considered this for a second. Having him study my face the way he examined a crime scene made me even more nervous. I jammed my hands into my vest pockets and felt the dead bud. Could Kirk be the one leaving rotting roses?

"Actually, that fits." His smile stretched to his eyes, which practically sparkled under the chandelier. Was he flirting with me, or did he really agree with Kirk? I wasn't sure that being compared with a fairy-tale character was a compliment.

"Thanks." I rolled my eyes.

"No. I'm serious. You have an airy quality about you."

"What's that supposed to mean?"

He unbuttoned the top button on his white dress shirt and rolled up his sleeves. For a minute I thought he was going to dive in and help with my flower arrangements. But instead he sounded flustered. "I didn't mean that as an insult. The opposite, in fact. You're not like most people I have to interview at crime scenes. You're very astute and yet it's evident in everything you do that you're an artist. Even in the way you move."

I wasn't sure how I felt having him dissect my personality. Suddenly I was very self-conscious. I took my hands out of the vest pocket and began snipping already trimmed hydrangeas. "How do I move?"

"I hate to say it because I can tell that you don't find the comparison with Snow White flattering, but you move with grace and intention. Even in the way you're cutting the flowers right now. Most people would grab the stem and snip it off. But you're almost cradling the flower and cutting it like a conductor directing a symphony."

Was I doing that? I stared at my hand. I didn't think there was anything particularly unique about the way I was cutting the stem, and I wanted to change the subject before my neck turned as red as my plaid vest. "Have you already interviewed Kirk?" I removed the dead bud from my pocket and handed it to him. "Someone keeps leaving dead flowers at the shop. There has to be a connection with Frank's death. Don't you think? What if it's Kirk?"

Whatever moment we had just shared evaporated. Detective Fletcher's attitude shifted. He turned to the door and then stared at the black bud in his hand. "We've spoken with Mr. Jaffe, but I'll follow up again."

"He just told me a few things that could be connected to Frank's death." I piled the tips of stems into a little ball in the middle of the countertop.

"Were you planning to elaborate?" He folded his arms across the front of his chest. I noticed that he had a small—maybe a quarter of an inch—tattoo on his left forearm. He caught me staring at it and pulled his sleeve down. "Ms. Johnston, do you have any other information pertaining to my investigation?"

Why didn't he want me to see the tattoo? He was a hard man to read. One minute he came across as friendly, almost flirtatious, the next he was stern and nothing but business.

"Yeah." I stopped snipping the flowers. "He told me that Frank was having financial trouble and had taken on a silent partner who was planning on funding the waterfront development with him."

He didn't respond, which I took as my cue to continue. I repeated everything that I had learned from Kirk about Frank's money issues. Then I explained that Mark was his secret backer, and I even filled him in on my suspicions of Kirk. When I finished he simply nodded and said, "Thanks."

The Riverplace Village business owners began to disperse. Mark and Nora left together. Elin gathered empty coffee cups and paper plates and joined us at the workstation.

She tossed the plates in the garbage and tied her blue and red shawl tighter around her shoulders. "Any news on the investigation, Detective?" she asked.

He shook his head. "Nothing I'm at liberty to share. Although I am here on a formal request. I need you both to head up to the station and get fingerprinted."

"Today?" The creases around Elin's eyes deepened.

"Actually now." Detective Fletcher tapped on his

watch. "We have a few more things to finish in the cottage this morning. I was under the impression that Officer Iwamoto had already gotten your prints, but it seems we had a misunderstanding, so I need you both to get printed as soon as possible."

"Can we take turns so we can keep the shop open?" Elin glanced at me. I could tell that she was as confused as I was about why we were being asked to get fingerprinted.

I decided that I might as well voice the question. I hadn't held anything back from Detective Fletcher yet and I didn't see any reason why to start now. "Is there a reason you need our fingerprints?"

"Standard procedure." He reached into his breast pocket and pulled out a white business card that looked exactly the same as the one he had left with us last night. "Here's the address and when you get up there tell them that I sent you in. They'll know what to do from there."

Elin held the card as if it might explode. "I'll go first if you're okay holding the fort, Britta."

"Of course," I said biting my pinky, an old nervous habit that I've never been able to shake. "Go ahead. I'll take care of everything here."

She picked a half dozen sunflowers from one of the buckets and tied them loosely with twine.

Detective Fletcher tapped his watch and gave her an expectant stare.

"If I have to go to the precinct I might as well bring something cheerful for our men and women in blue." She wrapped the sunny flowers in brown parchment. "I'll be back as soon as I can."

As she left Detective Fletcher removed the caution tape from the barn doors. "When your aunt returns be sure to go get your prints taken too, Ms. Johnston."

"I will, but can I ask you a favor?"

Rolling up the yellow tape into a ball, he waited. "Yes?"

"Can we drop the Ms. Johnston thing? Can you call me Britta?"

The corners of his lips tugged up. "Are you sure you don't want me to call you Snow?"

I furrowed my brow and scowled.

"All right, all right." Detective Fletcher tossed the used tape into the waste basket. "I'll call you Britta if you call me Pete." This time he actually smiled before he opened the door and disappeared into the cottage.

Was I imagining things or was there a little flirtation going on between us? He was so different from Chad. Chad was brooding and moody. He believed that to create true art one had to endure pain and suffering. I'd always believed the opposite, that art should feel unbound and free. Chad was serious and self-absorbed. I could tell that beneath Detective Fletcher's competent demeanor he had a playful side. What I couldn't tell was whether or not he was enjoying our friendly banter. Either way I was glad to drop the formality. Every time Detective Fletcher—Pete—addressed me as Ms. Johnston I felt like I was back in school.

I put the finishing touches on the bank arrangements. They had come together nicely. The blue and silver blooms gave off a lovely luminosity. When Elin returned I could drop them off on my way to get fingerprinted. As I wrapped sheer silver organza ribbons around each vase I kept replaying my conversation with Kirk. I'd been convinced that he had to be the killer, but his revelation that Mark was funding the development project planted more than a seed of doubt in my mind. What was Mark's motivation for joining forces with Frank? And could something have gone wrong in the partnership? So wrong that Mark could have decided to silence his boastful and brash business partner for good?

Chapter Eighteen

The rest of the day breezed by, between the steady stream of customers and private floral consultations. As late afternoon approached, customers streamed in and lingered over glasses of sparkling wine and gossip at the bar. I barely had a minute to breathe, let alone simmer on Frank's murder. Fingerprinting had been easy and painless, and our clients at the bank were as pleased with my designs as the law firm had been.

Sometime after four Officer Iwamoto gave us the all clear. "We're finished," he announced as I rang up a walk-in sale. Handing the customer a pretty vase of tulips and Stargazer lilies, I gave her instructions on caring for the flowers at home and turned my attention to Officer Iwamoto. "That's great," I replied, brushing pollen on my jeans. Lilies are exotic and intoxicatingly fragrant, but their pollen is notorious for staining hands and clothes.

"Does that mean we can resume our workshops tomorrow and that the launch party is a go?"

"I don't see why not." He glanced behind him. "Fletcher tells me I can call you Britta, although word on the street is that you prefer Snow."

"Where did you hear that? From Pete?" I pursed my lips together.

"No, from Kirk. He went on and on about how gorgeous you are—just like Snow White. Told me that you had to be her based on your outfit."

I looked down at my faded jeans spotted with yellow pollen, boots, and plaid vest. "This?" I waved one hand over my outfit. "This is about as far away from princess as it gets."

He grinned and elbowed me playfully in the waist. "Right, but according to Kirk you're dressed like the huntsman. He's convinced that it's a secret sign."

"That guy is crazy."

"I know, but don't you think we should play along? It would be pretty funny to go all in." He tapped the badge on his uniform. "You know they film *Grimm* here in Portland. I could be an Asian American police officer by day and a ninja warrior by night. It would be kind of fitting to have a real Snow White walking around in our midst. Imagine our dynamic duo."

"No thanks."

"Think about it." He winked. "Oh and hey, since you're on a first-name basis with Detective Fletcher now, you can call me Tomo."

"Tomo, that's a great name. Does it mean anything?"

"It means twin. My parents chose it to represent my twin cultures—Japanese and American. And honestly because I think they thought it would be a lot easier for my friends to say. My American name is Thomas, so it's not really a stretch to shorten it to Tomo."

"That's beautiful."

"What about you? Do you know the origin of Britta?"

"Yes, in Swedish Britta means strength or strong."

"That fits."

I wish, I thought, but smiled at Tomo. "What happens with the investigation now?"

"Now we sort through the evidence and interviews, review our list of suspects, and wait for lab results, fingerprints, and the coroner's report. Fletcher is old school. You should see the whiteboard that he commandeered in one of the conference rooms. It's plastered with photos and notes."

"Do you have any theories on who killed Frank and why?"

"A bunch, but we have to compile evidence and find tangible proof to back them up. This is when the real fun begins." He winked. "We'll keep you posted."

By the time the police cleared out it was time to lock up for the evening. Elin filled me in on her consultations. Not surprisingly she had landed both the wedding and the corporate party. The wedding would take place in late July at a winery that was housed in a converted barn. The bride wanted rustic arrangements and little bouquets in mason jars for each guest. The corporate party was for a local chocolatier. They wanted chocolate-themed flowers in dark browns and tans. My mind immediately began to dream up visions of chocolate sunflowers, burgundy dahlias, amber orchids, and bronze spider mums. The thought of chocolate flowers made my mouth water. Fortunately the client intended to bring us samples of their ornate truffles to weave into the designs. Perhaps Elin and I could have a tasting party for inspiration.

I went over the completed order forms with Elin. "Hey, it's been so busy that I never had a chance to tell you about my conversation with Kirk."

"Yes?" She thumbed through the stack of papers. "He's something, isn't he?"

"You can say that again." I rolled my eyes. "He's definitely not someone I'm interested in getting to know more, but he said that Mark was planning to invest in Jaffe and Associates' development plan."

Elin rested the papers on the countertop. "Mark? What?"

"I know. Doesn't that seem odd? What would Mark's motivation be?"

Her face clouded. "Mark?"

I shrugged. "According to Kirk, but who knows if he's a reliable source."

Elin considered my words and then returned to reviewing the paperwork. I wondered if I had made a mistake in telling her. I wasn't sure if it was sadness or disbelief but hearing that Mark could have been in partnership with Frank Jaffe had upset her. I dropped the subject and we concentrated on mapping out a plan for the rest of the week. Now that her workshops could resume, I would be spending the bulk of the day managing the front of the shop. Elin would help between classes and workshops, and could cover if I needed to run a delivery somewhere in the village.

We were about to decide whether to tackle the cottage tonight or save it for the morning when Nora rapped on the front door. "Hey, girls. I come bearing dinner." She held up a bag from La Comida, the Mexican restaurant down the street. "It's tamale Tuesday and I figured you might be famished after the craziness of . . ." she trailed off.

"You are a dear," Elin said welcoming her and the savory-smelling tamales in. "Britta, do you want to open a bottle of wine?"

"Sure." I walked to the wine wall and scanned it for something Spanish. My eyes landed on a bottle of Tempranillo with a gorgeous label of white and pink roses.

"Britta and I were just discussing whether we should start putting the cottage back in order, and I was about to say let's skip it and go get dinner, but now you've solved that problem," Elin said to Nora.

"I knew you couldn't pass up La Comida's tamales. I brought the works. Chips and guacamole, their famous chile verde salsa, and chicken and beef tamales." She reached into her black leather jacket and pulled out her cell phone. "I've got some jamming tunes and two hands to help. Let's eat and then you can put me to work."

"Nora, you are a godsend." Elin's voice cracked.

"Don't get all mushy on me, Elin." Nora brushed her off. "You'd do the same for me and everyone else in the village."

I uncorked the earthy bottle of wine and followed them into the cottage with three glasses. The space wasn't as bad as I had imagined it might be. Stinky fingerprint dust coated the worktop, desk, and some of the antique furniture. The chalk outline on the floor had been partially scrubbed. The evidence markers had been removed and the beheaded Deep Secret roses had been swept into a pile in the far corner of the room.

"It's not terrible, is it?" Elin commented, trying to brush away fingerprinting dust to make room for Nora's tamale feast.

Nora knew her way around the cottage. She walked to the desk and plugged her phone into a speaker. "What are you in the mood for? How about some Pink Floyd?" She didn't wait for an answer. Instead she clicked on a song and turned up the volume.

Pink Floyd's "Comfortably Numb" began to play overhead. The lyrics matched my mood. I felt comfortably numb. Being at Blomma was the most comfortable I'd been in years, and yet Frank's murder cast a numbing shadow over everything.

Nora returned to the workstation and removed steaming tamales and homemade chips from the brown paper bag. She scooped guacamole and green salsa into each to-go container and topped them off with handfuls of the deep-fried chips. My mouth salivated in response to the spicy scent of Nora's Mexican feast. The food smelled amazing and I was suddenly starving. I had forgotten to eat lunch this afternoon. This morning's Swedish pancakes were now a distant memory.

I poured us glasses of wine and passed them

around. Elin clinked her glass to Nora's and then mine. "To my favorite women. What would I do without either of you? *Skål!*"

"*Skål.*" I toasted.

"Nope." Nora shook her head. "I said no sentimental stuff tonight. You need to eat and then we need to get this place back in business. Cheers to that, right, girls?"

I wasn't about to argue with Nora if it meant diving into my tamales. Elin laughed and took a bite. I followed suit, removing the corn husk from one of my tamales and then stabbing it with a plastic fork. It had been steamed to perfection with a warm doughy exterior and spicy beef interior. I polished off the first tamale, pausing only for a sip of wine.

"Lay it on me," Nora said dipping a chip in creamy guacamole. "What's the scoop? I can't believe how long the police were here. They must have found something incriminating to have stayed for two days."

Could that be true? Having never been involved in a murder investigation I had no idea what was normal.

Elin swirled her wine. "They haven't said much. We had to be fingerprinted today."

"Yeah, me too." Nora nodded and chomped on a chip.

"You too?" Elin sounded surprised. "Do you think they fingerprinted everyone in the village?"

"It looks that way. Mark and Serene both stopped by for coffee today and they said they had to be fingerprinted too."

That was good news given that Mark had

launched himself to the top of my suspect list. Had he been asked to submit prints before or after I told Pete about his connection to the waterfront development?

"I've been trying to catch as much gossip as I can," Nora continued. "But I have to tell you murder has been good for business. Demitasse had our best day ever today. I ran out of milk at noon. I had to send one of my baristas out to get more."

"Frank's murder certainly brought many more people to the village today," Elin agreed. "I'm not sure that it is great for business though. One of my consultation clients today expressed concern about having her wedding flowers associated with a heinous crime. I can't blame her, although I did try to reassure her that our mission is to spread love." She focused on the deep wine in her glass and finally took a drink. "I'm hopeful that none of my customers coming to the preview workshops cancel, and I'm starting to get nervous for the launch party. What if no one comes? We've put in so much work. So many painstaking hours." Her eyes drifted to the mannequin.

"No way." Nora shook her head knowingly. "No way will anyone cancel. This is big news in Portland and if anything I'm betting my last dollar that this place is going to be a mob scene. It's going to be standing room only with people knocking one another out for your flowers."

"I don't want that either," Elin replied with a halfhearted chuckle. "I just want Blomma back to normal." Frank's murder was obviously unsettling, but again I wondered if there was something else bothering my aunt.

"We'll get it there," I said, reaching over and squeezing her arm.

"Yeah." Nora broke a chip in half. "And no more worrying. We're going to rock this place tonight."

I dove into my pile of chips, slathering them with the thick guacamole and green salsa. "What do you know about Mark?" I asked Nora between bites. "I heard that he was working with Frank on the development project."

Was it my imagination or did Nora flinch slightly?

"That's news to me," she said helping herself to another tamale. "Frank and Mark weren't exactly friends. In fact you might say they were the opposite. I can't imagine any scenario that would have brought the two of them together."

Elin topped off our wineglasses. "I agree. I always got the impression that Mark and Frank didn't see eye to eye, but Britta is right. I don't understand why Mark is pushing for us to sell. How long have we known him? Twenty years? He's never so much as mentioned the idea of selling the Riverplace Inn. If Mark is really committed to preserving Riverfront Village, why would he partner with Frank?"

Nora choked on a bite of tamale. She coughed and clutched her narrow neck. "Sorry, swallowed wrong," she finally said. "No, there's no way Mark would fund anything associated with Frank's name. I can't believe it. There must be some kind of mistake." She closed the lid on her to-go container and closed the subject.

We tossed our empty dinner trays and began cleaning up the cottage. I knew that Elin and Nora had been best friends for many years, but I couldn't shake the feeling that Nora was hiding something. Her reaction to Mark's involvement with Frank Jaffe had been strange. I couldn't imagine Nora hurting anyone, especially Elin, by staging the murder at Blomma. And I couldn't imagine what her motivation for killing Frank could be, but I was sure Nora was holding back. The question was what and why?

Chapter Nineteen

Once the cottage had been scrubbed and wiped down we opened the windows and lit every candle we could find. Nora's way of cleansing the negative energy from the space was to blast rock and roll as loud as the speakers would allow. Elin's was to craft a striking white bouquet. She placed it on a distressed whitewashed armoire near the spot where I'd found Frank's body.

"A remembrance for Frank," she said twisting the vase so that the flowers faced the front of the cottage. "I think we've done it. It feels much more like home in here now, doesn't it?"

I assessed the cozy cottage. Every surface had been polished with a natural wood oil. The floors had been mopped with lemon-scented industrial cleaner, and fragrant candles flickered beneath the warm open-timbered ceiling. I hated it but the first thought that crossed my mind as I surveyed our work was that it looked like something out of a fairy tale. No wonder Kirk had nicknamed me Snow. The cottage could easily belong to the fair-skinned princess from the fable. Not that I would ever admit that to Kirk.

Elin's face appeared lighter as she walked around the cottage and blew out each candle. Little puffs of smoke escaped from the windows. I felt content that with the cleaning, lingering scent of candles and the brilliant white floral homage to Frank, none of Elin's clients would feel squeamish about working in the cottage. There was no trace that any malevolent event had occurred here.

"Thanks for your help, and the tunes," Elin said to Nora, rubbing her left ear. I suspected that, like me, she would have opted for classical music over Nora's heavy guitar solos, but I knew that we both appreciated an extra set of hands and the mouthwatering Mexican feast.

Nora unplugged her phone from the speakers and tugged on her black leather jacket. "Anytime." She turned to Elin. "Hey, have you heard from Jon yet? He's been radio silent, which isn't like him."

"Who's Jon?" I interjected.

"The owner of Torch—the candle shop across the street." Nora flipped the collar up on her jacket. "He's been on vacation, but I thought he was supposed to be back a few days ago."

Elin nodded. "Yes, he was, wasn't he? Have you emailed him?"

Nora frowned. "Nope. But I'll do that when I get home. You two get some sleep. I'll catch you girls in the morning." She flashed me a peace sign and gave Elin a kiss on the cheek.

I closed the windows while Elin blew out the last

candle. "There's still so much to do before the launch, but what do you think?" she asked. "It's much better, isn't it?"

"No question." I popped my ears. "Nora likes her music loud." My ears continued to hum despite the fact that there was no music playing.

"I know." Elin rubbed her other ear as if trying to get the sound to stabilize. "I've told her a thousand times that she's not going to have any hearing left, but I don't think she cares."

"My ears might be ringing for days but I have to admit that the thundering drums and pulsing beats in Nora's music felt like they were pounding out all the bad vibes back here."

Elin laughed. "I know, but now we'll be shouting at our customers for the next few days. That's the running joke around the village. Demitasse is the best place to go for rich coffee and if you don't want to hear yourself think."

We surveyed the cottage one last time and left arm in arm. Sleep came easily for me that night, but it wasn't restful. I found myself waking almost every hour caught up in rambling dreams involving Snow White and an army of her seven dwarfs who were disguised as Riverplace Village owners. Kirk Jaffe was the big bad wolf who kept trying to lure me into a den tucked into Forest Park with promises of Demitasse lattes.

I finally gave up sometime after six and padded downstairs to the kitchen. It was my turn to cook for my aunt. I rummaged through her refrigerator and decided on a standby that I used to make for Chad on Sunday mornings—roasted red potatoes with bacon and herbs. Of course Chad never appreciated that I took the time to make him a hot breakfast. He would usually scarf down a bowl of the sizzling potatoes not bothering to look up from his manuscript and then leave for the library— or his love den—without so much as a thank-you or kiss good-bye. I would clean up his breakfast dishes, and spend the rest of the day leafing through flower catalogs or reading a romance novel.

It sounded so pathetic now. How could I have done this to myself? I took out my frustration on the red onions and green chives, chopping them into tiny shreds. I didn't even hear Elin enter the kitchen.

"My, someone is chopping with gusto at this early hour," she commented and pulled me from my self-loathing.

I held up the knife and stopped butchering the vegetables. "Guilty. I didn't wake you, did I?"

She wore a plush robe and fuzzy slippers. "Goodness no. If you were chopping that madly I think I might have to arrange some sort of intervention." She walked to the far cupboard, removed a coffee cup, and poured herself a cup of the dark brew that I had made before I got caught up in releasing some of my anger at Chad and myself.

"Have the potatoes offended you?" she teased as she took a seat at the round table in the center of the kitchen and cradled her coffee mug.

"No." I laughed and returned to dicing, but this time with much less force. "I'm trying to follow your advice and focus on the now, but I'm still so mad at myself for staying with such a loser for so many years. Cooking breakfast was just another reminder of how much time I wasted."

Elin took a sip of coffee. I wondered if she was buying herself an extra minute to consider her words. "Britta, it's only been a couple of weeks. I wasn't suggesting that you should be over Chad immediately. Grief takes time. It was more that I want you to know how much I love you, and what a strong woman I see on the inside."

"Thanks." I scooped the onions and potatoes into a cast-iron skillet with warm olive oil. They crackled in the heat and let out a pungent scent. I reached for a wooden spoon. "Do you think I'm grieving over Chad? Honestly I don't think I am. I think I'm grieving over myself."

She gave me an understanding nod. "I'm sure you are. It hasn't been easy for you. Losing your parents so young. It broke my heart."

"But I had you." I stirred the potatoes, allowing them to gently brown and then tossing chunks of chopped bacon into the pan.

Her smile faded. "Yes, we had each other. I don't know how I would have survived without you."

We both became caught up in old memories. Had I latched onto Chad because of my parents? I'd never thought of their loss impacting my love life before, but it made sense. I was young when my parents died. I had known that Elin loved me deeply, but their unexpected death had left a gaping hole in my heart that I had never found a way to fill. Maybe that's why I was drawn to the art of flower design. Creating beauty out of pain and sadness. Could that be why I fell for Chad? There was no denying that he had romanced me when we were young. Had I overlooked his tendency toward dark black moods and his self-absorption? Or had he changed too?

I sighed and gave the potatoes a final stir. Then I scooped them into two bowls and finished them off with salt, pepper, and fresh rosemary.

"Oh my," Elin exclaimed when I placed a steaming bowl in front of her. "These look divine."

"I figured it was my turn to cook for you." I took the seat across from her.

She rested her fork in front of her bowl. "Britta, I know you're caught up in your head about what went wrong with Chad."

"Is it that obvious?" I frowned.

"Maybe to me because I've known you your entire life, but not to anyone else." She paused and then met my eyes. "Britta, you are strong, and I have the sense that you've been trying to be strong for a while now, but it's okay to let go. I'm here for you. You know that, right?"

I didn't trust myself to speak, so I nodded.

"It's like what I say to our clients about flowers. The flower has to find you. You can't force yourself to love daisies if roses capture your heart. The same is true in the world of love. I know I probably don't seem like the right person to offer romance advice given I've been a happy spinster for all these years, but I think that in your heart you know the kind of flower that you're meant to be. Don't let one mistake detour you."

"Chad was kind of a big mistake," I said with a sigh as I stuck a potato with my fork and brought it to my lips to blow on it.

"Love is never a mistake, Britta, as long as we learn from it."

Her words struck a chord. What had I learned from Chad?

A lot actually. I had learned that I wanted more—needed more—from love. I deserved that. My work hadn't flourished. I had stifled my creativity. And for what? For an unhappy marriage and a bad match. That wasn't me. I had learned that I didn't want to close myself in and stay stuck. I wanted to blossom. I was blossoming. Maybe a bit later than some of my friends, but it was better than never, right? Plus some of the best flowers in the world were slow to bloom.

Elin gave me a knowing smile and began eating. She was definitely onto something. I made a promise to myself that anytime I began to sink into self-doubt or beat myself up over staying with Chad in the coming days, I would shift my focus to what I had learned and what I wanted next.

"You know, you should have been a therapist instead of a florist," I said to Elin.

"They're really one and the same," she said with a wink.

We dug into our potatoes and changed the subject to our game plan for the day. However, when Elin went to shower and I washed the dishes I thought about her love life. Why had she never married? Had it been because of me? She had taken me in without hesitation when my parents died, but I never considered how suddenly becoming the caregiver to a teary wide-eyed seven-year-old may have changed her life. Had she ever been in love? Not that I knew of. What about after I left for college and Minnesota? What about the photo of her and the handsome man on the dresser upstairs? She had blown it off when I'd mentioned it, but could she have a former love I didn't know about? I had complained about Chad being selfish. Had I been any better?

It wasn't the right time to broach the subject, but just as she had said she would be there for me, I intended to do the same for her. If anyone deserved love, it was Elin, and I was going to have to find a way to get my aunt to open up about her romantic dreams.

Chapter Twenty

By the time I placed the last fork in the dishwasher Elin had returned to the kitchen refreshed and ready to start the day. I threw a cream cable-knit turtleneck sweater over my T-shirt and tugged on my rain boots. The drizzle continued outside on Portland's wet streets. We splashed through huge puddles and kicked up wet leaves on our drive to Blomma.

"I'd forgotten how much rain Portland gets," I commented as we turned in to Riverplace Village.

"It's good for the blooms," Elin replied.

And good for me, I thought internally. I felt like the rain was slowly washing away the old me. "Uh-oh," I said pointing to the police car parked in front of Blooma. "I thought they were done yesterday."

"Me too." Elin frowned.

Tomo was waiting for us at the front door. He gave Elin a half bow and nodded to me. "Good morning, ladies. Sorry to bother you, but I have a request from Detective Fletcher."

"Come in, you're getting soaked," Elin noted and unlocked the front door.

It was true. Tomo's blue police uniform was splotched with fat raindrops, and his jet-black hair looked like he had just stepped out of the shower.

"Thanks." He held the door open for me. "I guess the wind is blowing the rain more than I thought."

Elin went to find him a clean towel. I flipped on the lights. "What's the request? Or should we wait for my aunt?"

He brushed rain from his broad shoulders. "No, it's for you."

"Me?"

"Yep. I'm here on other business but Fletcher asked me to stop in and see if you could meet him for lunch this afternoon—1:30 at the Riverplace Inn."

"Sure, I guess. Why?"

"It sounds like he has some more questions about roses, and word around here is that you're the rose expert." He wiped his damp brow with the back of his sleeve.

Elin returned with a towel. "Here, you look like you had a run-in with a storm cloud." She handed him the tea towel.

He mopped his brow and patted his hair with the towel. "Thanks. I think I did. I'm just not exactly sure how. I wasn't waiting for long. In fact I had knocked right when you two pulled up."

"It's supposed to get worse today," Elin said.

"Really?" I turned to her. "I hadn't heard that. I guess we won't be rolling open the garage doors today, then?"

Tomo brushed the towel over his shoulders. "Yeah. They're predicting a huge storm to roll in later. Fifty-mile-an-hour winds. The precinct is already prepping for it. It's all hands on deck today. We could lose power."

That wasn't exactly great news for Blomma. We were finally ready to open the cottage doors to the world. It would be a major bummer to have to cancel if we lost power.

"Welcome to spring in Portland." Elin held out a hand. "Here, I can take that." She pointed to Tomo's towel.

"Thanks again. I appreciate not having to go back to the station looking completely like a drowned rat." Tomo glanced behind him to the sputtering sky.

"You mentioned that you needed a favor?" Elin took the towel and hung it over her forearm. A puddle had formed around Tomo's feet, but Elin ignored it.

"Right." He snapped his fingers. "Well, I was telling Britta that Detective Fletcher wants to meet her for lunch. He wants some more information about the roses we found near the victim. Thinks they could be significant."

"Yes." Elin's eyes twinkled. "Lunch is a good idea. As you know, Britta is an expert when it comes to roses."

I started to protest, but Tomo looked at the vintage clock made from pressed flowers on the far wall. "Shoot. I have to get moving. The lunch is at

1:30 at the Riverplace. I'll tell Fletcher that you're a go, yeah?"

"She's a go," Elin answered for me and shooed him out the door.

"What was that about?" I asked after she shut the door behind him.

She mopped up the hardwood floor with the towel. "Nothing. I want to make sure that we're offering any help we can. The sooner they figure out who killed Frank the sooner things can really be back to normal." Her eyes held a hint of a glimmer.

"And?"

"And Detective Fletcher—Pete, as you call him—is quite handsome, don't you think?"

My mouth dropped open. "*Moster*, are you trying to set me up? We were just talking about how messed up I am over Chad."

"I know. I know. I'm not trying to set you up." She walked toward the workstation and tossed the wet towel into a hamper. "I was simply commenting on the fact that Pete Fletcher is attractive. There's no harm in lunch."

I wasn't ready to admit that I found Pete attractive too.

"Actually he reminds me of someone I used to know," Elin said taking out the file folder with the day's orders and stacking them on the counter.

"Pete?"

"Yes. He reminds me of someone I knew a long time ago." Her voice sounded nostalgic.

I wanted to ask more, but Nora burst in with coffees. "Hey girls, did someone call for coffee?" she sang out as she danced in, holding two paper cups.

"You're right on time as always," Elin said greeting Nora and taking one of the cups.

"Right on time? How did you call in an order? We haven't been here for five minutes?" I asked.

Nora ruffled her damp silver hair. "Your aunt has a standing order. I deliver her a piping hot latte at nine o'clock on the dot in exchange for my weekly flower arrangements." She handed me the other cup.

"That's a pretty good deal," I said to Elin and thanked Nora.

"No one in the village exchanges actual money," Nora explained. "We do everything on trade."

"Right." I took a sip of the coffee. It had a hint of nutmeg and cinnamon. "Mark mentioned something about a complimentary happy hour.

"Oh sure. The Inn hosts those for their guests, but Mark always extends the invitation to all of us as well. We've gone a few times, haven't we?"

Elin nodded. "Yes. Mark always puts out a lovely spread, and the view from the Inn is incredible. We'll have to bring you, Britta."

Nora agreed. "Let's do it. Girls' happy hour this week, what do you say? I'd love to go today, but one of my baristas called in sick so I'm going to be pulling shots behind the bar all day."

"Happy hour sounds wonderful, but we have a launch to prepare for, remember?"

"Right. Next week, then?" Blowing us air kisses, Nora backed out the door. "It's a date. Coffee calls. Catch you later."

Elin returned to the workstation. I followed after her. "It's so great that everyone in the village is connected and works in trade."

She handed me a stack of individual orders. "And?"

"And what?" I checked off the list of bouquets we had completed for the party. The sherbet arrangements were finished and waiting in the cooler. The garlands were nearly ready. We needed to add hops and a few fresh flowers tomorrow. Otherwise the main focus would be on the jewelry, dresses, and headpieces for the models.

"Britta, I can tell that your wheels are turning. What are you thinking about?"

"It's just that I keep coming back to the key. You're sure that no one is holding a grudge or could want to damage Blomma's reputation?"

She bent down and removed a collection of fluted frosted vases from beneath the counter. "You've met everyone. Honestly, I can't think of a single person in the village who I don't call a friend."

"Except Kirk Jaffe."

Placing the vases on the cement counter she looked thoughtful for a moment. "Yes, but Kirk isn't part of the village, and remember he doesn't have a key."

"What about Lawren?"

"Frank's assistant?" Elin frowned. "No, why would she have a key?"

I shook my head. "I don't know. I need to stop torturing myself."

She walked over to the flower buckets, removed an armful of peonies, and handed them to me. "These might help."

"Flowers always help." I laughed.

"My sentiments exactly." Elin kissed my cheek. "I'm off to the cottage to continue working on the dress. If you need anything, don't hesitate to call me." She picked up her coffee cup. "And, Britta, try not to worry too much. I'm sure there must be some other explanation as to how Frank's killer broke in and why they picked Blomma as their rendezvous spot."

I didn't want to harp on it, but the fact was there was no evidence of a break-in, no sign of a forced entry. There was no broken glass; Blomma had been perfectly intact. Whoever killed Frank must have had a key. Or Frank had a key and unknowingly let his killer in? I wanted to let it go, but I couldn't.

I needed a distraction and found one in dainty pale yellow peonies. I filled the tapered vases with greenery and the herbaceous peonies. The variety that Elin had picked was called Butter Bowl for its light pink outer petals and gorgeous spindly yellow center.

A few customers came in to place orders while I worked, which kept my mind focused on designs. Sometime after 11:00 a gentleman wearing a chocolate turtleneck that matched his skin and a pair of well-cut dark denim jeans sauntered into the shop carrying a box of taper candles. His short gray curly hair gave him a distinguished look that matched his angled jawline and handsome pecan-colored eyes. A small bandage stretched across the bridge of his nose.

"Why, I don't believe that we've had the pleasure of being introduced," he said shifting the box of candles into one hand as he approached the workstation and extending his free hand.

"I'm Britta," I said, shaking his hand, which was warm despite the chilly rain outside.

"Most excellent. Of course." He rested the candles on the counter. "I see the resemblance now. Same lovely bone structure, same skin tones, and yet your hair is so dark compared with your aunt's, but yes, yes I see that you share the same Scandinavian ancestry that's for sure." He stared at my face a moment too long, making me feel uncomfortable. Who was this guy?

"Thanks?" I replied in more of a question.

"Oh my, where are my manners? I'm Jon. Jon Jacques. I own Torch, the candle shop." He pointed with one long bony finger in the direction of Torch. He was tall, well over six feet, but with a thin, almost giraffe-like frame.

"Okay, right." I let my guard down.

"Your aunt has been talking about you nonstop. Can I please tell you how relieved everyone in the village was when we learned that the famous floral artist Britta was finally coming home after all these years?" His tone was dramatic, but his eyes twinkled.

"Sorry." I grinned and shrugged my shoulders. "I'm pretty sure that my aunt is extremely biased and I'm definitely sure that I am not famous."

"You are around here," Jon said sweeping his arm around the front of the shop. "The mere mention of the name Britta sends your aunt into story after story of her most famous niece the floral designer extraordinaire."

I laughed out loud.

Jon started at me from behind a pair of black

wire-rimmed glasses. "You think I'm teasing? Ask anyone, you are *all* that your aunt talks about."

"Well then I'm really sorry, because I can't imagine what she might have said, given that my life has been pretty dull up until now." Jon's playful attitude immediately put me at ease.

"So I've heard." He leaned across the counter. "Nothing happens in Riverplace Village. I mean there was that poodle incident a few years ago, and then there's always Mrs. Martenson, who owns one of the waterfront condos and has to stir up drama, but otherwise we could be in the middle of Idaho most days." He shuddered and reconsidered his words. "Okay, maybe not Idaho. Can you imagine being surrounded by potatoes? Fortunately the shops are much more refined here, but you catch my drift. Nothing ever happens. Nothing."

He wandered to the wall of flowers and smelled a pale peach rose. "I decide to treat myself to a getaway and am gone for two days and a murder takes place? Tell me what the fairness in that is?"

I got the sense that Jon was kidding, but I wasn't quite sure. "Yeah, I heard that you were on vacation. Were you somewhere fun?"

"No. Sadly nowhere exotic if that's what you mean." He didn't expand. Not that he needed to give me the details of his travels, but I found it a bit strange that he immediately shifted the conversation back to Frank's murder.

He placed his glasses on the tip of his nose just above the bandage. "Murder. An actual murder. Here at Blomma. Say it can't be so."

"I'm afraid it's true."

"How is Elin holding up?" He sounded genuinely concerned.

"She's okay. I mean I think we're still in shock, but she's fine. She's strong."

"Truer words have never been spoken." He placed his hand over his heart. "Your aunt means the world to me. If there's anything I can do, anything, you must promise to tell me. I know that Elin is one tough cookie, but I also know that she likes to play her cards close to the chest."

I couldn't debate him on that. Blame it on our hardy Swedish roots, but I knew something about playing things close to the chest too. It was one of the many things I intended to work on about myself now that I was starting over.

Pushing his glasses to the bridge of his nose, he dropped his voice to almost a whisper. "Have there been any other disturbances around here?"

"Huh?" I scrunched my nose. "Disturbances?"

"Nothing out of the ordinary?" He scoffed. "Aside from this nasty murder, of course."

"No. Why?" I thought about the black van that had been parked in front of his shop. An uneasy feeling assaulted my body. He couldn't be tied up with Frank's murder, could he? By all accounts he'd been gone. But what if that was a lie? I studied his calm face. He was attractive, with dark eyes and striking features. He didn't look like a killer. As if I knew what a killer looked like. My instinct told me that Jon was harmless, and yet until Frank's killer was behind bars, everyone was a potential suspect. What was the bandage on his nose from? Just a harmless cut? Or could it be from a scuffle or something more sinister?

For a moment I thought he might say something more. He stared at a cascade orchid that Elin had artfully accented with moss and rocks. "It's nothing." He tapped the box of candles. "Is she in the back? I have a delivery for her. She asked for tapers for a centerpiece workshop."

"Of course. Head on back. She's setting up for another class now."

"Lovely to meet you, Britta," he said reaching for my hand one last time. "I'm looking forward to getting to know you more." He kissed the top of my hand.

"You too," I said as he walked into the cottage and I returned to my peonies. My first impression of Jon was that he was warm and funny. He sounded like he was concerned about Elin, and had obviously known her for a while if he knew about me. Why had he asked about the shop? There had to be something that Elin wasn't telling me. I was probably being paranoid, but was it too convenient that he'd been gone during Frank's murder?

He'd said it himself. Nothing happened in Riverplace Village. Nothing happened until he was gone. I knew from our short interaction that surely he must also have a key to Blomma. I wanted to like him, but he had said he had been gone for two days. According to Elin he'd been on vacation for weeks. Was it a simple mistake or could Jon be lying? Had I just met yet another potential suspect on my ever-growing list?

Chapter Twenty-one

The rest of the morning passed in a blur of fragrant flowers and colorful bouquets. As predicted, the wind kicked up as the day progressed, making it impossible to open Blomma's giant garage doors. I enjoyed listening to the sound of rain lashing the windows and watching the wind bend the trees along the pathway outside.

Before I knew it, it was time for my lunch meeting with Pete Fletcher. I checked my appearance in the bathroom before I left. The cream-colored sweater contrasted nicely with my dark hair. My pale skin looked especially white. I dug through my purse and found my compact. Then I dusted my cheeks and added a touch of red lipstick, trying to convince myself that the only reason I was concerned about the way I looked was because this was a business lunch. Not because I had the slightest attraction to Pete.

My attempts at improving my appearance were

futile. The second I stepped outside the wind blew
my hair in every direction. Rain pelted my face
and coat. I hid under the hood of my red raincoat
and hurried down the flooding sidewalk. A moment later a sopping wet pug lapped at my heels.

The pug had on a black diamond-studded raincoat and paced in front of Demitasse's sweaty windows. This had to be Sticks, Nora's coffee-loving
pooch. I bent over and petted his soggy head. Sticks
responded by licking my hand with slobbery kisses.
"Hey, buddy what are you doing outside?" I said to
the friendly pup.

I was about to let him back into the coffee shop,
but when I stood up I realized someone was tower-
ing over me. Talk about bad luck. It was none
other than Kirk Jaffe. Sticks yapped at Kirk's feet.
Kirk responded by kicking him.

"Hey! Don't hurt the dog," I protested.

"I didn't hurt him. He's fine."

Kirk's treatment of Sticks only furthered my dis-
like of him. I patted Sticks on the head, opened
Demitasse's door, and pushed his rump inside.
Then I stood to face Kirk.

He blocked my path. "So, Snow. Are you another one of Portland's do-gooders? Out rescuing
poor mangy mutts in the storm?" He gave me a
lecherous stare. "You know what? Forget Snow. In
that coat you're more like Little Red Riding Hood.
Hope the big bad wolf isn't around anywhere."

How did he manage to make everything that
came out of his mouth sound sleazy? And why had
I bought a red raincoat? It had seemed like a good
idea when I was in Minnesota. A bright red jacket
to cut through winter's barren landscape, like a

single red rose budding on the vine. But with the way Kirk was leering at me I decided that I might have to ditch the raincoat for good when I got back to Blomma.

One fairy-tale nickname was enough. I didn't need two.

"Listen, Kirk, I'm late," I said, trying to skirt around him.

"Late for what? Got a date?" His beefy body took up most of the sidewalk and blocked my path.

"It's none of your business, but I'm meeting Detective Fletcher."

Was it my imagination or did he look scared? He moved to the side. "Have fun. That dude is a barrel of laughs."

I didn't want to risk getting stuck in a conversation with Kirk or chance his coming up with yet another annoying fairy-tale reference to describe me, so I continued on.

"Hey!" Kirk called after me above the wind. "I know you're trying to play it cool, but women can never resist the Kirkster. When you're ready for a real date, let me know and we can swap digits."

Had I been out of the game too long? Swap digits? The Kirkster? Is that really how people talked now? And come to think of it, who told Kirk that I was "back on the market"? I tried to shake off the rain and the thought of spending even a minute alone with Kirk and continued on to the Riverplace Inn.

The doorman ushered me inside and encouraged me to warm up in front of the fire. I thought he was simply being kind, but then I caught a glimpse of myself in one of the lobby mirrors. My ponytail had been teased by the wind and looked like a hairstyle from a fifties movie. I didn't need to worry about my skin lacking color. My cheeks were cherry red and splotched from the rain and wind. I did my best to tame my locks and wipe the rain from my face.

Pete was waiting for me at a table against the window when I entered the rustic dining room. The décor matched the rest of the hotel with natural and distressed wood, huge potted ferns and ever-greens, Edison-style light bulbs, and hand-loomed rugs. Our table offered a floor-to-ceiling view of the waterfront path and Willamette River. Although the clouds were so thick that it was impossible to tell where the path ended and river began.

"Did you swim here?" Pete stood and pushed out my chair for me.

"Thanks a lot." I tried to brush my wet ponytail knowing it would do little good. Then I removed my coat and hung it over the back of my chair. "It's wet out there."

He sat and smiled at me. "So I've noticed."

The way that Pete looked at me made me feel off-center. Unlike Kirk he was completely subtle. It wasn't anything I could exactly pinpoint. Maybe the fact that he held my gaze a moment longer than necessary, or how his scar indented when he smiled. Whatever it was made my hands quiver and my stomach flop.

"I meant our view." He tapped the window with his left hand.

"Got it." I grabbed my napkin and dried my hands on it before placing it on my lap. I tried to tell myself that my hands were clammy from Portland's weather, not because of Pete's broad shoulders and brooding eyes.

"Would you like a drink?" he asked handing me a lunch menu that had been printed on recycled wood paper.

"Water's fine."

"Don't let the badge stop you. I indulge in a lunchtime wine when I'm not on duty."

"No, really I'm fine. My head has been fuzzy ever since I found Frank. I had a half of glass while we were cleaning up the cottage last night and I feel like my head is still spinning." Or could it be the fact that I caught a hint of his cologne? He smelled like the forest—a bit like pine and a wafting campfire.

Stop it, Britta, I commanded, digging my fingernails into my napkin. What was my problem? Was this a natural reaction to getting a divorce? Maybe the fact that Chad had cheated on me had me hungry for male attention. Whatever it was I couldn't stop staring into his intensely brown eyes, which in this light appeared flecked with gold.

"I assure you, Ms.—I mean—Britta, that what you are experiencing is completely normal." He ran his hand along his auburn stubble.

"Really?" I twisted my napkin on my lap, hoping that Pete wouldn't notice.

"Absolutely. If you weren't thrown off by stumbling upon a murder you would quickly ascend to the top of our suspect list." He offered me a kind smile that made tiny beads of sweat form on the back of my neck.

"Can I ask you something?" I scooted my chair closer to the table. "I know that I'm here to talk to you about roses, but I keep obsessing about Blomma and maybe you can help put me at ease."

He filled our water glasses from a carafe on the table. "Shoot. I can't promise I'll be able to share anything pertaining to the case, but if your question falls into the realm of public domain I'll give it my best shot." His gunmetal gray dress shirt made his skin appear slightly tan.

"It's about the key. When I opened the shop that morning there was no sign that anyone had tried to break in. Same for the cottage. There were no broken windows. No signs that the door had been tampered with. Whoever killed Frank must have had a key, right?"

"That's one theory," he said and took a slow sip from his glass.

"Are there others?"

"Britta, you appear to be a quick thinker. I'm sure you must have formulated a few other theories."

I wished he wouldn't hold my gaze so intently. It was unnerving. "Well, I did wonder if Frank had a key."

"Yep. That's another theory."

"What's the other? You said you had a few."

He unbuttoned the top of his dress shirt and leaned back in his chair. "In my line of work everything is on the table until we have solid evidence to prove or disprove it."

"Like?"

He strummed his fingers on his chin. Again I wondered how he'd gotten the scar on his cheek. "One possibility is that you didn't lock up."

"But, I . . ." I started to protest, but he cut me off.

"I know you report having locked up, but it happens. People are so used to going through the motions that sometimes we forget."

I wanted to retort that I wasn't used to going through the motions. I was still learning the motions. And that I knew Elin and I had locked the doors, but he continued. "There's the possibility that you or your aunt let Frank in."

"What?" I gasped. "You can't really think that."

"I didn't say that I did. I said it was one of many theories that are currently on the table." He reached for his water again. "Frank could have stolen a key. He could have been meeting someone who had a key. The list goes on and on. Like I said, none of these ideas have legs until we find proof."

The waitress came by to take our orders. I decided on split-pea soup and a side garden salad. Pete ordered a grilled chicken sandwich and sweet potato fries.

"Do you think someone could have intentionally set Elin up?" I asked after the waitress left.

He tilted his head from side to side. "I suppose there's an outside chance that could have happened, but the crime scene says otherwise."

"What do you mean?"

"You're implying that someone planned this murder, but nothing about the crime scene points to that. This is off the record, and it doesn't go past this table, understood?"

I nodded, hoping my face looked solemn.

He leaned in. I tried to steady my breathing as I

caught another whiff of his cologne. "My guess is that this was a crime of opportunity. I don't think it was premeditated. There aren't any signs of that, and the way that the victim was killed also implies a moment of passion versus something that was well thought out."

A sense of relief flooded my body. If Pete didn't think that the murder had been premeditated it was unlikely that someone had been trying to sabotage Elin or Blomma.

"But why Blomma?" I asked, still puzzling over how the killer got in.

Pete shrugged. "Who knows? Everything we discussed still applies. It could be that our perp and victim met at Blomma, maybe more than once. Maybe your aunt was unfortunate in that the killer found a way into the cottage and used it as a secret meeting space."

I immediately flashed to my conversation with Elin where she had mentioned feeling watched and being convinced that someone had been peering into the cottage's windows.

"Britta, is there something you're not telling me?" Pete asked narrowing his eyes.

Was he a mind reader too? "It's probably nothing," I answered flattening my napkin in my lap. "Elin mentioned that she thought someone had been snooping around, and Nora brought up something about a competitor who has been feuding with my aunt. But every time I ask her about it she blows me off."

"Snooping around?"

"Yeah. She was sure that someone had been peeking in the windows, but every time she went outside to check there was no one around. She figured it was probably teenagers, or maybe the occasional tourist who was curious about construction in the cottage, but now I'm wondering if maybe there was more to it? What if the killer was checking to see if the cottage was empty?" My mind spun like crazy.

Our food arrived at that moment. My split-pea soup was as thick as the wall of clouds outside. It was loaded with salty bacon and tender carrots, and topped with house-made herbed croutons. Pete's grilled chicken sandwich and mound of sweet potato fries looked equally appetizing.

"Please, dive in." He nodded to my soup.

I stirred it and stared at the tumultuous thundering skies. Who could have been using the cottage? Nora, Mark, Jon, Frank, Kirk, Serene? Everyone in the village was a possibility. But why?

"There's no chance I'm getting this conversation back in control, am I?" Pete broke a steaming fry in two pieces and grinned at me. His scar transformed into a deep canyon when he smiled.

"What do you mean?" I blew on my soup.

"You're in another world, now. I can tell." He popped half a fry into his mouth. "I see it all the time with green cops. You get locked on to one idea."

"Is it that obvious?"

He munched the other half of the fry. "Yep."

"Sorry." I took a bite of the dense savory soup. It was warm and hearty, the perfect antidote to the crummy weather.

"Don't give it a thought, but maybe a change of subject will help." He reached behind him to his black overcoat which hung on the back of his chair. Then he removed a plastic bag containing one of the Deep Secret roses. "What can you tell me about this rose?" He slid the bag across the table.

I picked up the bag and examined the rose. "Like I told you when I found Frank, it's called Deep Secret. Although you should know this rose is different from the dead ones at the scene. I don't know if that's significant, but someone had to have spent a lot of money on the Deep Secret roses. Why would they put dead roses in the mix? It's almost like they were two separate bouquets."

He had taken out his notebook and sat with a pencil poised awaiting my response. "Hmm. Good point. According to Officer Iwamoto and your aunt, it sounds like you know all there is to know about roses. Is there any way to tell if they were part of the same bouquet?"

"No. It's just a gut feeling."

"Okay." He scratched his beard. "The question is why this rose? Why is it called Deep Secret? Could the rose hold a secret clue to why our victim was killed?"

That was a complicated question. Every rose had meaning. I started to tell him as much but his cell phone buzzed. He answered it and replied, "Okay, I'm on my way," and then hung up.

He stuffed his phone in his pocket and pulled on his coat. "Sorry I have to cut our lunch short. Something's come up. Keep the rose. Think about it. I'll be in touch."

With that he practically sprinted out of the dining room, leaving me sitting alone to ponder over roses—dead and secret roses.

Chapter Twenty-two

I finished my soup in silence and watched the storm outside. Could the roses scattered around Frank's body hold the clue to who killed him? Red roses signified romance and love. They were synonymous with passion and deep affection. Since ancient Greece the red rose has been a recurring symbol of love in mythology and literature. Red roses were tied to Venus (the goddess of love), found in the classics like Shakespeare, in poetry, and even in *Alice in Wonderland*. I thought of the scene where the queen declared that her card soldiers be beheaded for planting white roses and painting them red to try and fool her.

There was one person I knew who was obsessed with fairy tales—Kirk. Again and again I came back to him being the most likely suspect.

When I finished my lunch the waitress informed me that Pete had already paid. I bundled up for a chilly wet walk back to Blomma and stored the rose in my coat pocket. I planned to revisit my flower bible (a three-inch-thick notebook I had created while attending the Floral Institute) when I got home later and see what I could find on the meaning of Deep Secret.

As I wound my way through a small crowd gathered to hear an afternoon trio in the front lobby, I heard someone call my name. It was Mark.

"Britta, what brings you here?" He left his post in front of the fireplace and made his way to me.

"I was having lunch with . . ." what should I call Pete? A friend? A detective.

Mark didn't wait for me to land on the right word. "Excellent. I hope that your meal and the service exceeded your expectations." He wore a Riverplace Inn pullover jacket. I wondered if he was on his way out the door.

"Everything was wonderful."

"Excellent. Excellent." He clapped his hands together. "That's what I like to hear. Our priority is to offer our guests the most exquisite dining and exceptional service."

"You succeeded," I assured him. Then on a whim I asked, "Hey, do you have a minute to talk?"

For a minute I thought he might decline. He glanced at one of the arrangements that I had spruced up. "Is there something wrong with how we're displaying your pieces?" he asked.

"No." I lowered my voice. "I want to ask you something personal."

He looked taken aback, but motioned toward the hallway. "Of course, follow me."

We ended up in his office which, like most other rooms in the elegant hotel, had a view of the river-

NATURAL THORN KILLER 185

front. The walls were lined with awards and certificates touting the Riverplace Inn as a five-star venue for weddings, events, and luxury lodging. There were framed and autographed photos of celebrities and dignitaries who had stayed at the Inn, as well as thank-you notes from charity organizations and happy guests.

I took a seat in one of the comfortable plush chairs in front of Mark's warm pine desk. He clicked on the gas fireplace in the corner and sat behind the desk. The office reminded me more of a cozy hotel room with its Native American artwork and leather loveseat.

"Can I get you something to drink?" Mark offered, pointing to a matching pine side table that held coffee, hot chocolate, and expensive bottles of liquor.

"No thank you."

Mark strummed his fingers on the desk. I couldn't tell if he was nervous about meeting with me or if he needed to get back to work and wanted me to hurry up with whatever I had to ask.

"Thanks for taking a minute out of your busy day. I know this might be out of line, but I'm worried about my aunt and Blomma," I started.

Mark's eyes perked up with concern. "You're worried about Elin?" he repeated.

"Yes. She's really upset about Frank's murder, but I know that she's also worried about the future of Riverplace Village." I waited before expanding on the topic to see how Mark would respond.

He didn't take my bait. Instead he wrinkled his brow. "Why is she worried?"

I decided that I didn't have anything to lose and

trying to play coy with Mark wasn't working. "Well, she was already worried before Frank died, but I think she was pretty confident that everyone was going to stick together when it came to negotiating with him."

Mark nodded. "We were."

"But now people are saying that you and Frank were in partnership together."

His brow smoothed and his jaw dropped. "What? How did that get out?"

"So it's true?"

He let out a long sigh and pounded his forehead with one hand. "Oh man, I can't believe that Frank said anything. Who did you hear that from?"

"I don't know who said it first, but everyone in the village is talking about it," I lied.

"Oh no," he sighed again. Then he stood, walked over to the side table, and poured himself a whiskey. "You sure you don't want a drink?" he asked.

"No thanks."

He returned to his chair and swirled the glass of golden whiskey. "Damn. I can't believe that Frank talked. What an idiot. I told him we had to keep everything completely buttoned up."

"I don't understand. Why would you want to partner with Frank? Isn't the hotel a major success?" I pointed to the awards plastering the far wall. "From the looks of Frank's plans—at least what I saw—everything on the waterfront would be demolished."

"Yes, yes." He took a drink of the whiskey and closed his eyes for a minute. "It's not what you think."

I waited for him to expand.

He pounded his forehead again with one hand. "Damn, Frank."

This was not the reaction I had anticipated.

After an awkward pause, Mark knocked back the rest of his drink and sat up. "Look, Frank was in over his head. He didn't have the cash to develop the waterfront, but unfortunately he had me between a rock and a hard place."

"I'm not sure I get your meaning."

"He owned part of this hotel."

"Really?" No wonder Frank and Kirk had wandered around the Riverplace Inn like they owned the place. They actually did.

"Unfortunately, yes." Mark tilted his head back and let out another audible sigh. "I worked my way through the ranks here. The hotel had originally been owned by a larger chain, but they opted to sell about twenty years ago. At the time I didn't have the cash and I needed a financial backer. Frank wasn't my first choice. In fact to be honest he was my only choice. I went to every bank in town at the time but no one wanted to invest in an unknown. I was managing the hotel at the time but owning it is another story."

"So Frank offered cash?"

Mark stared at the last drop of whiskey in his glass. "Back then Frank was grabbing up any piece of property he could. Portland was not hot in terms of the real estate market in those days. In fact, that's one of the reasons I had such a hard time getting a loan. No one wanted to invest in the waterfront. It was run-down and vacant."

He stood and refilled his glass. "Frank agreed to a silent partnership. I got to run the hotel the way

I wanted, but with one stipulation—he had broader visions in mind. He saw Portland's potential before anyone else. I have to credit him with that. He predicted the boom that we are experiencing now. And part of our contract spelled out that should he ever want to sell I had to buy him out at a price three times higher than the going market rate."

"But I heard that Frank was having money trouble." I crossed my legs and noticed that the lily stains from earlier had sunk into my jeans. Yet another reason that florists rarely dressed up for work.

"He was." Mark held his whiskey glass to the light and studied its rich flax color. "That was the problem. He needed my cash to move forward on his development plans. Like an idiot I signed my life away two decades ago. Frank wanted out of Riverplace Inn. My loan finally came due. And paying three times market value for this property would have stung twenty years ago, but now it will drain me dry. Not only will I have to pay everything I have in the bank to buy out Frank, but I've run the numbers a thousand ways. In buying him out the only way to survive long term would then be to turn around and agree to his development deal."

"Wow." I let out a little gasp.

"It's bad, isn't it?" Mark tugged off his logoed pullover and hung it over the back of his chair.

"I don't understand why you needed Frank to be silent about this though?"

He placed the whiskey glass in front of him and hung his head. "If my fellow business owners learned about this, I would lose all credibility with them. Plus I've been working around the clock to try to find another solution. There are a few glimmers of hope out there. Unlike when I first bought the hotel, I have a history now. Banks are much more willing to have a conversation with me, but that doesn't mean that anyone is going to give me the funds. We're talking about paying millions of dollars over what the Riverplace is valued at today. I have to get someone to buy into its long-term potential. But at least they're willing to come to the table now."

I tried to make sense of everything that Mark was saying. "And none of the other village owners know about this?"

He looked up from his whiskey and met my eyes. "One of them does."

"Who?" I could feel my heart pulsing in my neck.

"Nora."

"Nora?" I couldn't mask my surprise.

"I suppose it's going to come out anyway. Nora and I have been seeing each other for a while. She wanted to keep it between us. Thought it would be better if things didn't work out. Then it wouldn't be awkward for everyone. No one would have to take sides, you know?"

Nora and Mark? I couldn't believe it. Nora was at least ten years older than Mark. Maybe more. Not that that mattered. She was young at heart and rocking her late fifties, but I would have never pictured the two of them together. Did Elin know? She and Nora had been best friends for years. If she knew, she had been extremely loyal to her friend and kept her secret—which wouldn't have surprised me.

"You won't say anything, will you?" Mark asked.

"No. I promise."

Mark's intercom beeped. I took that as my cue to leave, thanking him for his time, and assuring him once again that I wouldn't spread any more gossip.

As I exited the hotel into a squall-like wind I wondered if Nora had actually told Elin about her secret tryst with Mark. My hand went to my pocket and felt the Deep Secret rose. Nora had a key to Blomma, and she was having a secret fling with Mark. I knew that she was my aunt's dearest friend, but was there a chance that she had killed Frank? What if he had learned about her and Mark? What if she had killed him to protect Mark and the Riverplace Inn? What if the note I found in Frank's pocket wasn't for him? What if it was a note meant for Mark? I didn't want to believe it. I had already fallen in love with Nora's spunky personality. But keeping her love secret could make her a suspect.

Chapter Twenty-three

I had to think about how to bring up the subject of Nora and Mark with Elin and not betray their secret. There was no need to rush the conversation. I wanted to carefully craft my questions and wait for a natural opportunity to pose them.

Once I made it through the screaming wind and rain back to Blomma I found Elin and Serene chatting at the wine bar.

"Britta, you look terrible!" Elin exclaimed. Then she laughed and threw her hand over her mouth. "Sorry, I didn't mean that as an insult—you look wet."

"That's because it's a typhoon out there." I shook off my dripping coat and hung it on the hook near the front door. I took the Deep Secret rose out of my pocket and walked it over to the workstation.

Serene watched me as she cut open a case of wine. "Are you carrying around a dead rose?"

I chuckled. "Sort of. It's a research project."

"Is that to see how long your roses last before they die?" Serene asked.

"Something like that." I didn't offer more.

Elin caught my eye, but I gave her a look not to say more. Pete hadn't told me not to say anything, but given what I had just learned about Nora I didn't want to chance anything. If the Deep Secret roses were her and Mark's signature flower I wasn't about to share that with anyone else, except Pete or Tomo.

Changing the subject, Elin motioned for me to join them at the bar. "Serene is going to offer a complimentary tasting for my workshop this afternoon. Isn't that nice? I thought our clients would appreciate a bonus since we had to cancel and for braving this terrible weather."

"Good idea," I said.

Serene ran her hand over a label with a water-color design of a Tuscan villa. "It's good for me. I just got a few cases of this in from Italy. I think you're going to be able to move this quickly. But offering a taste always speeds that process up." She uncorked the bottle. "Speaking of tastes, who wants one? You're going to love this. It's a traditional Chianti—bold, fruit forward. I had it in Italy last month with . . ." she stopped in midsentence and dropped the corkscrew on the counter. It hit the distressed wood with a loud thud and then rolled onto the floor.

What had made her stop so abruptly? I looked to Elin, who appeared to be as confused as me.

Serene bent over and scrambled on the floor to retrieve the corkscrew. She set it on the counter and then shifted her pencil skirt back into place.

"Sorry about that. I thought that branch was going to slam into the window." She pointed to the front of the shop.

Elin and I turned. At that moment I saw someone in a dark coat run past the window. There was no sign of a giant branch though.

"I don't see anything," Elin said, voicing my thought.

"Huh." Serene continued to stare out the window. "It must have blown away."

I wasn't sure why but I got the sense she was lying. Granted there was debris on the sidewalk. Small branches and leaves were being tossed about like small boats on rough seas. But had she really been worried about Blomma being struck by an errant tree limb, or had she actually been startled by whoever ran past the window?

Serene poured three glasses of the Chianti. "Here, give this a try." She thrust the glasses at us.

Elin held her nose to the rim of her glass. "This is from Italy, you said?"

"Yes, a charming vineyard. I had a chance to meet the family while I was there. They have been cultivating grapes on the land for five generations now. One sip and it's obvious. You can taste the earth and the history of the soil in the grapes." She traced the label with her finger. I got the sense that she was reminiscing about her time in Italy.

"It's lovely," Elin said after tasting the wine. "I'm not sure that my palate is refined enough to be able to taste the dirt, but it's delicious nonetheless."

Serene cradled her glass as if the wine was precious cargo. "I'm glad you like it. I'll set up the tasting in the cottage." She began loading glasses into a box and left for the cottage.

I tasted the Chianti. Like Elin I found the wine to be smooth and bold with hints of tobacco and currants, but tasting the historic vineyard wasn't my skill set either.

Elin rested her glass on the table. "I should finish setting up too. Is there anything you need?"

"Nope. I should be fine. I'll make sure nothing blows away and be here ready to put something together for anyone who comes in in need of flowers to survive this blustery afternoon."

Only three customers came in for the remainder of the day. I had a feeling everyone in Portland was trying to hunker down and weather the storm from the comfort of home. The lights flickered a few times but otherwise, aside from an occasional crack of lightning or rumble of thunder overhead, Blomma stood as a sturdy safe harbor from the storm. I could hear occasional laughter from Elin's workshop as I used the time to continue prep for the launch.

I was about to lock up when Lawren scurried in. She was as tiny as a twig, and I was worried the gusts might sweep her away.

"Come on in," I said, holding the door open.

She shivered and darted her doe-like eyes from side to side. The girl either drank way too much caffeine or had a major anxiety problem.

"Are you still trying to find your wallet?"

"What?" She stared at me as if I was speaking a foreign language.

"Your wallet—remember? You were here looking for it?"

She tousled her wiry curls. "Oh yeah, yeah. I found that. It was in the backseat of my car. I should have looked there first. My mom tells me all the time that I would forget my legs if they weren't attached."

"I'm glad you found it." I didn't trust that she was telling the truth. Even when she had first come to Blomma in search of the missing wallet I had doubted her motives. How would she have lost a wallet on a wall of wine? Now I was convinced that she was looking for something else or just lying. She didn't even remember that she'd lost her wallet? No woman has her wallet go missing and blows that off.

"Did you need flowers?" I asked, pointing to a few bouquets that I had arranged earlier. It was important to have grab-and-go flowers ready for any customers who came in and didn't have time to wait for a personalized design. The cooler was packed with the arrangements for the party but I had managed to squeeze in five vases of varying sizes with springtime bunches. Based on a customer's needs and budget they could walk out with a bundle of happy rainbow-colored gerbera daisies for less than thirty dollars or a more elegant and expensive display of lavender larkspur, white gladiolas, variegated hydrangeas, and pink heather.

"What?" she asked, biting her fingernails.

"Flowers," I repeated. "Are you here for a bouquet?"

"Oh, no. No I was, um, well, I was in the village and I wanted to see how, um, everything was here. You know, with Frank."

Her stilted speech was another sign of her nerves.

"I'm not entirely sure what you mean about Frank. We're all fine, if that's what you're asking."

"Yeah, exactly. I just really have been worried, you know."

I felt motherly toward her. I wanted to sit her down with a cup of tea and try to get her to calm her breathing.

"Can I ask you something?" She bit her bottom lip as she spoke.

"Of course. Anything."

"Well, um, I was kind of wondering if." She paused and stared over my shoulder. "Well, I wanted to talk to you about something."

Did she know something about the murder? Before I could respond, Lawren flinched and let out a muffled squeal when Serene opened the barn door to the cottage and stepped inside.

"Shoot, I'm super late. I've got to go," Lawren squeaked out, then she turned and booked it out the front door.

"What was she doing here?" Serene's tone was like ice.

I wondered what was going on between the two of them.

"She came to see how we were doing. It was very sweet, actually," I replied, not mentioning how odd Lawren had acted.

"Right." Serene rolled her eyes and began rinsing wineglasses in the sink.

I flipped the chalkboard sign to CLOSED and walked back to the sink. "Do you know Lawren well?"

Serene scoffed. "As well as I want to. It's hardly

as if I have anything in common with that mousy little thing."

That much was true. Serene was sophisticated, dressed immaculately, and gave off a slight air of pretension. I figured that came with being a wine aficionado. Lawren, on the other hand, came across as meek and fearful. I got the sense that if someone yelled "Boo" she would shriek and then run and hide. They were certainly opposites. What I couldn't figure out was why Serene cared. It wasn't as if Lawren was any competition for her.

"Frank told her to jump and she would ask how high. She was his little lackey," Serene said with a snarl.

"Had she worked for him long?" I reached for a towel and helped her dry the wineglasses.

"No. I don't know why he hired her. He said she was a family friend or something. I think he owed someone a favor but she was worthless."

That was a strong sentiment for someone Serene claimed not to know or care about.

"How so?" I asked, returning two wineglasses to their shelf.

"She never got an order right. Never. Frank was pompous, but the man knew wine. He had stellar taste. Lawren does not. She couldn't tell you the difference between grape juice and a four-thousand-dollar bottle of Domaine Leroy's Grand Cru."

I wanted to admit that I probably couldn't either. Serene's visceral reaction to Lawren had me confused.

"That idiot constantly screwed up my wine orders. I lost so much money thanks to her." Serene placed the last glass on the shelf and grabbed her leather briefcase. "I'm off to a private event. Tell Elin that I'll check in later in the week."

She clicked across the gleaming hardwood floor on her stilettos, leaving me wondering why she was so hostile with Lawren. I'd heard conflicting reports about Frank, especially when it came to his spending habits. Could it be that Lawren was taking the blame for Frank's financial troubles? Maybe she had had to reorder cheaper wine in order to keep him on budget? I wasn't sure, but I knew that the next time I saw Lawren I was going to ask her what it was really like working for Frank Jaffe.

Chapter Twenty-four

The preview workshop was a success. Elin's students left with cheerful banter and gorgeous showpiece jewelry. The textures and tones in each student's design were dramatic and definitely would be conversation starters at any party or event. I took pictures of the students' designs with my phone. We could use them for marketing materials and online. Even though Elin was in her fifties she was totally connected. I had been following her on social media for a few years now. It was an excellent marketing tool and a quick and simple way to share flower trends.

"That was delightful." Elin's face glowed with excitement.

"It looks like a successful workshop," I agreed. "Everyone seemed very pleased with their final product."

"Britta, I can't thank you enough for allowing me to follow my passion. Being able to share what

I've learned and watch my students blossom is such a gift."

"You are a gift." I squeezed her hand. "I listened to everyone's comments as they were leaving and they are so inspired by you. It's not every day that you can walk into a shop like this and have no idea what you're doing and leave with a headband that looks like something off of a Paris runway. It's a talent you have, to be able to teach your art."

She patted my hand. "You are too kind, but I do love it, and I'm relieved to know that Blomma is in your capable hands."

She gathered her coat and put away the last of the supplies. "I forgot to mention that Jon and Nora want us to meet them for dinner tonight. Are you up for that?"

"Sure. That sounds great." Secretly I wondered if I could find a way to have a side conversation with Nora and ask her about Mark.

"They suggested the noodle shop. It's one of our favorites. Does that sound good?"

"Noodle shop, here in the village?" I didn't remember passing by a noodle place on my deliveries.

"No it's up a few blocks, closer to the police precinct. It's an authentic Japanese ramen shop. They also serve sushi and rice bowls. I think you might know the family who owns it." She winked.

"Who? Tomo?"

Elin wrapped her shawl around her shoulders and tied it in a slipknot. "The one and only."

"That sounds amazing." My mouth began to water. How long had it been since that bowl of soup for lunch? Suddenly I was famished.

We closed up Blomma for the night and linked arms for a blustery walk. The wind had let up a bit, but the rain fell in sheets. It dripped down the back of my raincoat. I was happy that I had opted for my knee-high rubber boots.

When we made it to the restaurant we were both soaked, but the scent of ramen and fried sticky rice perked us up as we stepped inside. The space was small with six two-person tables in the center of the room and booths flanking the far wall. An open kitchen was a blur of activity with a female chef shouting out orders in Japanese and line cooks dumping boiling pots of water straight onto the floor. Customers could watch the action close up at a long bamboo bar.

Nora and Jon, the owner of Torch, waved from a booth. "Over here, ladies!" Nora sang out.

Jon greeted us with a kiss on both cheeks. Nora scooted to make room for me next to her. Elin slid in after Jon.

"Isn't this cozy?" Nora said patting my knee. "I'm so glad you can join us. Usually we're a party of three but you round things out nicely. Doesn't she, Jon?"

Jon folded the tip of his black turtleneck and nodded in agreement. "Indeed."

"Did you hurt yourself?" Elin commented on the bandage on Jon's nose.

"Something like that," he replied with a hint of mystery in his tone.

"Jon, you're too much." Nora waved him off. Then she turned to us. "Do tell. What is the latest? I've been filling Jon in on the details. I still can't believe you missed the action." Nora had removed her black leather jacket. She was wearing a neon purple T-shirt that read VINYL—ALWAYS VINYL across the front.

"Or you could argue that you picked the perfect time to be gone," Elin said with a small sigh.

"Sorry." Nora reached for her arm and shot her an apologetic look. "I'm making light of what I know is a terrible tragedy. I supposed it's my coping mechanism, and of course there's no denying Frank wasn't exactly the most beloved man around."

"Please," Jon cackled. "That, my dears, is the biggest understatement of the century. Everyone loathed him. He was absolutely vile."

"But that doesn't mean he deserved to die," Elin interjected.

I sat back and listened to them discuss Frank. Neither of their reactions surprised me. And yet I found myself watching their body language intently. Then I scolded myself. These were Elin's closest friends. I trusted her judgment. Why was I questioning whether her friends could be involved in Frank's murder?

In an attempt to refocus, I studied the menu. From miso broth infused with garlic butter, pork, corn, and bean sprouts to shoyu with eggs, fish cakes, spinach, and nori, my stomach gurgled with anticipation. Chad had never been adventuresome when it came to eating. Elin had exposed me to world cuisine from a young age. When I was little we had a tradition where we would try a new restaurant once a month. From Indian to African, we sampled every variety of food that Portland had to offer. Not Chad. He used to complain when I would make a traditional dish like Swedish meatballs. I could hear him saying, "Britta, what is this? Why can't we have plain old American meatballs?"

The ramen menu would have sent him into a full-blown panic attack. I smiled at the thought.

"What's the grin for?" Jon leaned across the bamboo table and winked. "Daydreaming of a dashing gentleman?"

That made me laugh out loud. "The exact opposite." I tapped the menu. "I was thinking about how much my husband—soon to be ex-husband—would hate this."

"She is one of us, isn't she?" Nora nudged my waist.

"Britta?" I heard a man's voice call out as more of a question and looked up to see Tomo standing at our table wearing a black apron around his waist and holding an order pad.

"Tomo?" I mimicked his surprise.

"What are you doing here?" he asked.

"Drooling over the menu." I motioned to his apron. "The better question is what are you doing here? Aren't you supposed to be on a murder case?" I glanced around the room to see if Pete was here too. To my disappointment there was no sign of him.

"No. My parents own the place." He nodded toward the open kitchen. I caught a better glimpse of the head chef and immediately saw the resemblance. "One of the waiters came down with the flu, and I had the night off, so I told them I could jump in."

"My aunt mentioned that this is your family's restaurant," I said nodding to Elin. "But I thought you said your dad was a cop."

"Was. He *was*. He got injured a while ago and took early retirement." Tomo's eyes clouded and he glanced toward the lively kitchen again.

"I'm sorry to hear that."

He flipped the order pad to a blank page. "It's okay. What can I get you?" He looked completely different in his skinny black jeans, flannel shirt, and Chuck Taylors. I noticed that he had a black stud earring in his left ear.

"One of everything?" I asked the table.

Jon clapped his hands. "Yes! Let's be entirely uncivilized this evening. Extra spoons and chopsticks all around. We can pass bowls and decide which ramen we like best, what do you say?"

Everyone agreed. Tomo smiled. "It's a good idea, but I can guarantee that you won't be able to agree on a favorite. My mom's ramen is the best thing in town. She won't even let me touch her secret family recipe and I'm her only son."

He left to put in our order. Nora let out a low whistle. "He's a cutie. I bet he would help you forget your husband."

Elin wrinkled her brow. "He must be at least ten years younger than Britta."

Nora put her arm around my shoulder. "We are women of the twenty-first century, aren't we, Britta?"

I nodded.

"Since the beginning of time men have dated women much, much younger." She glared at Jon.

He threw his lanky arms up in protest. "Don't look at me."

"It's true," Nora insisted. "I for one am over it. We can rock, girls. We don't have to sit back and wait for our husbands to leave us for some leggy blonde with an augmented chest. We can flip the tables, can't we, Britta?"

"Sure." I wondered what Nora's background was like. Had her husband left her for someone younger too? Or had Elin explained what happened with Chad and me in perfect detail? Nora's girl-power pep talk also had me more convinced that Mark had been telling me the truth earlier.

"But I'm not ready to date yet," I said.

Nora squeezed my shoulder and then removed her arm. "That's fine. You take your time, but don't wait too long. That Tomo is adorable. Some lucky lady is going to scoop him up."

Elin saved me by changing the subject and asking Jon about a Japanese-style beer on the menu. She patted my leg under the table. I shot her a look of thanks. Discussing my failed love life wasn't high on my list of dinner topics. But since Nora had been so vocal about dating a younger man, I intended to use that as my opportunity the next time we were alone to see if she would open up about Mark. I was growing attached to Nora, and didn't want to believe that she could be a killer. However I never thought I would be in my thirties, technically homeless, and on the brink of divorce. I was going to have to keep an open mind because for the moment there was an outside possibility that one of my dinner companions could be a killer.

Chapter Twenty-five

Tomo delivered a tray of steaming ramen bowls that could have been framed and displayed in an art gallery. They were lush with ingredients and color, piled with noodles floating in a savory broth and topped with chopped fresh herbs, bean sprouts, julienned carrots, boiled eggs sliced in halves, and mounds of seared and shredded meats.

"Britta, my mom made this for you. I told her you were a friend." He placed an oblong white ceramic bowl in front of me. Then he pointed to the kitchen, where his mom, who barely stood tall enough to see over the bar, gave me a wave and then a bow. I did the same.

"Tell her thank you. This looks too good to eat," I replied.

"She will be happy to hear that." He gave me an impish smile. "You know it's considered rude in our culture if you don't finish the entire bowl."

I stared at the bowl of ramen in front of me, which could easily feed our entire table. "Really?"

"Nah. I'm just messing with you." Tomo winked and bid us good eating.

"See." Nora nudged me again after he left. "He brought you a special bowl. I do believe that young man is smitten."

Jon silenced her by saying. "Nora, dear, leave the poor girl alone. Not everyone has to have a hot-and-heavy romance like you." His thick wire-framed glasses had slipped to the tip of his nose.

His words quieted her. She twirled ramen noodles around her chopsticks and dropped the subject. Jon shot me a look from across the table as if to say, "you're welcome." I appreciated his intervention, and wondered if he knew about Nora and Mark.

If Elin knew about Nora's "hot and heavy" romance, as Jon had put it, she didn't give any indication. "Isn't this the most beautiful bowl of ramen you've ever seen?" she commented opting for a fork over chopsticks.

We all agreed and dug in to Mrs. Iwamoto's masterpieces with gusto. The broth had a kick from the Asian spices and a slight tang from the fish sauce. It was simple and yet layered with flavor. Every time I took a bite I tasted something new. I devoured the bowl and couldn't believe my own eyes when I finally put my fork down and realized I had eaten almost all of it.

Tomo checked in to see if we wanted after-dinner sake or tea. We declined. It was late and there was no way I could put anything else in my stomach.

"I'm impressed, Britta," he said stacking my nearly empty bowl on his tray. "I really was kidding about offending my mom."

I placed my hand on my satiated stomach. "I know, but it was so amazing that I couldn't stop myself."

He swelled with pride. "I'll tell my mom."

"Can I come meet her?" I asked.

"Sure." Tomo loaded the other bowls on the tray and waited for me to squeeze out of the booth.

Mrs. Iwamoto was short in stature with a blunt-cut bob and makeup-free skin. Despite her size she had command of her tiny kitchen.

"Watch your toes," Tomo cautioned.

Boiling pots of noodles took over each burner on the industrial gas stove. The galley kitchen's cement floor had a long drain running through its center. When a pot of noodles was ready one of Mrs. Iwamoto's cooks would grab it from the flames, hold a long-handled colander over the drain, and dump the water directly on the floor. No wonder the bamboo counter seating was packed with customers, I thought, as a handful of people let out a cheer watching steam rise from the floor. This was like a Broadway production.

Mrs. Iwamoto wiped her hands on a black towel hanging from her petite waist, and skirted around bubbling pans of broth and a cook chopping meat with a giant cleaver.

"Okaasan, this is my friend, Britta." Tomo introduced me.

"Nice to meet you, Britta." Mrs. Iwamoto's skin

was dewy and her eyes were bright. "Did you like the ramen?"

"It was the best thing that I've ever had in my entire life." That wasn't even an exaggeration. I knew that I was going to dream about her noodles for days to come.

She smiled. "You come anytime and I will make more for you."

"Thank you. I will definitely be back. You'll probably get so sick of seeing me that you'll have to ban me from the restaurant."

"Never. You are family when you are here. You are always welcome." She gave me a small bow and walked over and tapped one of the line cooks on the shoulder. Apparently she wasn't pleased with his sautéing technique, because she took the pan from his hand and demonstrated with an elegant flip of the wrist how she wanted him to do it.

"She is amazing," I said to Tomo as he walked me to the front door where the rest of my party was waiting.

"And she likes you." He fiddled with his earring.

I wanted to ask him about his father, but I didn't want to pry.

"Hey, I texted Detective Fletcher to tell him you were here, and he asked me to tell you that he's going to swing by Blomma first thing in the morning to talk to you about those roses."

"Right, okay." I'd almost forgotten about Frank's murder in the afterglow of Tomo's mom's delicious meal. "That's fine. Tell him I'll be there," I said as we left the restaurant. That meant that I had some research to do.

By the time we got back to Elin's I was wiped out. I decided to call it a night. I would most likely be up early anyway. I could pull out my binder in the morning and see what—if anything—I could find out about the Deep Secret rose.

Chapter Twenty-six

Indeed the next morning I woke before the sun. I was still on Midwest time. At some point I figured it would wear off, but for the moment I enjoyed being awake in a quiet house with the silence of the morning to myself. Careful not to disturb Elin, I found my flower bible, tucked it under my arm, and tiptoed downstairs to the kitchen. Once I had a pot of coffee brewing for Elin and a strong cup of tea steeping for me, I took over the kitchen table.

My flower bible had been my go-to source of information when I'd attended the Floral Institute. I hadn't touched it for years. Brushing dust off the cover, I flipped it open and was flooded with memories.

Studying at the Floral Institute had been a dream. It was like a chocolatier receiving a golden ticket to Willy Wonka's factory. I remember feeling so excited on the first day of class that I couldn't sleep

the night before. My days at the Institute had revolved around flowers, from memorizing the color
wheel to understanding how to balance different
textures and learning the history of different wedding traditions to building a portfolio of my designs. It had been a magical time.

I got caught up in memories as I leafed through
photos of the first corsage I made and old pressings of heirloom roses. I'd always been drawn to
roses. My instructor used to say that every florist
needs a flower muse, and roses were mine. Maybe
it was due in part to the fact that I'd grown up in
Portland surrounded by wild roses blooming on the
side of the road and spent summers picnicking in
Portland's stunning Rose Garden. But as I looked
through my earliest designs it was evident that roses
were everywhere.

Turning to the back of the spiral-bound notebook, I found the section I was looking for on the
history of roses. I had taken extensive notes in
class about each rose's origin and specific meaning. Deep Secret was the darkest of all roses. It
originated from Germany and was known for its
exceptional fragrance. Deep red, with virtually
black buds, the rose had a continual bloom, making it an excellent option for cut flowers. Its young
foliage turns a glossy olive green with age. There
wasn't anything else particularly unique that stood
out to me about the rose. I had jotted down notes
about growing conditions and where best to plant it.

My tea was ready, so I took a break and poured
myself a cup, adding a splash of cream and spoon-
ful of sugar. Returning to my flower bible, I read
through other entries I had included on roses and

found a tiny note in the margin of one of the last pages. It said, "Best revenge rose—Deep Secret." Then it went on to list a flower shop in Florida that specialized in revenge roses. It certainly wasn't my style, but there were some florists who offered novelty bouquets like bunches of dead roses that they would ship to an ex or an enemy. Immediately I thought of the dead roses I had found near Frank's body.

I wondered if the flower shop in Florida was still in business. I had taken these notes almost fifteen years ago.

Elin interrupted my thoughts. "Good morning, you're up early and already working?" She raised an eyebrow and poured herself a cup of coffee.

"Just trying to see if I could find anything else for Pete." I showed her my notes and told her about the shop in Florida.

She looked thoughtful as she studied my notes. "You know, this reminds me of something. There is a florist here in town who does this kind of thing. I think it's quite tacky, to be honest. I know that there's money to be made on this sort of cruelty, but not for me. As you know, I believe in spreading light into the world. Lord knows we don't need more darkness." She cradled her earthenware mug. "I wonder if Darren could have anything to do with this. I should have thought of it before."

"Darren?" I took a sip of the hot tea.

"He owns Drop Dead, Gorgeous, a novelty shop that sells dead flowers." She held up a finger. "Hold on a minute. Let me get my iPad." She hurried to the living room and returned with her iPad. Then she pulled up the Drop Dead, Gorgeous website, which had photos of rotting and wilted flowers on the front page and text about how they would cram dead flowers into a box with absolutely no care so that they would look as terrible as possible on arrival. Bouquets of their decaying flowers sold from twenty dollars for a dozen to over a hundred and fifty dollars for one hundred dead roses. Who would spend that kind of money on decomposing flowers?

"Drop Dead, Gorgeous is here in Portland?" I asked Elin. This had to be the florist that Nora had mentioned earlier. Why hadn't Elin said anything to me about him?

She nodded. "Darren is my nemesis. He feeds off of Portland's quirky culture. Believe it or not, he always manages to secure a booth at all of the big trade shows. He even had a booth at last year's wedding show."

"Dead flowers at a wedding show?" My mouth fell open.

"Not exactly." She scrolled through her iPad and found photos of Drop Dead, Gorgeous's wedding page, which touted statistics about how many marriages ended in divorce. It went on to offer an assortment of divorce and breakup flowers. "It wouldn't be so bad if he wasn't so obnoxious. I filed a formal complaint with the organizers after last year's show. I have no problem with his business, but it has no place at an industry show. What poor bride-to-be wants someone thrusting a dead rose and a business card at her while shouting, 'It's not going to last, honey—call me when you're ready to kick him to the curb and I'll send him a box of rotting roses'?"

"Did he do that?"

"Absolutely. His booth at the wedding show was all black with stinking, spoiled bouquets. I had the bad fortune to be directly across from him. He spent the entire weekend shouting insults and forcing dead flowers into everyone's hand."

"At the bridal show? That's terrible."

"Exactly. I understand that there's a place in the market for everyone. He's welcome to have a booth at a Halloween show or any novelty convention, but he has no place in this industry." Elin's voice was hard and angry.

"I'm going to have to fill Pete in. I wonder if whoever bought the flowers we found at Blomma bought them at Drop Dead, Gorgeous."

"It's highly likely." Elin clicked off the iPad. "Although I wish him good luck trying to get any information out of Darren. That man is . . ." She clenched her teeth. "A nightmare."

Somehow I had a feeling that Pete's badge would grant him access to any information Darren might have on who purchased dead flowers.

"Why didn't you say anything? Is Darren who Nora mentioned a few days ago?"

She nodded and stared at the iPad. "I didn't want you to worry. I know you have a lot to think about with leaving Chad and coming home."

"I've been worried, though! I found another dead bud in a vase in front of the shop and handed it over to Detective Fletcher."

"You didn't tell me?"

"I know." I sighed. "I could tell that you were holding something back, but we're supposed to be here for each other, right?" I reached for her hand and met her eyes.

"Right."

We finished our drinks, had a simple breakfast of toast with butter and jam, and then parted ways to get ready.

Pete's unmarked car was waiting in front of Blomma when we pulled in to a parking space a half hour later. Yesterday's storm had rolled through leaving a trail of debris in its wake. Cloudless skies and sun greeted us as we got out of the car. The sidewalk in front of Blomma was going to need some serious cleanup today. Wet leaves, branches, even a bit of trash blown by the wind had landed on the cobblestone walkway.

"Oh my, everything is soggy," Elin commented as she unlocked the door and flipped the sign to OPEN.

I followed her inside expecting to see Pete exit his car. However, it sat empty. I wondered where he went. I was eager to fill him in on what Elin and I had learned this morning. It seemed like a solid lead and potentially the evidence he and Tomo had been waiting for.

"Let me work on cleaning up out front," I said grabbing the broom and industrial dustpan that she kept in the storage closet.

"Thank you. I'll bring the yard debris bin around from the back."

I pulled on a pair of thick gardening gloves and opened the garage doors. The air smelled clean and fresh, as if renewed from the storm. Blue jays squawked in the trees above me as I began sweeping the leaves and branches into a pile. Elin rolled the large green bin to the front of the shop and then crossed the street to go chat with Jon, who was also cleaning up his storefront. In fact, everyone had opened their shop doors and emerged from their cocoons. The cobblestone pathway was abuzz with activity as business owners sprayed down the sidewalk and scooped up soggy storm debris.

"Morning, Britta," Pete called as I stuffed slimy wet leaves into the bin. He had come from Demitasse and was holding two paper cups in his hands.

"Hey." I closed the lid on the bin and yanked off the damp gloves.

"I brought you a coffee," he said, holding one of the cups out for me.

"You didn't have to do that." I took the coffee. Everyone in Portland seemed to drink coffee around the clock. No wonder Nora had had so much success with Demitasse. Like Italians with wine, I had a feeling that Portlanders drank more coffee than water.

"I was right there. It's no problem." He made it sound like no big deal. "Do you have a minute to continue our conversation from yesterday?"

"Yeah." I motioned inside. "Tomo told me that you were going to come by."

"Right. What did you think of the ramen?" He followed me in through the open garage doors.

"It was amazing. I loved it. I can't wait to go back." I walked to the workstation, set my coffee down, and grabbed my flower bible.

"Good. Maybe we can grab lunch there sometime." His voice held the same casual tone. Was he asking me out or just being friendly? Either way my heart gave a little thump.

I took a deep breath in through my nose, trying

to shake off the unsettled feelings that swelled inside me whenever I was around him. Then I opened the notebook to the section on roses. I showed him pictures of the Deep Secret rose, we went over its characteristics, and then I told him about Darren and Drop Dead, Gorgeous.

Pete's semi-aloof attitude shifted. He scribbled a note in his notebook and strummed his fingers on his chin. "Drop Dead, Gorgeous. That's an ominous-sounding business name to a guy in my line of work."

"I know. Isn't it terrible?" I told him about Elin's complaints about Darren's booth at the bridal show.

"That's low." Pete scowled and shook his head. "I'm not exactly the romantic type, but harassing young brides at a wedding show, that's almost arrest-worthy."

It made me think about Chad. Even though I was furious with him for cheating on me, I would never send him dead flowers. What kind of person would do such a thing, unless in total jest?

"And there's nothing else specific about the roses we found at the crime scene, right?" Pete asked staring past me to the buckets of flowers.

"Not as far as I know, sorry."

"Don't be sorry. This is a huge break, potentially." He picked up his coffee. "I appreciate your help, Britta." For a minute our eyes met and my heart thumped erratically. What was it about Pete that threw me off balance? He was handsome and intelligent, but it wasn't just that. I felt like I had known him for years and yet at the same time he was so reserved that I felt like I didn't know him at all.

I wasn't in any kind of position to fall for some-one right now. I had to work on myself. Pete Fletcher was uncharted territory for me, and I felt slightly out of control whenever he was close.

He broke the moment and headed toward the garage door. "I'll be in touch."

"Thanks for the coffee," I called after him.

"It's the least I could do for breaking our lunch date." He winked. I watched him stroll to his car, his long athletic legs moving in an easy rhythm. Then I chided myself. Get back to work, Britta, and stop daydreaming about the detective.

Chapter Twenty-seven

Storm cleanup took another hour. By the time I had dumped the last pile of squishy leaves into the recycling bin my cheeks were blazing and sweat dripped from my forehead. The physical exercise felt exhilarating and got me out of my head, at least momentarily.

Our second preview workshop wasn't until late afternoon, so Elin and I fell into a comfortable tempo as we snipped flowers, filled vases, and tied bows. Blomma burst to life as we finished each bouquet. I appreciated Elin's advice and input. "What do you think about pairing these poppies with some clematis and fruited boughs?" I asked, placing a pale pink poppy with a long curved stem into a ceramic vase.

Elin wrinkled her brow and thought for a moment. "I like that, but what about a different vessel?" She reached under the counter and handed me a vintage glass vase. "Try this. I think the poppies will have room to stretch out and look almost wild in this vase."

She was right. I finished the unique design with purple berries and dried milkweed pods.

"Yes, that's it," she exclaimed when I finished the arrangement.

Her delight was short lived because a beefy man wearing black from head to toe stormed into the shop. I guessed him to be about my age, although thanks to the extra weight he carried around his middle and his jaundiced puffy face, he looked older.

"Elin, I want a word," he shouted as he thudded toward us.

"Darren of Drop Dead, Gorgeous," Elin whispered to me.

Of course. His shirt read: "Flowers are ~~red~~ dead." This was Elin's infamous dead flower rival.

"What did you do, Elin?" Darren spit as he spoke. "Send a detective my way, snooping around, asking questions. You're the one with the rotten corpse here, not me."

"Darren, I don't believe that you've met my niece, Britta." Elin kept her tone even and calm.

A trail of tiny spider veins running across Darren's blotchy face pulsed with anger. "Huh?" His beady eyes landed on me. "Hey."

"Nice to meet you," I replied, standing shoulder to shoulder with Elin.

"Cut the crap," Darren growled. "I know that you're out to get me and I can tell you that it's not going to happen. Sales are through the roof. Business is booming at Drop Dead." He paused and darted his buglike eyes around the shop. "Doesn't look like the same can be said for this place. Is that why you sent that detective my way, Elin?"

It was obvious that Darren wasn't the kind of guy who would listen to a rational explanation. He looked like he was ready to pounce on whatever Elin said.

She walked over to the flower wall and removed a handful of creamy daffodils. Returning to the workstation, she began trimming the flowers. "I assure you that nothing could be further from the truth, Darren. I'm focused on what we're doing here at Blomma."

The veins bulged on Darren's cheeks. "Right. Cut it out, Elin. I know it was you who tried to get me banned from the bridal show."

"That's different," Elin kept her composure. "As we've discussed in the past, Darren, you and I have different philosophies when it comes to flowers. I believe that it's my duty as a florist to stay positive and share joy. I'm part of my clients' most significant moments in life—births, weddings, times of sorrow."

"Yeah and I'm there when your little happy world falls apart. That's not real life. Real life sucks, and *my* clients know that."

"That's where we differ," Elin said with a solemn smile. "I certainly don't wish you ill, but when it comes to events like the bridal show I don't think there's a place for darkness and death. I told you that in person and I stand by that now."

I was impressed with her calm resolve.

Darren became more agitated. "Right, so that's why I got a visit from the police detective this morning? Don't try to pretend like it wasn't you. I know you sent him to me."

Elin focused on the daffodils. She smoothed their delicate petals. "Yes. The police have asked us for any leads we may have in their investigation, including how two dozen dead roses ended up in our cottage."

"Don't look at me like that!" Darren flicked his hand in the air and snapped. "You're trying to get me in trouble. I know it."

"We were merely doing our civic duty. There is only one shop in Portland that sells dead flowers. It's that simple."

If Elin was intimidated by his overbearing presence she wasn't letting it show.

Darren, on the other hand, had scrunched his face so tight that I thought he might actually burst a vein. "This isn't over, Elin. You started a war and you're going to get one. You better watch out. I hear there's some big party here tomorrow night. Better get ready for a party crasher!" He turned and stalked out the garage doors.

"Wow," I said, watching him almost knock down a woman walking two small terriers on the sidewalk. "He is something."

Elin held up one of the daffodils in her hand. "Isn't he? I don't even know why I'm trimming these. We're done with the morning's orders, but I had to do something with my hands." Her hands were shaking.

"You handled him beautifully," I assured her.

"Darren likes to hear himself talk." She began twisting the daffodil stems together and wrapping them with a matte green ribbon. "There's no point in trying to argue with him. That's what he wants."

"I got that impression, but what about his parting comment. Should we be worried about him starting a 'war' with Blomma?"

Elin shook her head. "No, I don't think so. Hopefully he'll forget about us and be on to his next target before you know it."

She finished the mini-bouquet and placed it in a container of water in the cooler. "Let's give this away to the next customer who comes in. Consider it a gift from Darren."

Her tone was lighthearted, but I was worried. Darren's unstable behavior and promise to engage in battle left my stomach feeling fluttery, and not in the good way like when I was around Pete. Could Darren have killed Frank? I wasn't sure if the two men had even known one another, but Darren obviously held a grudge against Elin. Could he have murdered Frank to get back at her?

"Britta, are you okay?" Elin asked, closing the flower cooler.

"I'm fine. I was just thinking about Darren. Is there any chance that he and Frank knew each other?"

She shrugged. "Not that I know of, but that doesn't mean anything. Portland is a big city. We might feel like we're tucked into a small town here in the village, but Frank owned property all over. He could have known Darren. They could have worked together. I wouldn't put it past Frank to have ordered rotten roses from Drop Dead, Gorgeous."

Now I had another suspect to add to my list. Wasn't the ultimate goal to narrow down suspects, not keep adding them? I didn't know if Darren had ties to Frank Jaffe, but I was going to let Pete know, and the only good thing about having another suspect was that it gave me an excuse to call him.

Chapter Twenty-eight

The remainder of the day involved deliveries, final prep for the party like coordinating with the caterer who was creating a custom menu of flower-inspired hors d'oeuvres, and sketching out plans for a client wedding and corporate chocolate party that Elin had secured earlier. After a one-on-one meeting with a client the next step was to create a tentative design and cost estimates. Since we dealt in whatever was blooming at the moment, it could be challenging to budget and prepare a plan months in advance. The wedding was in mid-July so our designs revolved around flowers, shrubs, and berries that we knew would be in season. However the growing market could always change. Another round of storms like yesterday's could affect pricing and what wholesale flowers we could secure at the market.

Elin included language in every contract about substitutions based on availability. Rarely had she encountered a client who was angry about having to swap a specific flower in an arrangement, but it had happened from time to time, and we tried to do our very best to ensure that the final bouquet matched our preliminary designs.

I enjoyed the process of putting a proposal together for clients. It reminded me of being back in school as I cut swatches of ribbon and snapped pictures of columbines and purple basil. With charcoal pencils I drew rough sketches of my vision for the bridal bouquet, which involved cascading spray roses, chocolate and dark pink cosmos, and clustered florets of lavender larkspur.

"What do you think?" I asked Elin when she peered over my shoulder after coming in to the front of the shop for a cup of tea. She had been working around the clock on finishing the floral gown.

"I think we will have one happy bride." She picked up a sketch of one of the centerpieces with rustic tall-stemmed dark purple stock which not only would look dramatic in the clear hurricane vases I had picked out, but would also give the centerpieces a spicy clovelike scent.

"It's better than a bouquet of black roses from Darren's shop, right?" I joked, trying to make light of the earlier tension.

"Yes, that goes without saying, doesn't it?" Elin smiled and placed my sketch back on the stack of drafting paper on the countertop. "I'll be in the cottage if you need me."

"How is the dress coming along?"

She tucked her hair behind her ears. "I'm not sure. It's starting to take shape, but it's a challenge in terms of structure and movement. I won't be able to put any of the flowers on it until tomorrow night when we actually get the model into the skirt."

"Is there anything I can do to help?" I arranged the pencils in the shape of a star on the top of the workstation.

"No. Not at the moment." She pointed to my sketches. "These are a tremendous help." With that she poured herself a mug of tea and returned to the cottage.

Once I had a completed set of designs I bundled them in a pale pink file folder with Blomma's logo stamped on the front and tied it with one of the swatches of ribbon I wanted to use in the bridal bouquets. When the bride-to-be came back in for her next consultation she would leave with sketches and a complimentary centerpiece. Like the mini-bouquets that Elin created for every initial client meeting, we also made small centerpieces to give each client a sense of height, texture, and fragrance. It was another simple yet personal touch that set Blomma apart from other flower shops.

Tomo poked his head in as I filed the designs away. "Hey, Britta!" he grinned and held up a paper bag.

I waved him inside. "How's it going?"

He placed the bag on the countertop. "Great. I have a special surprise for you from my mom."

"What is it?"

"Open it. You'll see." He nudged the bag toward me.

I opened it to find a small paper quart container

usually used to store ice cream. It was cold to the touch. "What is it?" I asked again.

"Just open it," he said with another grin. After seeing him out of his uniform last night, he almost looked like he was dressing up as a police officer for Halloween today with his blue short-sleeved shirt and shiny badge.

I lifted the lid from the container. A deep black frozen custard filled it to the brim, topped with a sprinkling of black sesame seeds. "Is this ice cream?" I asked.

He nodded. "Yeah. It's the best. You're going to love it. My mom doesn't make it very often, but when she does it sells out before the lunch rush is finished. When she told me she was making it last night I told her to save me a couple of containers. I brought one for you and Elin and I saved one for Detective Fletcher too. I can't wait to see his face when he tries it."

I loved that Tomo was so proud of his heritage and his mother's exquisite cuisine.

"Is it savory?" I asked swiping my finger over the top of the custard.

"Just taste it." Tomo sounded impatient.

I licked my finger. The creamy custard was slightly sweet with a hint of vanilla but a salty finish. It wasn't like any other ice cream I had ever tasted.

"Well, what do you think?" Tomo handed me a spoon.

"It's delicious, but it's hard to describe. It's very different from American ice cream."

"Right?"

I took the spoon and went in for more. With each bite I enjoyed the ice cream more and more. The subtle sweet vanilla and deep sesame flavor mingled nicely, and the occasional crunch of the seeds was an unexpected treat.

"You like it, right?"

"I love it." That wasn't a lie. "Tomo, you've been so great about sharing Japanese food, now we are going to have to make a Swedish feast for you. How do you feel about whitefish?"

"Let's do it. I'm up for anything." He flashed me a thumbs-up. Then his cherubic face turned more serious. "Honestly, Britta, I really appreciate you being open. Not a lot of the men and women in blue are super excited about trying eel or red bean sprout pudding."

"I am your girl when it comes to international cuisine. After being stuck married to a man who only wanted to eat meatloaf and green bean casseroles for five years my taste buds are practically singing every time I see you."

"That's right. I keep forgetting you were married."

"Technically I *am* married," I corrected him, wishing it weren't true. If only the situation with Chad could resolve itself magically without my ever having to talk to him again.

"Yeah, Fletcher mentioned something about that yesterday." Tomo was casual, but my stomach did a flop. Did that mean that Pete had been discussing my love life with Tomo?

"You better eat that before it melts." Tomo pointed to the black custard.

"Hey, I wanted to ask about your dad. You mentioned that he was hurt. Was it in the line of duty?"

Tomo crumpled the bag that he had used to deliver my ice cream. "Yeah."

"Sorry. I didn't mean to pry. We don't have to talk about it." I stabbed the spoon into the silky custard.

"No, it's cool. It's fine." He rolled the bag in a ball between his hands. "He was shot last year. Someone tagged our ramen shop. My dad happened to be the nearest responder. When he arrived on the scene he was thinking he was going to have to chase off a bunch of kids, but it was more serious than that."

"That's terrible."

He squeezed the bag with one hand. "Yeah. We're not sure if the tagging was racially motivated, but we were the only shop hit. My dad didn't wait for backup. He went after the group of guys, who were wearing masks, and chased them up Front Street. They had a car waiting. I have no idea why, but one of them shot my dad as they flew past him. He was on foot and alone. It doesn't make any sense." He sighed.

"I'm so sorry." I knew that I had already expressed my condolences, but I felt terrible for Tomo.

"It was touch-and-go at first. The surgeons weren't sure that Dad was going to make it, but he came through. It's been pretty rough ever since. He was shot in the back. Lost a kidney, has been doing rehab three days a week, still doesn't have full range of motion in his lower half."

"Oh my gosh."

Tomo nodded. Then with one fluid sweeping motion he stepped back and shot the paper bag into the garbage can with a perfect swish. "I'm going to find the guys. I was already motivated to follow in my dad's footsteps, but after what happened last year I'm not going to stop until we bring them to justice."

I swirled the slowly melting ice cream with my spoon. "Do you have any leads?"

"Nothing solid. I've been tracking taggers around town though. There have been twelve other incidents in the past year, concentrated on this side of the river. I know it has to be the same group, and I have some suspicions about who may be involved, but we haven't been able to make an arrest yet. Most of the businesses that have been hit have been owned by minorities. I'm sure that my parents were targeted because they're Japanese, but my superiors don't agree."

"That's awful, and such a surprise here in a place like Portland. Let me know if there's anything I can do to help." The noodle shop wasn't far from Blomma. I wondered if any businesses in the village had been tagged. I didn't want to upset Tomo, so I decided I would have to ask Elin about it later.

"Thanks. I appreciate that." Tomo smiled. "I have to get back to the beat. See you later."

"Wait, there's one more thing" I said, scooping ice cream onto my spoon. "I wanted to tell Pete that Darren from Drop Dead, Gorgeous was here a little while ago."

Tomo stopped. "Really? What did he want?"

I glanced around to make sure Elin wasn't

nearby. I didn't want to worry her with my theory that Darren was trying to sabotage Blomma. She was still in the cottage, so I explained my suspicions and told Tomo how angry and threatening Darren had been.

"That's weird that he came here. I was with Fletcher when he questioned Darren. He didn't say a word about Blomma or your aunt. He's a professional. Why would Darren have come straight here?" Tomo made a note on his phone. "I'll let Fletcher know. He might want to come ask you about it."

"I'll be here." I savored the milky ice cream. "Gorging myself on your mom's dessert."

Tomo laughed. "Awesome, see you later."

Elin's special guest students began arriving shortly after Tomo left. I directed them to the cottage and hung back for a minute, watching her greet them with a welcoming hug and pair of gardening shears. Tonight's class was on succulents. The oversized island in the center of the cottage had an assortment of water-retaining plants like aloe, cacti, sedums, and agave. Elin would teach her students how to arrange the fleshy drought-resistant plants in pots filled with small rocks and stones and low containers. Succulents are extremely difficult to kill, and require very little maintenance, making them a perfect houseplant or focal point on a coffee table or windowsill.

Catching my eye, Elin clipped the root of one of the ornamental plants and encouraged her students to gather round the island to get a closer look. I waved and ducked out. The day's orders had been delivered, both of the new contracts had designs and sketches ready to go, and I couldn't decorate for the launch party until tomorrow. I tidied up the shop and reviewed the order forms for the next day. Then I used the downtime to post pictures of some of the arrangements we'd made as well as workshop photos on Blomma's social media.

With that complete, I checked the clock on the wall. Elin's workshop would run for another hour, so I decided to take an evening walk along the waterfront. I turned the sign on the door to CLOSED and changed into tennis shoes. Then I grabbed my raincoat—it was the only non-parka I had—and stepped outside into the early spring air.

Every storefront in Riverplace Village had a pile of debris or green recycling bin in front of the entrance. I was impressed by how quickly the cobblestone path had been cleared and remnants of the storm's damage had been swept away. As I passed Demitasse I spotted Nora standing on a step stool and stacking brilliant white coffee mugs in the shape of a pyramid in the front window.

She positioned a cup at the top of the stack and waved for me to come inside. When I opened the door Sticks ran to greet me. He nuzzled up to my leg and snorted.

"That is quite the stack you have," I said to Nora, careful not to let the door slam behind me. Sticks was wearing a black leather collar with metal studs.

"What do you think?" She stepped off the stool and appraised her work. "We have a friendly window competition in the village each season. This year I intend to win! Your aunt has smoked all of us every year."

"Really? Is there a prize?" Sticks panted at my feet. I bent down to pet him.

"He likes you." Nora ran her fingers through her spiky hair. "Bragging rights, girlfriend."

"How did you manage to stack them that high?" I asked pointing to the mugs.

She brushed her hands on her skintight leopard pants. "It wasn't hard, and I'm not done yet. I was hoping maybe you could make some garlands to hang on either side of the coffee pyramid. Then I'm going to scatter coffee beans all along the windowsill."

"Great idea." I studied the pristine display. "What about cherry blossom branches? We could hang them from the ceiling, almost as if the blossoms were dripping down into the coffee mugs."

"That's perfect." Nora folded the step ladder. She walked to the espresso bar, returned the ladder to its spot, and grabbed a ten-pound bag of coffee beans. "Want to help me toss some beans around?"

Part of me wanted to decline. The purplish light and sinking sun were calling me. A walk might help clear my head, but this was also my chance to ask Nora about her relationship with Mark, especially since Elin wasn't around.

"Sure," I replied.

She ripped open the bag and the scent of coffee hit me like a tsunami. Sticks let out a low bark and pawed at Nora's legs.

"Those smell amazing." I laughed as Sticks tried to climb up her to get at the coffee. "You weren't kidding about having a four-legged coffee hound, were you?"

"Off, Sticks." Nora snapped. "He's addicted. It's a serious problem." She shook a bunch of beans into her hand and held her palm out. "See how they're starting to get a matte finish? Coffee beans should be glossy. It's the oils that make a great cup. These are stale. That's why I'm using them in the display."

She tossed a handful in front of the coffee pyramid. I did the same, and thought about how best to broach the subject of Mark.

Nora gave me the perfect in by mentioning Tomo. "I saw that young cop coming out of Blomma with a silly grin on his face a while ago. Are you sure you're not up for robbing the cradle? I can tell you from experience that dating a younger man has some wonderful benefits."

"I'm sure." I sprinkled beans on the window ledge. "Actually, since you mention it. I've been wanting to ask you about something."

"Shoot."

"Well, I heard that *you* are dating someone younger."

She spilled the bag of beans on the floor. Coffee beans scattered in every direction and hit the cement floor like popcorn popping. Sticks yelped with delight and chased the beans. "How did you hear that?" Nora asked.

We both bent down and began scooping beans into a pile. "I wasn't trying to pry into your love life. It came up when I was asking about Frank and Kirk Jaffe."

"You've talked to Mark, then?" Nora squeezed a handful of beans. "Have you said anything to Elin?"

"No, I promise. I haven't said a word to any-one."

She tossed the beans toward the front window with little care. "Shoot. I should have known this would happen."

Sticks chomped a coffee bean and then spit it out on the floor. "Leave it!" Nora commanded. Then she scooped Sticks up. "I'm going to put him in my office. Hang on a second."

A pug who liked coffee and wore leather, how perfectly Portland, I thought as I waited for Nora to return. She was back in a second. "So you haven't told Elin yet? I thought you two were best friends," I asked scooping beans into my hands.

Nora rubbed her eyes and smeared her black eyeliner. "We are."

I thought that might be the end of our conversation. She picked up more of the beans and threw them at the window.

"Damn. I should have told her."

"Is there a reason you didn't? Mark said that you guys wanted to keep things on the down low with the other village business owners."

Nora stood and rubbed a coffee bean between her fingers. "Yeah, that was part of it. We're just having fun right now. It's not serious, but we both are old enough to know that these kinds of things don't always last. Neither of us want to create drama in the village. If they don't work out, who cares? We're adults. If it doesn't work out with Mark I know that we'll both be professional and it will be much cleaner if no one else around knows."

She repeated Mark's words to me almost verba-tim.

"And that's why you didn't want to tell Elin?" I asked.

Nora tapped the coffee bean on her teeth. "No, it's more complicated with Elin."

"Why?"

"I didn't want to break her heart again."

Again? What? I felt like Nora had thrown me off balance with her words. When had Elin had her heart broken? And why had she never said anything to me?

Chapter Twenty-nine

Picking up as many beans as I could I sprinkled them in the window, and then turned back to Nora. "I don't understand," I said to her. "What does your relationship with Mark have to do with my aunt?"

Nora frowned. "Your aunt has never mentioned anything about Eric?"

"No. Who is Eric?" I couldn't believe that Elin would have kept her romantic life separate from me.

Sighing Nora flicked the coffee bean at the window. She pointed to the espresso bar. "Let me make you a drink."

I was about to protest that it was too late in the day for more caffeine, but Nora walked behind the stainless steel espresso machine and brought out a bottle of white wine and two tumbler glasses.

She tucked them under her arm and nodded at one of the bistro tables. Its chairs had been stacked upside down on the tabletop, I assumed so that the floor could be scrubbed. "Can you take those down?" Nora asked.

I moved the chair and Nora placed the wine on the center of the table. "Sit," she commanded. I sat as she filled the tumblers with wine. Handing me a glass, she sighed. "Elin has never mentioned Eric?"

"No." I shook my head, and set my glass on the table. I wasn't in the mood for wine. I wanted to know what Elin hadn't been telling me.

"Maybe you should talk to her about this," Nora said, taking a long, slow drink of the buttery yellow wine.

"You can't leave me hanging." My foot bounced on the floor.

She drummed her black fingernails on the bistro table. "You're probably right. You know having you home has been the best thing for Elin. You have no idea how good your timing was."

I wanted to remind her that I had nothing to do with timing my return. She could thank Chad and his wandering eye for that.

"It would be good for her to talk to you about this. I can't believe she's held on for so long. She needs to let go."

Thoughts assaulted my brain. What had Elin held on to for so long? And why hadn't she said anything to me?

"Your aunt and Eric were engaged many, many years ago."

"I never knew that she was engaged."

Nora nodded. "She was. She and Eric were deeply in love. They planned to get married, and then move to London. He had been offered a job with one of England's premier publishing houses. And Elin was up for an adventure. This was before she bought Blomma. Having lived her early years in Sweden, the idea of returning to Europe was fine with her."

"Then what happened? They broke up?" I asked.

"Not exactly." Nora took a swig of wine like she was downing a shot of whiskey. "They were set to sail off into the sunset. In fact Elin had her bags packed, her passport and work visa ready to go, and then a week later your parents were killed."

"Oh." Her words felt like a punch in the stomach.

She squeezed my hand with her black, Halloween-inspired nails. "It's not your fault, honey. I'm sure that's why she's never said anything."

I thought about the picture I'd found on Elin's dresser. She looked blissful and carefree in the photo. That changed because of me. My stomach swirled. I felt sick.

"I don't understand. Why did they have to break up though?" I asked Nora, trying to hold back salty tears.

"Because of you. Your aunt didn't hesitate for a moment when she was named your guardian. She already adored you, and as I'm sure you've heard she and your mother were more than sisters. They were best friends. It never crossed her mind to give you up."

"But Eric?" I already knew what Nora was going to say.

She tapped her wineglass. "Eric wasn't ready. It wasn't just you. I think that you were his out, but it had to be more than that. Elin and I have talked about it over the years. He wanted her to come to London, but you had just lost both of your parents. She had lost her sister, best friend, and brother-in-law. She refused to uproot you like that, to tear you away from Portland, school, your friends. She thought that would have been the worst thing for you, and I know that she was right."

My throat closed as salty tears clouded my vision. Elin had given up her life—her love—for me?

"Don't take it to heart, Britta." Nora placed her hand on mine. "She loves you more than anything else in the world. She doesn't blame you."

"But . . ." I couldn't formulate a sentence. My nose dripped and tears streamed down my cheeks.

Nora jumped up and returned with a stack of napkins. "I'm sorry. I'm sure this can't be easy to hear, but I promise you that Elin would have never done it differently. She loved every minute of raising you and watching you grow. You are her pride and joy. You have to know that. Hasn't everyone in the village said the same thing?"

I dabbed my eyes and blew my nose. "Yes, but to give everything up."

"She didn't. She's never seen it that way. She's always said that losing her sister was the most bittersweet experience. It left a gaping hole in her heart, but gave her you."

This made me sob even more. I couldn't stop the tears from falling or my shoulders from heaving over. I had been young when my parents died and while I had always missed not knowing them, Elin had given me a full life. But at what price? She had lost her sister and given up love for me. The weight of her sacrifice made my heart feel heavy.

Nora looked worried. "Britta, you can't blame yourself. Elin made a choice. She knew what she was doing, and like I said, we've both wondered if Eric wanted out. I don't know. I do think they were in love. I don't doubt that he loved her, but he made a choice too. He put his career first."

"And that was it?" I asked, wadding the napkin into a ball and reaching for another. "Did they ever talk again?"

"Well, yeah." Nora sighed, took a drink, and re-filled her glass. "That's why it's complicated with Mark. You see, Mark and Eric are cousins."

"Really?" The photo flashed in my mind again. That's why the man in the picture had seemed vaguely familiar. He and Mark were cousins. I couldn't believe it.

She nodded. "They grew up more like brothers here in Portland. Mark is twelve years younger, and Eric was like an older brother to him."

"That's a small world."

"Not really. Elin had graduated from the Floral Institute when she and Eric got engaged. She was planning to open a small boutique in London. When things changed after your parents died Mark was the one who recommended Blomma's space." She paused and took a long sip of her wine. "He was just starting out at the Riverplace Inn and the lease for Blomma was open. He called Elin and helped her get her first loan."

"Wow, that was kind of him." I swallowed back another round of tears.

"A lot of this I've learned from Mark. It wasn't all him. He was acting on Eric's behalf, but Eric made him swear never to tell Elin. He was worried that if Elin knew that it was him, she would turn down the help. That's another reason I think he really did—does—love her."

"Does?"

"They didn't keep in touch. It was too painful for your aunt, but Mark kept Eric up to date on how things were going at Blomma and for Elin. Neither of them married. Eric built his career in London, climbing up the publishing ranks until he was named editor in chief of the house three years ago. Last summer he came to Portland for a book convention. Mark told me that he was going to be in town, but asked me not to say anything to Elin. I couldn't keep that promise. She's my oldest friend." Nora threw her head back. "I think I made a mistake by telling her, Britta. Mark was probably right. He thought it would be better to keep them apart after all of these years, but I thought it was better to let her decide."

My mouth felt like cotton. "And, what did she decide?"

"She was stoic about it at first. She claimed that those memories were long in the past, but I know her better than that. She met him for a drink. He apologized. He explained why he had opted to go to London without her. He told her that he had never stopped loving her and that there wasn't a day that went by that he didn't think about her."

"Are you serious?" I couldn't believe everything Nora was telling me. And yet I thought back to my conversations with Elin for the past year and how I had been worried about her. I felt like she had been holding something back, and now I knew what it was.

"He asked her to come back to London with him. I think it stirred everything up for her again. It was like no time had gone by and she was back in her twenties having to make huge choices. She told me that she'll never leave Portland. I do think that she's happy here, but ever since seeing Eric again she's been different. Distant. Quieter. I don't know exactly how to explain it, but I can tell that he reopened an old wound."

"You're right. I've felt it too. I thought it was me—you know, from being gone—that maybe it was her getting older or too many gloomy Portland days. This makes so much more sense."

"Seeing him again after all those years really set her back. She hasn't been the same since. I feel terrible, I should have listened to Mark and never said anything about Eric being in town."

It was my turn to console her now. "You couldn't have known, and I think it would have been much worse to keep that from her. You did the right thing."

She ran her fingers through her spiky hair. "I hope so."

"I still don't entirely understand why you kept your relationship with Mark a secret from her. Because of Eric?"

"Exactly. Mark and I started out having a fun fling. It's turned a bit more serious, but I don't know that it will last. I'm flighty and he's stuffy. They say that opposites attract. That could be true in the bedroom, but time will tell if this turns into anything more." She winked. "I was planning to tell Elin but after her disastrous reconnection with

Eric it felt like I would be rubbing it in her face, especially since Eric and Mark are cousins."

"Right." I nodded, trying to absorb everything. Where did this leave us with Frank's murder?

Nora stood and gathered the tumblers and bottle of wine. "I just saw the time, I've got to get a move on. I'm meeting Mark for dinner."

I followed her to the espresso bar. "Can I ask you one more thing?"

"Shoot, honey."

"You don't think there's any way that Mark could be involved in Frank's murder, do you?"

She rinsed the glasses in the sink. "Mark? Never! He wouldn't swat at a fly. Why do you ask?" She looked genuinely surprised that I would suggest such a thing.

"No reason." I decided I had enough information to process for tonight. Frank's murder could wait. I needed to figure out how to get Elin to open up, and assure her that she had a solid shoulder to cry on.

Chapter Thirty

After I left Demitasse I needed a few minutes of fresh air to clear my head. Fortunately Elin's class still had at least a half hour to go. I continued along the cobblestone path and past the Riverplace Inn. Once I turned onto the riverfront path I was greeted by the Willamette's swollen muddy waters. Between the melting snowpack in the Cascade Mountains and the rash of spring storms that Portland had experienced, the river was running at record levels. It had flooded the far end of the pathway, so my only option was to walk west.

With the churning river to my right I headed toward the city, past runners out for early evening jogs and tourists who had come to get a firsthand look at the post-storm damage. Pink and white cherry blossoms looked like snow on the pathway. I had to maneuver around some broken limbs and intermittent puddles where the river had splashed through the embankment. A couple walking five dogs tried to control a wad of tangled leashes as they passed me. The woman hollered an apology when a fluffy husky stopped to lick my pant leg. I bent down to pet him and was greeted with a wet sloppy kiss on the lips.

"I'm so sorry!" The woman tried to pull him away from me.

"Don't give it a thought, he probably smells Sticks. I love dogs," I told her and patted the husky on the top of his head before continuing on.

"Of course you love dogs," a deep and familiar voice sounded behind me and made me stop in midstride.

I turned to see Pete. He was wearing a charcoal overcoat and holding a bag from Torch.

"Hey, what are you doing here?" The sound of geese fleeing from a toddler chasing them made me turn toward the river. The fading sunlight hit the swollen water giving it a rakish glow.

He motioned to the stream of people running and strolling around us. "Last time I checked this was a public path."

"I didn't mean that." I buttoned my coat. The air held a chill.

"What, are you worried that I'm tailing you?" He winked, which made my heart rate quicken.

"Are you?"

"I don't typically make a habit of following attractive women who love dogs."

Had he just called me attractive? I swallowed and tried to smile naturally, but had a feeling my face was probably betraying my feelings. "I was just at Demitasse with Nora's dog Sticks. He's adorable. Almost like a mini version of her, and she wasn't exaggerating about the coffee thing. The dog loves java."

Two women walked by us holding paper cups from Nora's shop. Pete laughed. "Sticks and everyone else in Portland." He studied me for a moment. "Nice coat, you look good in red."

My heart flopped. "Thanks." I changed the subject and pointed to the matte black shopping bag with a white silhouette of a candle and the word TORCH spelled out in flames. "Were you in the market for candles?"

"Something like that." He glanced at the bag. "Mind if I walk with you for a stretch?"

"Not at all." If I was being honest with myself that wasn't entirely true. Being around Pete had me feeling completely confused. We had quickly developed an easy rapport. Was it too soon? I didn't trust myself yet, and I didn't want to rush into anything. Yet, Pete made me feel so comfortable it was hard to resist his company.

He fell into step with me. I willed my heartrate to steady itself. "To be honest, I'm in the market for information, and I've found sometimes the best way to get a business owner talking is to do some shopping."

"Did you mean to rhythm just now?" I teased.

"Was that a rhythm? I didn't notice." His eyes stayed focused ahead, but I could tell from his tone that he was kidding.

"Did you find what you were looking for at Torch?" I was acutely aware of the proximity of our bodies as we walked toward the Hawthorne Bridge.

"I found a nice set of votive candles."

He didn't strike me as a candle kind of guy.

As if reading my mind he continued. "They'll make a nice present for my favorite lady."

Favorite lady? Had I misinterpreted our flirtation? Did Pete have a girlfriend? My heart sunk and my cheeks flamed. It was silly. I was still married, had yet to receive Chad's copies of our divorce papers, but hearing that Pete had a woman in his life was a disappointment. My attraction to him was probably nothing more than a welcome distraction from my impending divorce and Frank's murder, but learning that he was taken was depressing.

Pete was oblivious to my reaction as he continued. "I did learn a few interesting pieces of information from Jon while I was picking out candles though."

"Really?" Was he going to share the information with me?

"You've met Lawren, right?"

"Yeah. Why?"

He kicked a two-foot branch from the path and watched it tumble down the grassy bank. "I'd be curious to hear your impression of her."

"She seems pretty timid to me. Not that I can imagine working for someone with Frank's demanding personality, but from the brief interaction I saw between them it looked like Frank ordered her around and she jumped at his every command."

"Mm-hmm." Pete moved to the side to make room for a young mom pushing a baby jogger to pass us. "Anything else?"

I thought about her weird search for her wallet. "There is her missing wallet. She burst into Blomma the morning I found Frank and claimed that she had forgotten her wallet, yet she kept looking for it on the wall of wine."

Pete nodded slightly. "Yes. That is odd."

"What did Jon say? I didn't know that he and Lawren were even acquainted."

"Neither did I. That's why perusing Torch for candles for my mom turned out to be highly beneficial. Not only do I have a Mother's Day present weeks early but I learned that Lawren had been begging everyone in the village—including Jon— for a job."

His mom was his favorite lady? I almost slipped on a pile of wet leaves. Pete caught me with his free arm. "You okay?"

His touch made the tiny hairs on my arms stand at attention and sent warmth spreading through my body. "I'm great," I said trying to sound neutral. The news that his mom was the recipient of his candle purchase made me feel light on my feet. "Lawren asked Jon for a job?"

"Yep. What about you? Did she approach you or your aunt about a position at Blomma?"

"Not that I know of." I shook my head. "I can ask Elin, but as far as I know Lawren never mentioned anything about a job. Was this before or after Frank was killed?"

"That's one of the things that I'm trying to figure out. According to Jon, Lawren asked him weeks ago."

"Can you blame her? I wouldn't have lasted five minutes working for Frank."

"Jon agreed. He made some pretty major accusations that I'm going to have to follow up on."

"Like what?"

"That, I'm afraid, is confidential." We had made it to the base of the Hawthorne Bridge. Cars and bikes zoomed above us on the truss bridge. The Hawthorne was the busiest bicycle bridge in the city. Close to ten thousand bikes passed over it daily. Farther down the path tourists were waiting to board the *Portland Spirit,* a riverboat that took passengers on dinner cruises along the Willamette. Across the river a submarine sat permanently tied to the dock. It was part of OMSI—Oregon Museum of Science and Industry. Visitors could board and tour the retired military vessel.

Pete looked at his watch and then pointed up the street. "I have to leave you here. Thanks for the walk and talk, Britta."

I needed to get back to Blomma too. The workshop should be wrapping up soon, and I wanted to be there to take photos of the students' succulents and help Elin clean up. As much as I had enjoyed spending a few minutes with Pete I felt more confused than ever. Had Lawren gotten fed up with Frank's treatment of her and gone in search of a job? Could she have snapped? Pete had mentioned that he thought the crime scene was that of an act of passion not something premeditated. But did Lawren even have the physical strength to kill him?

I knew one thing. Tomorrow I was going to check in with Jon and see if he would tell me what accusations he made about Frank. For the moment my focus had to be on Elin. She was hurting and I had to find a way to break through her steely exterior and talk to her about Eric.

Chapter Thirty-one

Once we had sent the last of Elin's students out the front door and picked up the cottage, we headed for home. I kept the conversation light as we drove along the Willamette River. I knew I was going to have to choose my words carefully so as not to betray Nora and to create a space for Elin to open up.

At her house I offered to make dinner and sent her off to take a bath. I decided to make a Swedish meatball soup. It was a recipe I had created to appease Chad's bland palate, but it was comforting and homey, which is exactly what I needed for my conversation with Elin. I started by sautéing onions, mushrooms, carrots, celery, red potatoes, and fresh herbs in olive oil. Then I added beef stock and let that simmer while I started on the meatballs. Making meatballs is second nature to me. For the soup I wanted mini meatballs, so I crushed crackers into a mixture of beef and pork and bound it together with an egg. Then I rolled little one-inch meatballs and dropped them into a sizzling pan of oil. Once they had been browned on all over I added them to my soup stock and brought the pot to a boil.

By the time Elin came downstairs with cheeks rosy from the bath and wrapped in her robe, the soup was ready to serve. I finished it with a splash of heavy cream, fresh chopped rosemary, and black pepper.

"Hungry?" I asked placing a bowl with a slab of rustic bread in front of her.

"Famished. This smells wonderful, Britta. What is it?"

"It's sort of a mashup recipe. I call it Swedish meatball soup." I ladled a bowl for myself and joined her at the table.

She dipped her spoon into the soup. "If it tastes as good as it smells we might have to package this and sell it at Blomma."

"Soup and flowers. Hmm? I don't know about that combination."

"Maybe not." She laughed and blew on her spoon.

I couldn't decide how best to steer the conversation toward Eric. Elin and I had been close my entire life, and now sitting across from her I struggled to find the right words. How could I ever thank and repay her for what she had done for me?

She must have picked up on my unease, because before tasting the soup she gave me a concerned look. "Is something bothering you?"

Without giving myself time to chicken out, I set

my spoon on the table and said, "I know about Eric."

Elin's face dropped. She dumped the soup on her spoon back into her bowl and placed her hand over her heart. "I see."

"I'm so sorry, Aunt Elin."

"Why would you be sorry, dear? It has nothing to do with you."

"It has everything to do with me. You gave up love and marriage for me."

She patted her chest. "No, no, never. I didn't give up a thing. I got you." Her eyes misted.

"Why haven't you ever said anything?"

She inhaled deeply then took a bite of the soup. "There wasn't much to say. You were so young when Eric and I parted ways and then later when you were old enough it didn't matter. It was so long ago and I never wanted you to think exactly what you're saying now. It wasn't a choice, Britta. It was always you. Eric knew that. I never hesitated. I never even gave it a thought. When Anna and Diego died it became you and me. We were a team, and nothing was going to tear that apart."

"Yes, but you were in love."

"I was." Her voice sounded as misty as the tears forming in her eyes. "Eric will always have a piece of my heart. I admit that, but you *are* my heart, Britta. To lose everyone you loved and then lose me. No. Never. And this might be hard to believe, but I needed you as much as, if not more than, you needed me."

Tears streamed down her face. My eyes were wet too.

"That was a terrible time. I'll never forget getting the call." She reached for her napkin to dab her eyes. "Your mom and I had been shopping the night before. She was helping me pack for London because she was a good sister, but I knew that she didn't want me to go. She never said anything, but I think that she had reservations about Eric."

"Why?" I bit into a hot meatball. It reminded me of childhood dinners enjoyed at this same table. How had I not known that Elin was hurting?

"Oh it's hard to put into words. Anna and I weren't just sisters, as I've told you before. She was my best friend, she was my mentor, my confidante, my mom after our parents died too. I wanted to believe that it was that she didn't want me to be far away from all of you, but with time I think that some of the questions she asked me about Eric were her way of trying to nudge me into reconsidering."

I thought about some of the questions Elin had asked me when I first brought up the idea of moving to Minnesota with Chad. She had done the same thing. I remember her saying things like, "Have you considered leaving your friends here in Portland?" and "How does Chad feel about you starting your own shop?" At the time I had figured she was helping me process, but now it was suddenly clear that she'd been worried about me, just like my mom had worried about her.

"Then a day later they were gone." She snapped her fingers. "In one terrible moment everything changed, for both of us."

Hot tears pooled in my eyes. That day was forever etched in my memory, too. My parents had been on their way home from dinner when a drunk driver slammed into their car, killing them both instantly. Elin had been babysitting me so that they could have an evening away. I remember the sound of her screams and how she dropped to her knees when she got the call. She didn't have to tell me they were gone. I knew. It was evident by her empty stare and the way that her mouth tried to form the words.

Now as an adult I could only begin to imagine how hard that must have been for her. How do you tell a child that her entire world has been ripped away from her? How do you begin to mend the pieces of that kind of loss? I wasn't sure how she had done it, but she had found a way to hold both of us together. She would stroke my hair while I sobbed on her shoulder. Leave little notes on my bedside table and tucked into my lunch box. We celebrated bittersweet holidays like my parents' birthdays and the anniversary of their death by planting flowers of remembrance in her garden. Their death shaped me, and Elin helped me grow through it—grow with it.

"Britta, do you know how proud your parents would be of the woman you've become? They loved you so much. I've always tried to live up to their legacy, but it hasn't been easy. They left huge shoes to fill."

"But you did," I managed to squeak out between sobs and wiping my dripping nose on the back of my napkin. "You gave me a wonderful life. That's one of the reasons I feel so bad that I never knew how much you lost too."

She reached for my hand. "I don't know what I

lost. I don't know how it would have turned out with Eric. In hindsight I don't think he was ready. I think that the accident was a way out for him."

"Have you kept in contact?" I knew the answer, but I didn't want to mention how much Nora had shared. Elin hadn't questioned how I knew about Eric, but she must have guessed.

She let my hand go and took a taste of her soup. "Not really. He tried to keep communication open, but it was too hard for me. He's been in London for years. Many years. I've been here. The distance kept our lives separate." Taking another bite she paused for a moment. "He came this summer though. I don't know if it was good to see him or if it made things worse."

"Why?"

"He's never married either. Every year on the anniversary of when he proposed to me, he sends me flowers. It's the only contact we've had. I've never responded. You can't go back in time, and I didn't see a point in opening an old wound. But I did enjoy knowing that red roses would arrive on my doorstep like a gift from the past every year. I often thought I would know that he had moved on or finally married when the roses stopped, but they didn't."

"And then you saw each other in person this summer."

She nodded. "I hadn't seen him in twenty-five years. Twenty-five years is a long time, and yet the minute we met it was as if no time had passed. He was the same as I remember him, maybe a tad grayer around the edges, but I would have recognized him anywhere." She stared off toward the window and into the night sky for a moment. "Seeing him brought a flood of happy memories back, and the same feelings I had had when I said yes to his proposal. I was twenty-eight years old when your parents died. It's hard to believe that time trudges on, and yet seeing Eric made me feel young again."

I ate my soup and waited for her to say more. It was evident in her body language, the way she kept clutching her heart, and staring longingly into space, that she was still in love with him.

"But that doesn't change the fact that we're in very different places now—literally and figuratively. He's established in London. He won't leave, and neither will I. Portland is my home and Blomma is my heart. I think that he has some regrets. That tends to happen as we age. Having a longer lens provides a clearer vision into our past. I got the sense in talking with him that he imagined a different life. I think he would have liked to have married, had children, but the years faded away."

I'd never seen Elin like this. I understood why Nora was trying to protect her. Regardless of what my aunt was saying I knew that her heart was tender in a way I had yet to experience. Her body shifted as she spoke about Eric and reflected on the past. Years seemed to slip off her skin. Only a true and intense love could create such transformation. Had I ever felt that way about Chad? I didn't think so. Which was worse, mediocre love or unrequited love? If we could both capture our love lives in bouquets what would they be? Mine would probably be a vase of cheap, dyed carnations, and Elin's something red and full of fiery passion.

"And you?" I almost whispered. "Do you have regrets?"

She clasped her hands in front of her. "Britta, we all have regrets. Of course I've wondered over the years what happened to him and occasionally allowed myself to imagine—fantasize really—what our life might have been like together. But that's not real. That's not how the world works."

"Are you sure that there's no chance of a reconciliation? Things are different now. Portland has a direct flight to London. It's only a ten- or twelve-hour plane ride. I'm here now and can cover the shop while you're away."

"Maybe, but there's more to consider."

"Like what?"

"Like you. Like Blomma. My life here. What's the reality of making a long-distance relationship a success? London and Portland, regardless of a direct flight, are almost five thousand miles apart. Trust me, I looked it up many years ago. I don't know that I want to open myself up to just have my heart broken again."

I appreciated her honesty and knew that she was sincere, but part of me wanted to shake her. What was the risk? She had spent the last twenty-five years being heartsick. I wanted her to take a leap. I wanted her to shine, to see her cheeks glow with happiness at the mention of Eric's name. I couldn't repay her for taking me in and raising me, but I could nudge her toward finding her own happiness.

She tapped her spoon on the edge of her bowl. "Eat up. Your soup has probably gone cold."

I knew that was her way of dismissing the subject. I would for now, but hearing her talk about Eric made me sure that they were meant to be together. Elin had been there for me, now it was my turn to do the same for her. I didn't know how, but I knew I was going to find a way to facilitate their romance. And I had a feeling that I would find a willing partner in crime in Nora.

Chapter Thirty-two

The next morning was the big day. We had a ton of work to do before we officially opened the cottage to the public. I wanted to talk to Jon, so I made a beeline for Torch the minute I saw him flip on the massive wooden candelabras that flanked his front door.

Like Nora he had updated his storefront to reflect the changing seasons. Pastel flameless votive candles flickered with warm pink and yellow light. He had arranged them in the shape of tulips.

"Britta, did you feel your ears burning? You are just the person I wanted to see." Jon held the door open. He wore another turtleneck, this time a dark navy blue, with jeans that looked as if they had been freshly ironed.

"Really? What do you need?"

He swept his hand across the window display. "I'm inviting spring to officially return, and was hoping you might be able to supply me with some living tulips to accompany my little light show. And to be honest I'm ready to win this season's window contest."

"Sure. Do you have color preferences?"

Jon picked up one of the two-inch votives. From a distance it was impossible to tell that their flames were fake. The gentle battery-operated light flickered like a real flame. Once again I was struck by the contrast of Elin's and my romances. Hers was a low-burning flame whereas my relationship with Chad had never even sparked. Why had I stuck with a dud? I was tempted to make a dismissive gesture, but realized that Jon was staring at me.

"Anything with this color scheme will be delightful." He returned the votive to its spot in the tulip and motioned me to the back. "Come, come. Do tell me what's new in the world of flowers?"

"Not much." I couldn't make my eyes focus. Torch was a sensory delight. Shimmering crystal chandeliers hung from the exposed wood-beamed ceiling, along with lights carved from deer antlers, rustic iron showstoppers that looked as if they belonged at a feast from the middle ages. Candle holders of all shapes and sizes were displayed by height in collections on deep walnut dressers. The entire far wall was made of rustic barn doors where Jon had mounted shelves to illuminate another assortment of candleholders. It smelled equally as enchanting. There were candles spun from beeswax, hand-dipped in paraffin, and molded into elaborate works of art. From forest pine to Bing cherry there were scents for any mood.

I stopped and lifted the lid on a candle labeled Spring Rain. Inhaling the scent I was immediately transported to a few days earlier when the storm had rolled through.

Jon gave me a nod of approval. "Isn't that wonderful? The candlemaker is local. She believes in using only natural products in her candles. No GMOs or synthetic scents. She's my best seller. You have exquisite taste, my dear." His dark bony fingers massaged the top of a lush candle. "Try this."

I took the tin he handed me and sniffed it. "Oh, what is that? It's so familiar." I stuck my nose closer. "Cloves?"

"Close. Cardamom and orange essence."

"It's amazing." I let my nostrils linger on the welcoming scent for a minute before returning the candle. "Your shop is beyond beautiful. I can't figure out where to look."

"You're not alone." He moved with lionlike grace. His lanky body skirted past stacked displays with ease. "I love watching first-time customers. Most of the time they don't even purchase. They spend hours perusing and touching."

"But they don't buy anything?"

"No, but I never give that a thought. I encourage them to immerse themselves in my world of light that I've created. I see it as my responsibility as a light worker to allow them the space to drink it all in. In fact I encourage touching, smelling, and browsing. None of my products are off limits, unless it's a snotty nosed kid with sticky hands. They might not buy right away, but once they've experienced Torch they'll come back." He sounded completely sure of himself without being pompous, a tricky thing to pull off.

"Very wise." I followed him as he clicked on an

antique stained-glass Tiffany lamp and plugged in a string of Edison-style bulbs that lit up the cash register—also vintage.

"However, I digress. You wanted to see me?"

"Yeah, I was wondering about Lawren."

"Little Miss Mouse." He lit a candle in a four-inch round tin. Immediately the smell of fresh-cut grass hit my nose.

"Is that what you call her?"

He made a sweeping gesture in the air. "Only in fun. You've met the girl, yes?"

"Yes."

"Well am I right, or am I right?" He winked and turned on eighties music. The stylized pop sounds of Michael Jackson's "Beat It" sounded out of place in the elegant almost museumlike light shop.

"Don't like my tunes?" He pretended to be injured. "Listen, dear, I'm a gay black man who lives in Portland—the land of indie alternative music." He shuddered. "You have to give me something." He grinned.

"You won't get any complaints from me. I love retro music."

"Did you just say retro? Out!" He pointed to the door. "Out of my store. Michael Jackson is a classic. Classic. You need to choose your words much more carefully the next time."

I laughed. "Sorry. My bad."

He strummed his fingers on his chin for a moment. "Fine, I'll give you a pass this time, but consider this your warning. Understood? Torch is a sacred space when it comes to eighties dance music and show tunes. How do you feel about *The Music Man*?"

"Never heard of it."

Gasping, he placed the back of his hand on his forehead. "We're going to have to remedy that aren't we? Between your aunt and her boring classic music and Nora's Pearl Jam what is a music-loving man to do?"

"Like I said at dinner the other night, I'm always up for trying something new. Name the day and I'll come listen to *The Music Man* or whatever else strikes your fancy."

A funny smile spread across his angular face. "Be careful, my dear, I'll hold you to that. I have a collection of musicals that would make most Broadway producers green with envy."

"I'm in."

He laughed. "I keep changing the conversation, don't I? What about Little Miss Mouse can I help you with?"

"Honestly I'm not sure. Pete—Detective Fletcher."

Jon clapped his hands. "Nice try." He winked. "Yes, what about *Pete?*"

I was sure a blush must be creeping up my cheeks, and Jon confirmed it. "No need to blush, dear. I've seen the way that the detective ogles you. I'm confident the feeling is quite mutual."

Part of me wanted to do a little dance. Jon noticed it too. Maybe my flirtation with Pete wasn't all in my head. "Anyway, Pete mentioned that Lawren had asked you for a job," I continued.

"That's right."

"He said something offhand about an accusation."

Jon glanced toward the front of the shop, as if to make sure that we were alone. "That's right." He leaned across the register. "I tease about her being mousy, but I feel sorry for the poor girl. So much so that I've been trying to decide if I should add a few evening or weekend hours for her."

"Why?"

"Well, not only did Frank fire her, but he tried to hit on her."

"He did?" Frank had been obnoxious, but I found it slightly surprising that he would have made a pass on someone so young.

"Apparently he lunged at her. She told me that she had considered going to the police but she didn't have any proof. It would be his word against hers, and who would believe her over the all-powerful Frank?"

"Did you believe her?"

Jon paused for a second. "I can't imagine why she would make something like that up."

He had a point there.

"So do you know if this happened before or after he fired her?"

"I'm not sure. She was sketchy on the details. I think it was upsetting her to talk about it, but come to think of it I remember her saying something about quitting. I wonder if she meant that or if she just got her words jumbled up."

Had she let something slip? If Frank had tried to hit on her that could be a motive for murder, but it seemed like a big leap especially given Lawren's small stature and low confidence. I couldn't picture her stabbing Frank, and yet it wasn't out of the realm of possibility either.

"The poor thing claimed that Frank was trying to ruin her reputation. Apparently he had started a smear campaign. He told her that he was going to go door to door and let every business owner in the village know that he had fired her. He swore she would never work in the village or Portland again."

Suddenly Lawren was looking more and more like a potential killer. Hitting on her and trying to make sure he put her permanently out of work. Both of those sounded like viable motives to me.

"Does that brain of yours ever turn off?" Jon asked, peering at me from beneath his wire-rimmed glasses.

"Not really. I wish it did."

"Don't say that." He patted my hand. "A woman of beauty and intellect is a wonderful gift."

"Thanks." A bell jingled on Torch's front door. "I should get going, and it looks like you have a customer," I said to Jon. "You told all of this to Pete, right?"

"Right." He escorted me to the door and greeted the customer with a welcome hug.

I crossed the street back to Blomma. Had I finally learned once and for all who had killed Frank Jaffe? Lawren had a solid motive, she easily could have ducked back into the shop, and if she had caught Frank off guard she most likely could have stabbed him with one sharp jab. Plus she had been acting so skittish searching for a lost wallet on a wall of wine. I didn't know what she was really looking for, but it had to be a clue. She must have left something behind when she killed Frank. I had to find it and get it to Pete ASAP.

Chapter Thirty-three

In between tying bouquets and taking customer orders I searched every square inch of the wine wall without success. If Lawren had stashed something among the bottles of wine she had hidden it well. I removed bottle after bottle on the off chance that she had tucked a note or something else incriminating under one of the bottles.

"What are you doing?" A woman's voice sounded behind me as I stacked a bottle of Beaujolais on the wine bar. I turned to see Serene entering through the garage doors. She sounded almost angry as she approached me rolling her wine cart. I wondered if she was upset that I was messing with her display.

"Just a little cleaning. Tonight's the big launch party so I want to make sure that everything is sparkling." That was a small lie. I did want Blomma to shine tonight, but Serene's wine practically gleamed.

"Dust?" Serene's immovable brows almost arched. "Are any of my bottles of wine dusty? I can't believe that. I'm meticulous about cleaning every time I restock. If you're not satisfied with my work, please let me know. Elin has given me free rein with Blomma's wine, but if you have feedback or suggestions on my display, I'm all ears."

She was irritated. "No, no. Like I said it was slow and I needed a project. Honestly I haven't even needed to use this." I held up a clean dust rag.

"Have you put everything back in the same place?" Serene's tone was short and crisp. "I have everything arranged in a specific order based on variety, blend, and vineyard." She untied her trench coat and began checking each bottle.

I felt bad. Serene was obviously not pleased that I had tampered with her product. "Yes. I've taken one bottle out at a time and put it back in the exact same spot."

She paced in front of the wall as if making sure that I wasn't lying. "Good. Hours of work went into putting this together."

"I'm sorry—I was really trying to help."

"Sure." She smiled through her clenched jaw.

"I'll let you take it from here," I said nodding at the bottle of Beaujolais.

"Thanks." She picked up the bottle and cradled it like a baby before returning it to its spot on the wall.

I could tell that I had offended her. She took her wine seriously. While I sketched out some rough ideas for a new spring window display I watched Serene check off her inventory sheet and twist bottles so that their labels were perfectly centered. I wondered if she was slightly obsessive-compulsive. That would make even more sense as to why she was irritated with me fiddling with her display.

When she finished she clicked across the cement floor and handed me an invoice. "I'm done. Tell Elin that I'll be back for the party by six thirty at the latest."

"Is there anything I can help do to prep?" I asked, filing the invoice.

"No, I have everything under control." She gave me a firm look and yanked her cart out the garage doors.

Wow, she was really upset with me. I was going to have to make amends. The last thing I wanted was to have our wine steward stalking around every time she saw me. I returned to my sketches and mapped out a spring in bloom design to show Elin. In my vision I thought we could create a window display from the ground up so to speak, with a layer of organic dirt and bark, sprouting up to seedlings, and then stretching into gorgeous, lush blooms to the top of the window. I hoped that Elin would like the concept, as I was eager for a fresh project and excited to try something new.

With that complete it was time to focus on decorating for our botanical couture bash. The students who had participated in the preview workshop would be showing off their one-of-a-kind wearable floral art.

Wearable floral art was a new trend that many people in the industry credited Elin with starting. Whether used as an accent on a runway show or as party favors for guests, floral jewelry was all the rage these days. However, crafting a structure that allowed movement and stability was a challenge. Part of tonight's launch would include Elin teaching a mini-workshop on the mechanics of building signature couture flowers as well as sourcing the right materials for each student's piece. She was a genius when it came to layering botanical fabrics so that they could move and flow without falling apart. Her avant-garde headpieces had been worn on catwalks and featured in fashion magazines around the world.

Flowers had a long-standing history with fashion. In the 1600s French women wore tulips like precious gems. Delicate lacy flowers were woven into fabrics of both men and women's attire in the middle ages. Flowers brought a certain light and romance to clothing and were often more expensive than actual jewels. Elin was reviving the trend and the fashion industry had embraced her vision.

Media and press had been invited to the soirée. Thus far every reporter had RSVP'd with a yes. It was going to be a packed house. I wondered if we would have had the same turnout if Frank hadn't been killed. How many members of the media saw tonight's event as an opportunity to rehash his brutal murder? I hoped that it wouldn't take away from the stunning party we had planned.

Elin was still working on putting the finishing touches on her masterpiece—the full-length floral gown that was sure to be the star of the show. I took on the task of decorating the front of the shop. First I rearranged the furniture and placed the fragrant sherbet bouquets throughout the room. Then I strung fresh snaking hop vines and rosebuds into the garlands Elin and I had made earlier in the week. Stringing these from the ceiling, I tied them so they crisscrossed the space and hung low enough for our guests to appreciate their beauty, but not so low that anyone would bump their head.

Next I positioned black iron candelabras that we had borrowed from Jon and pale pink and peach taper candles on the bar, the workstation, and coffee table. I wrapped twinkle lights between the bottles of wine and weaved them through the buckets of fresh-cut flowers. Blomma had never looked lovelier. There wasn't much more I could do for the moment. The caterer would arrive later, as would our models and string quartet. Right before the guests arrived we would roll out our floral carpet.

Elin came in from the cottage just before four. She held a canvas bag in one hand and rubbed her eyes with the other. "I'm calling it quits. I can't see straight. Cross your fingers and toes that the gown holds up."

"I'm sure it will. Don't worry." I unplugged the lights and flipped the sign on the door to closed.

"Everything looks wonderful, Britta. You've outdone yourself."

I waved her off. "It's nothing. I can't wait to see the cottage and gown."

Elin held up her index finger. Her eyes looked weary, but I could tell she was excited too. "Not until tonight. I want it to be a surprise."

"Are you ready to take off?" We had opted to close early to give ourselves time to run home and change.

Elin nodded. "I'll meet you outside."

"Okay." I went ahead of her. To my surprise Tomo was crossing the street. "Hey, what are you doing here?" I called.

He nodded to Torch. "I'm on follow-up duty for Detective Fletcher. I hear there's a big bash at Blomma tonight. Everyone in the village is buzzing about it."

I bit my thumbnail. "I know, I hope everything goes smoothly."

"I'm sure it will." He gave me a reassuring nod.

"Are you going to come by?"

"Am I on the invite list? From what I've heard, it's the most exclusive ticket in town tonight."

"Yeah, right." I winked. "You should come. I meant to invite Pete too."

"We'll be there, don't worry." He continued on to Torch.

Elin and I packed the Jeep with supplies. The caterer, Nora, and Serene would all be back a little before six to set up. That gave us two hours to shower and change. Typically Elin teaches workshops in her jeans and cable-knit sweaters, but tonight was a special occasion. It was the official launch of the cottage. We had hired local high school students as models who would display our haute couture flowers while circulating through the cottage and flower shop with trays of flower-themed appetizers and drinks.

I dug through my closet to see what I had to wear. Like Elin's, most of my wardrobe was geared toward function and comfort. However I did have a few dresses that had rarely been worn. In fact each of them looked brand new as I laid them on the bed and tried to decide which one would be the most flattering.

After trying each of them on, I opted for a red knee-length cocktail dress with simple black beading around the waist and a flare skirt. I paired it with open-toed black heels and a black cashmere scarf. I pinned my hair behind my ears with antique silver clips and highlighted my cheekbones with blush. Then I applied a shimmery silver eyeshadow and red lipstick. Stepping back to observe myself in the long mirror, I was pleased with my reflection. The dress accentuated my waist, and its flirty skirt made me feel like I was ready for a party. However I couldn't help but hear Kirk's teasing in my ear. I could already picture him calling me Snow. *Gross.*

I met Elin in the kitchen for a quick snack of crackers, cheese, and fruit. Who knew if we would have a chance to eat anything later? I almost didn't recognize her when she came down the stairs wearing an ankle-length green organza skirt, ballet flats, and a flowing ivory tank and matching sweater.

"You look amazing," I said.

She studied me. "And you are a vision. The red is so striking with your skin."

"You're biased."

"Maybe." She kissed the top of my head. "But I have to say we look ready for a ball, don't we?"

"Is this a ball? I thought it was a flower show." I crunched a cracker.

"It's the closest I'll ever get to a ball."

I laughed and spread goat cheese and chives on another cracker. "Me too. Are you ready for tonight? This is a long time coming. I'm so proud of you, and so glad I'm here to be a part of it."

Elin helped herself to a slice of pear and hunk

of Brie. "Britta, I would be lost without you. I'm the lucky one to have *you* here."

"Well if nothing else at least we both love what we've accomplished, right?" I joked.

"That reminds me, I have something special for you." She stood up and went into the living room. Then she returned with a Blomma box. "Here, open it."

"You didn't need to get me anything," I said.

"I know, but I wanted to make something for you, and it appears that I planned it as if I knew what you were going to wear."

I opened the box to find the most dainty flower headband I had ever seen. Elin had weaved variegated holly leaves with rosebuds and just a touch of Queen Anne's lace to give the headband texture and a pop of white. "This is beautiful. It's too pretty to wear," I replied as I gently removed the headband from the box.

"No, it's meant to be worn. That's the whole purpose of tonight's show." She held out her arm to display a bracelet and matching ring that she had made out of pastel succulents. They reminded me of something a garden fairy would wear. "We have to showcase our art tonight."

"I've never worn something as magnificent as this," I said placing the rose headband on my head.

She clasped her hands together. "Oh, Britta. It's wonderful. Exactly as I imagined. You look like a princess. Go see in the mirror." She pointed to the half bathroom in the hallway off the kitchen.

I followed her advice and went to see her creation. She was right. I looked as if I was wearing a bed of delicate roses on my head. The brilliant red roses and Queen Anne's Lace contrasted against my dark hair. I wondered how Elin had managed to design something that fit my head perfectly. Had she snuck in and measured my skull at night? The headband was snug without feeling too tight or restricting. I didn't need the clips to hold my hair back, so I removed them and left them in the bathroom

Elin's eyes looked dewy when I returned with the headpiece in position. "You really are a vision, Britta. You're going to be the star of the show."

"I don't know about that," I protested. "But speaking of the show, we should probably get back shouldn't we?"

Glancing at the clock above the stove, Elin polished off a piece of cheese. "Yes, we should."

We walked arm in arm to the Jeep, feeling like queens and ready to welcome the world into Blomma's cottage. I just hoped that everything would flow seamlessly tonight. Frank's murder was old news and now it was time to start fresh.

Chapter Thirty-four

When the party started Blomma had been transformed into something out of the pages of a fairy tale. It was impossible not to feel like a character from one of the Brothers Grimm stories as I practically floated from guest to guest. Every light and candle in the shop and cottage had been illuminated, casting a warm glow throughout the space. A plush red carpet greeted everyone as they entered the shop through the garage doors. It ran through the front and extended into the cottage, as if marking a path. We had scattered white rose petals on the carpet, giving it a dramatic flair, and wrapped posts with more of the garland to create a visually stunning entrance.

Serene stood guard at the wine bar, pouring glasses of wine in gold-rimmed goblets. Nora had set up a coffee tasting station in the front seating area where she treated guests to tastes of a special cherry blossom blend she had created just for the launch party. A string quartet wearing top hats and boutonnieres made of roses played on the sidewalk out front.

Models wearing ornate dresses and headpieces constructed entirely out of flowers and greenery worked the room with trays of appetizers—all shaped like flowers. There were daisy puffed pastries with cream cheese and a raspberry center, watermelon and white cheddar cheese tulips, sunflower truffles, salami roses, and miniature terra cotta pots filled with dip and spouting with vegetables.

I couldn't keep a happy grin from spreading across my face as I circulated around the room and chatted with clients and the press. Elin showcased her techniques in the cottage, creating individual rings for everyone who came in.

"This is quite a success," Nora whispered as I walked past the coffee station. "You and your aunt sure know how to throw a party. The only thing I would change is that I would lose the stuffy quartet for an electric guitar." She winked. Elin had made her a custom piece of floral fashion, too. Nora wore a floral choker with spiky tendrils and Black Magic hollyhocks. It matched her jet-black leather dress and studded black boots.

"What are people saying?" I asked, declining the tasting cup that Nora extended. I was already riding high on the happy energy of the night. I didn't need caffeine to enhance my experience.

"They're saying this is the best show that Portland has ever seen."

"Well, it is unique."

"No, not flower show—fashion show. Do you see

that woman hanging around near the musicians?"
She gave a subtle nod in the direction of a tall elegant woman dressed in man's suit. Somehow she
managed to make the suit look feminine and powerful at the same time.

"Yeah," I replied.

"That's Misty Haze." Nora poured cream into a
silver carafe.

"Who is Misty Haze?"

"She's the editor in chief of *Mod*."

"What's *Mod*?"

"Girl, where have you been?" Nora looked exasperated at my lack of knowledge. "Oh, that's right,
you've been out of the loop for a while. *Mod* is only
the biggest fashion blog on the planet. Misty lives
here but spends most of her time in Paris and New
York. It was a stroke of luck that she happened to
be in town for Blomma's launch, and I can tell that
she is loving this."

I glanced back in Misty's direction. Her severe
face and pouty lips said otherwise. "That's happy?
She looks like she's waiting for a root canal."

Nora topped off a tray of tasters as a group approached us. "No, she's thrilled. I promise."

I left her to explain the specialty roast and
headed in Misty's direction, but was cut off by a
grubby hand grabbing my shoulder.

"Hey Snow." Kirk Jaffe leered at me with a crooked
grin. "I see you dressed for the part tonight. How
about you and I sneak off someplace a bit quieter?"

"No thanks." I freed myself from his grasp. "I'm
good."

"You *are* good." He made a weird motion with

his eyes. If this was his attempt at a pickup line he was failing miserably.

Fortunately I spotted Tomo and Pete making their way toward the cottage, so I ignored Kirk and hurried to catch up with them.

"Hey, who are you hiding from?" Tomo asked when I squeezed in between them. They were both wearing street clothes. Tomo wore skinny jeans and an untucked flannel, like he had at his parents' noodle shop. He blended in perfectly with Portland's young hipster crowd. Pete had on a pair of black slacks, a gray shirt, and a tie the color of my dress. "You two match," Tomo commented.

"Indeed." Pete raised an eyebrow and stared at me so intently that the room started to sway. "I like the flowers."

"Thanks." I wondered if my voice sounded as weird to them as it did in my head. Absently I touched my hand to my rose band.

"Seriously, who are you trying to ditch?" Tomo glanced around the crowded room.

"Kirk Jaffe," I said, glad that Pete's focus had steered away from me. "He's the worst."

"He's crushing hard on you." Tomo laughed and then proceeded to block me with his bulky body when Kirk pushed through the crowd toward us.

Pete stiffened. "Is he bothering you, Britta?"

"No, I mean, yeah, but it's nothing I can't handle."

"You sure?" He watched Kirk try to cozy up to Lawren, who was hovering at the far end of the bar, looking nervous as always.

"Positive."

Tomo snagged three glasses of wine and handed

them to us. "This is some event you and your aunt have put on, Britta. My mom is planning to stop by in a while." He couldn't keep his eyes off one of the models who was wearing a cascading skirt of yellow, peach, sky blue, and red gerbera daisies. Her hair was tied in two long braids with matching daisies. "Do you care if I grab one of those cupcakes?" He pointed to the tray of vanilla cupcakes frosted with Swiss buttercream and adorned with succulents that the model was holding.

"You're not on duty. You don't need to ask permission," Pete responded. We both watched Tomo approach the model. His technique was much more subtle than Kirk's. I heard him compliment her on her skirt.

"I don't think it takes a detective to figure out that he's not really interested in her cupcakes," I said to Pete.

His crooked smile left me wanting to clutch the bar to steady myself. "Nope. But I can't blame him. There are beautiful women floating all around this place." There was no mistaking that his words were meant for me. He held my gaze, letting his eyes linger on me. Heat rushed up my spine. Is this how Elin felt around Eric?

"You aren't on duty tonight?" I asked, nodding at his wineglass.

"Not officially, but each of my suspects in my homicide investigation is here. Quite interesting, don't you think?"

I surveyed the room with him. Sure enough Lawren, Serene, and Kirk were all at the wine bar. Nora was pouring coffee in the front of the shop, while Jon was chatting with Misty from *Mod*, and

Mark was waiting in line for a pizza flower crisp. They were wontons cut and fried in the shape of a flower, filled with marinara sauce, and decorated with sprigs of Italian parsley and fresh basil leaves. I hadn't seen either of the men come in.

"Are you any closer to figuring out who killed Frank?" I asked.

He glanced at the bar. Was he looking at Lawren? I couldn't tell. "Close. We're very close."

"I heard about Lawren," I said, hoping that he might open up.

"Oh?" He tasted his wine, but didn't appear impressed by the flavor.

"Is there something wrong with the wine?" I asked.

"Not at all." He turned and stared at Serene for a moment. She caught him looking at her and gave him a flirty smile. He raised his glass to her in a toast and then turned his attention back to me. Was he interested in her? Was I so out of practice in the dating world that I was misinterpreting his signals?

"Don't you think that being fired and having Frank threaten to make sure that she never worked in Portland again is a strong motive for murder?" I could barely make out Lawren in the throng of people tasting wine at the bar. She hadn't touched her drink and appeared to be alone. What was she doing?

"Perhaps." Pete didn't sound convinced.

"But you said yourself that you thought it was a crime of passion. Don't you think that if Lawren discovered that Frank was going to axe her that could have sent her over the edge?"

He stepped closer to me. I could feel his breath on my neck and smell his minty soap. "I think this is supposed to be a party and a celebration, Britta Johnston. I think you should sip your wine and enjoy the evening. Leave the investigation to me."

For a minute I thought he might kiss me. I could feel my body being pulled toward his as if there was a force field between us. His eyes held a longing. My heart beat in rapid, erratic bursts. But then someone pulled me away.

"Are you Britta?" One of the models wearing a hat of palm leaves and ostrich feathers tapped my shoulder.

"Yes."

"They need you in the cottage. They're about to go live."

"Go live?" I hadn't heard anything about a live shot.

"Yes, Elin said to come find you." The model's gazelle-like posture made me straighten my back.

Pete took my drink. "You better go, duty calls."

The model whisked me away before I could protest. I'd never been on TV before, let alone live TV. What would I say?

The cottage was packed and bursting at the seams. Elin stood behind the island, which was littered with twine, wire, floral tape, and a brilliant collection of flowers, greenery, ribbons, and feathers. A news crew had set up in front of her. A photographer was snapping still shots of her at work as a TV reporter was getting in position next to her.

"Britta, good! Come join us." Elin waved.

I squeezed through the onlookers. "I don't want to be on TV," I whispered.

"You have to. We're a team." She turned to the reporter. "This is my niece, Britta, who I was telling you about."

In one quick flash the reporter swooped over to me, and had me slide a wire down the back of my dress and clip a small mic to my chest. "Good. Let's roll."

She took her handheld microphone and addressed the camera directly. "I'm here live at Blomma for the launch of their cottage couture line. This is where fashion meets flowers." Her voice turned severe as she stared into the camera and continued, "And the site of a gruesome homicide earlier this week."

Elin was brilliant on camera, answering each question flawlessly and showing off her artistic talents by whipping up a seedpod-and-poppy bracelet for the reporter while she spoke. I, on the other hand, was terrible. My answers felt stilted and I wasn't sure where to look. The reporter must have realized that I was far from a natural and motioned for the camera to return to Elin.

The interview built to the grand reveal. Elin clapped her hands and nodded to the antique desk where a temporary screen had been erected to hide the showpiece—Elin's floral dress. A model stepped out from behind the screen and the entire crowd inhaled collectively. Flowers cascaded from her bodice out into a massive hoop skirt. I could smell the fragrant bunches of lilacs hanging from her narrow waist. Misty Haze and every other reporter snapped dozens of photos as the model floated through the room. Elin's creation was more stunning than anything I'd ever seen on a catwalk or in the pages of a fashion magazine. The crowd must have agreed because they "oohed" and "aahed" when the model brushed past them, and squeezed in to get a closer glance at the floral structure.

Once the reporters left, Elin continued to make custom floral jewelry for every guest. I returned to the front to make sure everything was running smoothly. The rest of the evening was a happy blur. Our clients were thrilled, we'd garnered some great press, and Nora was right. On her way out the door Misty from *Mod* magazine pressed her business card in my hand and said, "I love what I've seen here. This is cutting edge. I want to do a full-color feature on the shop."

I couldn't believe my ears. A feature in *Mod* would be huge for Blomma and for Elin!

Nothing could bring me down—I floated throughout the room. The only thing that made me feel a twinge of sadness was when Pete came to say goodbye for the evening. He'd been called back to the station, but promised a makeup lunch soon. When the last guest left, the shop looked like it had been hit by a hurricane. We had a ton of cleanup to do, but Nora wanted to celebrate.

Nora placed her hands on her hips. "Leave it. We'll help you clean in the morning, but the night is young and we have to go have a celebratory round of drinks. Plus I don't know about all of you, but I'm starving."

It was just Mark, Jon, Elin, and me left.

"I don't know," Elin hesitated.

"Come, come. Nora's right. An evening such as

this requires a bottle of bubbly," Jon said, as he urged Elin toward the door.

"Or two!" Nora chimed in.

"Britta?" Elin turned to me for support.

"No way, I'm with them. Cleanup can wait."

Realizing she was outnumbered Elin agreed. "Okay, but at least let me go close up the cottage. The lights are still on and I have candles burning."

"You go," I insisted. "I'll close up the cottage, lock up here, and then come meet you all. Where are you going?"

Nora grabbed Mark's hand. No one even flinched. I wondered if Jon had suspected that they were a couple, too. "The Riverplace Inn. We'll save you a seat and have a cold glass of champagne waiting for you."

Elin hesitated, but I made eye contact with Jon, who caught my meaning and linked his arm through Elin's. "Your lovely niece is right. Shall we?" He pointed to the door.

I grinned as the four of them chattered about how much good press we'd received and speculated on whether or not it might bring a new round of customers to the village. I tossed a few empty coffee cups and appetizer wrappers that had fallen on the floor and rearranged the furniture. Then I made my way to the cottage.

As Elin had said, it glowed with flickering candles and twinkle lights. The island was a mess of flower supplies, thorns, and stems. Cups, plates, and napkins had been left around the room. I did a quick sweep and tossed them into the trash. The good news was that we didn't have any workshops slated for tomorrow, so we could spend the day getting everything back in shape. I wondered if the press coverage would mean more orders or the phones ringing off the hook tomorrow. Maybe tonight really was going to be the start of something new for Blomma.

I blew out each candle and unplugged the twinkle lights. As I was about to flip the switch for the overhead chandelier I head a crash in the front. Had I locked the door after everyone left? I froze for a second and listened.

Another crash sounded. Was it wine bottles shattering?

Someone was in the shop. What should I do? Was Darren here to get his revenge as promised? He had never showed at the party.

I scanned the dimly lit cottage. My eyes landed on Elin's old rotatory phone on her desk. I tiptoed over and dialed Pete's number. He didn't answer.

When his voice mail came on I whispered. "Pete, it's Britta. I'm cleaning up in the cottage but I think someone is in the shop. I keep hearing crashes and bangs, but I'm scared to go check because I'm here by myself."

Another giant crash made me jump. What was going on in there?

I crept behind the barn doors and considered my options. I could wait for Pete or someone else to arrive. I had left the lights on in the front. Blomma was a wall of windows, so whoever was banging about in there had to risk being seen. Could it be Darren? Maybe he'd come to sabotage us after seeing the news.

That made the most sense. I could feel my muscles relax. Suddenly I felt silly having called Pete. Darren didn't scare me, and catching him in the act would give us proof once and for all that he'd been behind leaving the dead flowers. Yet again, there was a chance that he had killed Frank.

I decided to try and get a peek. If I could see who the culprit was then I could decide whether to hide out in the cottage or confront whoever was smashing wine bottles. Suddenly the shop was plunged into darkness. I definitely wasn't alone.

My heart pounded and sweat poured from my forehead.

I stuck my head farther inside. A slice of moonlight illuminated the front of the shop. My eyes tried to adjust to the darkness.

A silhouette stood by the bar holding a bottle of wine. Then a hand smashed it on the table. I flinched. I must have made a sound because the person whipped around in my direction. Was that Serene?

It couldn't be. Why would Serene smash bottles of her wine?

My mind moved like honey. I tried to make sense of what was happening but the next thing I knew Serene grabbed another wine bottle and walked straight toward me. Before I could pull the door shut she lifted the bottle in the air and smashed it on my head. Then everything went dark.

Chapter Thirty-five

"Britta, Britta?" A muffled voice roused me.

I tried to sit up but a wave of nausea assaulted my body. My head throbbed.

"She's okay!" the voice hollered.

I peeled one eye open. Big mistake. The light made my head pulse.

"Easy, easy. Sit tight," the voice said. It sounded familiar but I couldn't place it.

What happened? Where was I?

I reviewed my last memory. I'd been at Blomma. The party. We'd had the launch party and I stayed to clean up. Then my mind was flooded—Serene. Serene was smashing wine bottles. Had she smashed me on the head?

Again I tried to sit up. My head felt like it was on a Tilt-A-Whirl. I rubbed the base of my skull. Was there a lump forming?

"Careful, Britta, take it slow." This time I recognized the man's voice. It was Pete.

I squinted, trying to let in the least amount of light possible. "Serene. Was Serene here?"

He put his arm around my back and helped steady me. "Yes. We've got her. I want you to take it easy though. You had a nasty blow. EMS is on the way. In fact I think I hear the sirens now."

"I don't need an ambulance," I protested, but as I opened my eyes all the way wavy lines clouded my vision.

"You do. It's not a choice." Pete's voice was kind but firm. I could smell his earthy cologne and feel his breath.

"What happened?" I rubbed the bump.

"Try not to touch it. That will just make it worse." Pete moved my hand away. "I was on my way back here anyway, but when I got your call we hopped in Tomo's squad car and flew here. Got here just in time. Serene was sprinting toward the river."

"Why? I don't understand." I could hear fuzzy sirens in the distance. "Was it Serene?" I repeated.

"It's too early to know for sure. As soon as EMS gets you stable I'll interrogate her, but my best guess is that she came back here looking for something. That note that we found in Frank's coat pocket most likely. Her prints came back on it, but so did yours and your aunt's. Since Serene works here and had served wine the night of Frank's murder that wasn't enough evidence to go on. But we had learned that the two of them were having an affair."

"Frank and Serene?" She must have really hit my head because nothing Pete was saying was making sense.

"Yeah. Apparently they traveled together. She was in Italy with him last month."

Blue and white lights flashed outside. The sound of the siren's wail made my head feel it might explode.

"Tell them to kill the siren," Pete called to an officer standing at the door. I hadn't even noticed that anyone else was here.

I thought back to the conversation we'd had about wine tasting and how Serene had stopped herself when she mentioned Italy. I had thought it was because someone ran by the front windows and she was nervous, but now I realized it had to have been because Serene almost let it slip that she'd been with Frank. Was that why she'd been so irritated with me cleaning the wine bottles? Did she think she had stashed the note there?

"It turns out they were using the cottage for their secret trysts," Pete continued. "Serene had a key."

"And she was the one peering in the window? Trying to see if Elin had left yet?"

"That's my working theory. We'll see what she has to say."

The EMS workers raced in with a stretcher. I dug my heels in and begged them not to take me in the ambulance, but Pete wouldn't hear of it. "They'll get you checked out, Britta. You're in good hands. I'll let your aunt and everyone else know. See you at the hospital later." He clapped one of the first responders on the back as a cue to wheel me away.

At the hospital the emergency room doctor was extra precautious. He ran a number of tests including a spinal X-ray and CAT scan before ruling that I had a mild concussion. "We want to keep you overnight to observe you, but otherwise with a week of rest and some ice and Advil you'll be as good as new."

Elin, Jon, Nora, and Mark crammed into my tiny room with flowers, candles, and even a steaming mug of Demitasse espresso. A stern nurse shot Nora the evil eye when she tried to hand me the coffee. "Absolutely not," the nurse said taking the mug.

"Don't let that go to waste, honey," Nora retorted to the nurse. "At least enjoy it yourself."

I thought I saw the young nurse smile as she took the coffee and left me to my visitors.

Elin's face was blanched. She sat on the bed next to me, rubbing my calves. "When Pete said that you'd been injured my heart stopped. I couldn't imagine . . ." she trailed off.

Jon placed a firm hand on her shoulder. "Britta's made of the same Swedish steel. I'm guessing she'll be back to building gorgeous bouquets in no time, isn't that right?" He winked at me.

"I'm fine. I promise," I reassured them and then we broke into a heated discussion about Serene and Frank.

The bandage from Jon's nose was missing and if I wasn't mistaken I thought I saw a small scar on the left side.

Jon must have noticed me squinting. "Is it obvious?"

"No, why?"

He gave me a sheepish grin. "Had a bit of touch up done. My plastic surgeon swears that you'll never be able to see the stitches once the swelling is completely gone." He turned to show us his profile.

"A nose job!" Nora punched him in the shoulder. "I thought you had a hot date in Bermuda or something. A nose job!"

"I thought you were the killer for a while there," I admitted with a chuckle. Bad idea. Movement made my head throb.

Jon burst into hysterics and Nora and Elin looked at me as if I were speaking in tongues. "A killer? *Moi*? How positively perfect."

"Come on, cut me some slack. I hadn't met you and you waltz into the flower shop sporting that bandage. I thought maybe you got into a fight with Frank before you killed him. And there was that weird black van parked in front of Torch." Even as I tried to explain my rationale it sounded pretty far-fetched.

Nora threw her head back and cackled. "Jon a killer. I love it, girl! Remind me to tell you about the time I called Jon to help me with my spider infestation. The man refused to kill a single spider. Not a single one." She punched his shoulder again.

Jon dabbed the side of his nose. "Maybe Britta is right. What if the nose job was to disguise my appearance?" His eyes twinkled. Then he frowned. "What black van was in front of the shop?"

Elin raised her index finger. "I can answer that question." She looked at me. "Darren."

"You think that was Darren?" I asked, rubbing the base of my skull.

"I'm sure it was Darren. He drives a black van,

and as you well know he's been casing Blomma for weeks."

Nora reached for Elin's hand. "Why didn't you let us help? We would have run his big pudgy body straight out of the village, wouldn't we, Jon?"

Jon gave her a nod of solidarity.

Elin smiled as the nurse returned to shoo everyone out. "Visiting hours are over, folks. We need to let our patient rest."

"Can I stay? I'm family," Elin asked the nurse, who gave her a nod.

Jon and Nora left with another round of wellwishes. Elin kissed the top of my head. My flower headband must have been left at the scene. "I can't believe that it was Serene. I trusted her. And her and Frank? I can't picture it."

"I know. She was so polished, and Frank was so . . ." I trailed off, not finding the right word in my hazy fog.

"Horrid," Elin offered. She tucked my feet into the blankets.

"Horrid." I tried to smile but pain shot from my cheekbones up to my forehead. "How do you think Lawren fit into it? Do you think that Serene got jealous? Remember that night how he pinched Lawren's waist and kept calling her honey? Could the love note have been meant for her? Maybe Serene read it and snapped."

"It's possible." Elin fiddled with her succulent bracelet.

I knew that my synapses weren't firing at full speed, but Elin looked disturbed. "Is something bothering you?"

She sighed. "That note was for me, Britta."

"What?" She couldn't have possibly been involved with Frank Jaffe.

"No, no." She waved her hand in the air. "I see what you're thinking. Not Frank. The note was from Eric. The roses—the Deep Secrets—those were for me. Remember how I told you that Eric has sent me flowers every year?"

I rubbed my temples and nodded.

"Those are our roses. Deep Secret. He sent me the note and the roses. They arrived the afternoon that Frank was killed. I put them in the cottage."

"Oh." Of course. Why hadn't I thought of that before? "That makes sense. If Serene and Frank were supposed to meet in the cottage what if she found the roses and note? She must have jumped to the conclusion that Frank was having an affair with someone else."

"My thoughts exactly." Elin reached over and fluffed the pillow behind my head. "Can I get you anything?"

"No, I'm fine." My head hurt as the pieces of Frank's murder finally began to fall into place. "You know at one point I considered everyone a suspect. Mark, Jon, even Nora."

"I didn't want to believe that any of my friends could have done it, but the same thoughts crossed my mind." Elin handed me a glass of water. "You should drink this."

I took a sip of the water. "And what about the dead roses at the murder scene?"

She pursed her lips together. We both said, "Darren" at the same time.

"You think?" I asked handing her back the water glass.

"I'm sure." She set the glass on the nightstand next to the bed. "I've been wondering if maybe he was the one hanging around and peering in the cottage windows."

"Why didn't you say anything?"

"I didn't want to worry you." She sighed. "It started after the bridal show. Darren was upset with me. He feels like I'm intentionally trying to put him out of business, which as you know is not the case. Although I do firmly believe that his novelty and negative flowers have no place at a bridal show. He's been sending me a dead bouquet once a week since I stated my position to the organizers. Like I said before, he's harmless. And he's wasting his money. If he wants to use his time to deliver his product to Blomma, more power to him. It's not going to intimidate me."

"For sure, but I don't understand why you didn't tell me." I rolled my neck from side to side. "Aren't we supposed to be a team?"

She laced her hand through mine. Her skin was warm and comforting. "We are." She squeezed my fingers tight. "Britta, I'm sorry. I've kept so much in. I didn't want to burden you, but having you home has made it so clear how much I need you."

"I need you, too, *Moster*." I clasped her hand.

"There's something else I want to ask you," she said as she stroked my palm. "It's about Eric."

"What?"

"He'd like to come for a visit. He wants to meet you." Her tone was timid, but laced with enthusiasm.

I removed my hand from hers so that I could sit

up a little. "Of course. Yes, I would love to meet him. When can he come?"

"Are you sure?" Her brow furrowed. "It's been a long time and so much has happened."

"Yes, I'm sure. I want to meet him and obviously he wants to see you again."

A blush crept up her cheeks. She looked at her feet. "Well, it would be nice to see him."

The nurse poked her head in the door and tapped her watch. "Almost time for bed."

"Would you like me to stay?" Elin asked.

"No, I'll be fine."

"Rest up. I'll be here first thing in the morning."

My eyes were heavy and a headache had begun to spread down my neck. I must have drifted off because I was roused sometime later when I heard the rustling of sheets and the sound of the single chair in the room sliding across the floor.

I opened my eyes to see Pete curled up in the chair. His long leg stretched under the bed. "Hey, how did you get in? I thought visiting hours were done."

Pete grinned and pulled out his badge. "Not for me. I'm here on official police business."

"You are?" I knew I was groggy and hoped that his questions could wait until morning.

"No. But no one needs to know that." He winked.

"Is that even legal?"

"To visit someone at the hospital?" He glanced behind him toward the hallway. "The last time I checked, yeah."

"You know what I mean."

"Actually, I don't." He strummed his fingers on his chin. "Is there a piece of news or lingering evidence you're holding back?"

"No. I'm just so glad it's done, but I still can't believe it was Serene."

He cleared his throat and reached into his coat pocket. "Right, I thought you might want to see this." Removing a photograph, he handed it to me and scooted his chair closer.

"What is it?"

"Take a look."

The photo was of a barely clothed Serene and Frank toasting with glasses of wine on an Italian terrace. "I don't understand," I said studying the picture.

"Lawren, you know, Frank's assistant, handed this over to me."

"When?"

"Tonight. She found it in a file of his paperwork and was going to confront Serene. Apparently she thought she had tucked it behind a bottle of wine at Blomma, but then couldn't find it. She's been looking all around for it. Wanted to have proof before she came to us."

So that's what Lawren had been looking for.

"For someone quiet and mousy she had some moxie. She told Serene she had proof. It sent Serene over the edge."

"Where was the picture?"

"She found it in a stack of résumés in her car."

I rubbed my temples. I knew it had been a long night and I had suffered a bump on the head, but I couldn't picture Lawren confronting Serene. "What made her tell Serene?"

Pete shrugged. "People do surprising things. I think she'd had enough of Frank's demands and abuse. She said Serene was threatened by her. She was pushing Frank to fire Lawren."

"Do you think that's why she killed him?"

"Most likely. We're working from the theory that she found him in the cottage with roses and the note and jumped to the conclusion that he was meeting Lawren for a secret tryst."

My mind tried to connect all of the dots.

"Go back to sleep, Britta." Pete patted my leg. "You're exhausted. We can talk more tomorrow."

I allowed my eyelids to droop and drifted off to sleep content knowing that Pete was watching over me. With Serene arrested, Frank's murder solved, and a successful launch Blomma's future looked like it was about to bloom, and I couldn't help wondering if my budding romance with Pete Fletcher just might be as well. That could wait for tomorrow, but tonight I was content and eager to start my new life in the Rose City.

Please read on for floral tips and recipes from

A TOUCH OF BLOMMA!

Take a stroll through Riverplace Village with Britta. You'll get a taste of the sensory delights that line Portland's waterfront village and learn why being back home again has made Britta ready to plant permanent roots.

BLOMMA'S FLOWER TIPS

Love Juice—Aunt Elin's simple solution for preserving fresh-cut flowers. When purchasing flowers at your local floral boutique or picking them from your garden be sure to immediately place them in warm water. While they are soaking, mix one cup of tepid water with a teaspoon of sugar, bleach, and lemon juice or vinegar. Stir the mixture. Then cut a half inch off each flower stem at an angle. Fill a vase with tepid water, add the love juice, and arrange the stems. Love juice will help extend the life of your arrangement. Change out the water and repeat the process every three or four days.

Shun the Light—To ensure a long-lasting and fragrant bouquet be sure to keep your fresh-cut flowers away from the direct sunlight. Elin and Britta recommend storing floral arrangements in a cool space, like a garage or basement, overnight. Enjoy your colorful bounty on your dining room table or in your entryway during the day, but then move it into a cold and dark space overnight. Your flowers and your wallet will thank you.

Blomma's Featured Wine and Flower Pairing— Wine and flowers are the perfect pairing. A lush bouquet or sweet centerpiece can enhance a bottle of bubbly or glass of vino. Blomma's featured wine is a Northwest pinot noir. This complex and romantic red wine is known to have hints of berries, cherries, and even a touch of the forest floor. Britta suggests pairing this wine with a bohemian-style woodland creation filled with fresh evergreen branches, succulents, Hypericum berries, deep red roses, and eucalyptus.

A TASTE OF BLOMMA

Aunt Elin's Swedish Pancakes

This quick and easy Swedish favorite is a treat for breakfast or any time of the day.

    1 cup all-purpose flour
    2 eggs
    1 cup milk
    1 teaspoon sugar
    ½ teaspoon salt
    1 teaspoon vanilla
    2 tablespoons butter, melted

Whisk eggs, milk, flour, sugar, salt, and vanilla together in a mixing bowl until the batter is thin. Heat butter in a small frying pan over medium heat. Pour ¼ cup of batter into hot pan. Swirl pan in circular motion until the batter coats the surface evenly.

Cook for approximately 2–3 minutes. Flip with spatula and cook on the other side. Serve hot with butter, fresh-squeezed lemon, and lingonberries or lingonberry jam.

Makes 8–10 pancakes.

Please turn the page for an exciting sneak peek of

Kate Dyer-Seeley's next Rose City mystery

VIOLET TENDENCIES

coming soon wherever print and e-books are sold!

Chapter One

Portland was flush with spring color, blooming roses, bright flags flapping from the boughs of Navy ships docked along the waterfront, and neon carnival signs, doting the banks of the Willamette River. The end of the unrelenting rainy season brought a celebration like no other to the city— Rose Festival. The festival spanned three weeks from the end of May through mid-June, attracting visitors from all over the world who joined in Portland's annual street party at the queen's coronation, milk boat races, starlight run, rose show, and the *pièce de résistance*, the Grand Floral Parade. This year, Blomma, my Aunt Elin's boutique European-inspired flower shop where I had been working for the past few months, had been chosen as the showcase florist for the Rose Festival. It was a huge honor. And a huge undertaking. In addition to managing our regular clientele at the

shop, we had been spending every waking moment at the float barn preparing our float.

This year's theme for Rose Festival was Shine,
and we intended to make our float do just that.
Elin had sketched out a design plan that mirrored
her artistic, Swedish style. Many float designers
opted to adorn their moving masterpieces with
Portland's signature flower, the rose. Not Elin.
Blomma's float would consist of giant violet garlands that stretched across a ten-foot bridge constructed from grape vines. The float would be lush
with purple violets, dark greenery, and earthy
vines, with touches of brilliant white violets to signal the return of spring. Elin had opted for the
dainty flower because they were often one of the
first to push through the ground in April. Her vision for the float was to create an Oregon forest-
scape that was just beginning to bud to life.
Assuming we could pull it off, her ethereal float
could have a good shot at winning the judge's
award for most outstanding. There were also awards
for craftsmanship, best depiction of whimsy, life in
Oregon, and community spirit. Winning a coveted
award would be a boost for our growing flower
shop and wine bar.

When it came to materials, the rules for the Grand
Floral Parade were simple—everything must be organic in nature. Seeds, bark, leaves, berries, flowers,
and moss were all acceptable. Gluing thousands
of tiny seeds by hand was a painstaking process,
but I hoped that our efforts would be worth it. As
of late, our biggest challenge (other than black,
sticky fingers) was procuring enough product.
Nicki Parks, the float barn director, had told me in

passing that each float used enough flowers to send someone a dozen roses every day for thirty years. That didn't even begin to account for the industrial-sized buckets of tapioca pearls, onion seeds, and cranberries lining every square inch of floor space in the float barn, along with stacks of twenty-foot evergreen boughs, corn stalks, and pumpkin vines. Trying to add up how many thousands of seeds and berries were being used in float production made my head spin.

Focus, Britta, I told myself as I surveyed the wholesale flower market. I had offered to make the trek to Oregon's largest flower trading market to see if one of our long-standing suppliers happened to have twelve dozen Shasta daisies in stock. We had received a last-minute call yesterday from a frantic bride whose florist bailed on her with her deposit. She needed six bridesmaid's bouquets, a bridal bouquet, boutonnières, and headpieces for the flower girls by tomorrow, and her budget was minimal given that her original florist had taken off with the cash she had put down for her wedding day flowers. Elin and I both had a soft spot for brides-in-need so we agreed to do our best. I had explained that the likelihood of finding enough Shasta daisies wasn't high given that the Grand Floral Parade was in three days. Every flower in the state had been purchased and accounted for. However, she had sounded so dejected on the phone that I couldn't turn her down. I assured her that I would give it a shot and that we could create something just as lovely with equally inexpensive white carnations and hints of greenery if necessary.

The trading floor was a mob scene as always, de-

spite the fact that the sun had yet to rise. Working
early hours was part of life as a professional florist.
The market opened at five and stayed active until
mid-afternoon, but any self-respecting florist knew
that the freshest and rarest stems would be gone
within the first hour. Usually I enjoyed strolling
through row after row of clementines, dahlias, and
California figs. The fragrant scent of jasmine and
the constant sound of vendors bartering were like
home to me, but today I was on a mission. I squeezed
past a florist I recognized who worked for one of
the big national chains and made a beeline for the
back of the humming warehouse. When I spotted
the sign for Abundant Gardens, I nearly broke into
a sprint.

"Morning, Britta," the owner greeted me with a
smile, tucking a pair of sheers into his overalls.
"You look like you're in a hurry."

I felt a blush creep up my neck. My skin is naturally pale, which means that the slightest hint of
color makes my cheeks look like two ripe cherry
tomatoes. Elin had always told me that my porce-
lain skin was a gift. She also had been a fierce pro-
ponent of using sunscreen.

"Britta, our Scandinavian skin is like an orchid.
We must treat it gently and shield it from too
much sun," she had cautioned. It was wise advice,
especially in our line of work, where visiting local
farms and outdoor growers' markets came with
the territory.

"Sorry," I said to the owner of Abundant Gardens. "I'm on the hunt for Shasta daisies. Desper-
ate bride."

He gave me a knowing nod. "That's why I prefer working in the field and on this side of the business. Don't have to deal with any crazy brides. Or worse, their mothers." He winked.

"Oh, I could tell you some stories."

"I bet you could." He pointed behind him to a black plastic tub with bunches of white daises. "And, you're in luck. How many do you need?"

"Can I have all of them?"

"Consider it done. You want me to wrap them up?"

While he bundled the Shasta daisies, I mentally reviewed my day. First, I would head to Blomma and assemble the bridal bouquets and our recurring corporate orders before we opened for walk-in customers. Typically, Elin hosts custom workshops in the cottage attached to Blomma, but we had put those on hold for a week until we were finished with the float. She would oversee volunteers at the float barn this morning, and then we would swap places in the afternoon. With only three days to go before the big event, the organizers were allowing designers and volunteers to work late every night. We would grab a quick bite of dinner and spend the rest of the evening twisting grape vines and stringing evergreen branches into tight bundles. The float prep-work had to be completed by Friday. That's when the real fun would begin. The actual flowers would be the very last thing to go on each float. No floral designer wanted a droopy tulip or wilting rose on their float. The Friday before the parade would be a mad dash to the finish as everyone raced against the clock and the elements to cover their structure with fresh flowers.

Elin and I had decided we wanted to create a test
garland of violets tonight. Just so that we could put
together step-by-step directions for the volunteers
who would help with the finishing touches.

I thanked my friend for the daisies and headed
for Riverplace Village. It was a short drive from the
flower market. The village was located on the west
side of the Willamette River with cobblestone streets,
charming shops, and an elegant, yet laid-back vibe.
The small community of business owners in Riverplace Village were a tight-knit group. Most of the
shops and the world-class Riverplace Inn had been
operated by the same owners for decades.

Blomma sat at the corner of the village with welcoming brick-red, windowed garage doors that
could be rolled up in the spring and summer
months. In honor of Rose Festival, we had draped
the front windows and door with strings of pink
lights and filled the front display cases with pastel
bouquets of roses in soft peach, creamy whites, yel-
lows, and pale pink. As I pulled the car into a parking space in front of the shop, I wanted to pinch
myself. I couldn't believe I was so lucky.

Of course, when I first made the decision to return home to Portland, I hadn't considered it
luck. Quite the opposite. I had discovered that my
deadbeat husband, Chad, had been having an affair instead of working on the next great American
novel, as he promised. It turned out that his late-
night trips to the library didn't involve writing.
That is unless you counted terribly cheesy poetry
"writing." At first, I'd been hurt and embarrassed,
but after the shock wore off I recognized that his

infidelity was actually a blessing in disguise. I'd been miserable for years. And, as much as I hated to admit it, part of that blame was on me.

After attending the Floral Institute, I had imagined myself opening a shop much like Blomma where I could leave my flower mark on the world, but instead I'd ended up in Minnesota working for a lifeless wholesaler. Chad couldn't take a traditional job because he claimed it would interfere with his creative process. That left me as our sole provider. Every time I suggested that Chad find a part-time job to help ease our financial burdens, he would have a burst of energy and swear that he was days away from finishing the book. Shocker. That never happened. Leaving Chad and the Midwest had been the best decision I had made in a long time.

I shook myself from my thoughts and turned off the car. Then I removed the bunches of daises from the back and went to open Blomma's front door. Immediately I was greeted by the scent of honeysuckle and sweet roses. I flipped on the lights, but kept the sign on the door turned to CLOSED. The chandeliers overhead cast a warm glow on Blomma's hardwood floors. Cozy furniture had been arranged in the front of the shop. Perfect for customers to take a break and breathe in the scent of flowers after a busy afternoon shopping in the village, and for casual meetings with potential clients. There were tins of fresh-cut stems and succulents displayed on tables. The back of the space housed a concrete workstation and sink, a display case with pre-arranged bouquets, and a wine bar, complete with a wall of Northwest wine available to purchase by the glass or bottle. Elin had learned early on that flowers and wine were an excellent pairing. Our customers often came in looking for a gift and wound up lingering over a glass of Oregon pinot noir at the bar while waiting for us to create a gorgeous arrangement.

The cottage was attached to the main building through two sliding barn doors next to the wine bar. It reminded me of a childhood fairy tale with its exposed timber beams and stone walls. Whenever we hosted classes and workshops in the cottage, clients gushed about the space, saying it felt as if they were stepping into a rustic European castle. This morning, I left the barn doors shut and focused on our rush bridal order.

Before I even began gathering supplies to create the bouquets, I quickly filled a bucket with warm water and mixture of "love juice" to process the daises I had bought at the market. It's critical when working with fresh flowers to trim their stems and douse them in a healthy bath of water, sugar, bleach, and vinegar. This preserves the life of the flower and ensures a long-lasting bloom. Once I had the vibrant, white daises soaking, I removed a pair of shears, wire, scissors, and a silky forest green ribbon from the workstation. For the bridal party, I wanted every bouquet to be symmetrical with a tight weave and exposed stems. Once I wound the bouquets with wire and wrapped them with the ribbon, I would finish them with a small bow and drape the ribbon on both sides to give the inexpensive flowers an elegant look.

Soon I was immersed in the creative process. Any worry about the Grand Floral Parade and our float faded away as I trimmed stems and plucked off any imperfections in the daisy's petals. Flowers were art and an expression of the soul. It was my job as a floral artist to infuse love and joy into every arrangement. I had found my true purpose, my calling. This was exactly where I wanted to be, and nothing could change that.

Connect with

Visit us online at
KensingtonBooks.com
to read more from your favorite authors, see books
by series, view reading group guides, and more.

for sneak peeks, chances to win books and prize packs,
and to share your thoughts with other readers.

facebook.com/kensingtonpublishing
twitter.com/kensingtonbooks

Tell us what you think!
To share your thoughts, submit a review,
or sign up for our eNewsletters, please visit:
KensingtonBooks.com/TellUs.